TWENTY-THREE MINUTES

J.C. DE LADURANTEY

TWENTY-THREE MINUTES

iUniverse books may be ordered through booksellers or by contacting:

iUniverse
1663 Liberty Drive
Bloomington, IN 47403
www.iuniverse.com
844-349-9409

Because of the dynamic nature of the Internet, any web addresses or links contained in this book may have changed since publication and may no longer be valid. The views expressed in this work are solely those of the author and do not necessarily reflect the views of the publisher, and the publisher hereby disclaims any responsibility for them.

Any people depicted in stock imagery provided by Getty Images are models, and such images are being used for illustrative purposes only. Certain stock imagery © Getty Images.

ISBN: 978-1-6632-2661-7 (sc)
ISBN: 978-1-6632-2662-4 (e)

Print information available on the last page.

iUniverse rev. date: 07/26/2021

ABOUT TWENTY-THREE MINUTES

For almost seven years, Howard Hamilton has his dream job. He happily works at the Orchard Hill Police Department, can go home for lunch, and takes pride in getting off on time and returning to his family. Now that he is on the day shift, however, his view of police work is changing. Nothing seems to be like actual police work. Can he eventually get back to his night shift and the actual work out there?

Before he can return to his coveted shift, he must deal with a former OHPD Officer who was arrested for narcotics trafficking and is pulled into his web of unlawful activities. Now he wants Howard to oversee a big drug bust to pay him back. Howard wants nothing to do with it until he finds that the shipment is headed to Orchard Hill and their schools.

In the meantime, he must run interference for a ticket happy motor cop who is writing citations to mothers at a local school. As a new Training Officer, he is assigned a trainee with ties to a local gang. He must deal with a detective investigating a suicide that Hamilton thinks is more than just someone killing themselves. But how can he challenge the very person who was selected over him for a position in detectives?

The average time spent on a call or observation is approximately twenty-three minutes. How can he go back to the easy life of the night watch where he goes from incident to incident and not get caught up in the day watch maggot work of the day shift?

AUTHORS NOTE

Among the many who can claim to be middle and upper class, there is a point in life where one dreams of doing something they have never done. While commonly called a "bucket list," it marks a point where we have almost accomplished everything in life, but then again, not that one thing left on the list.

In March of 1975, seemingly decades ago, but it could also have been yesterday, I was a Sergeant watch commander in the renowned and infamous Rampart Division of the Los Angeles Police Department. At the time, Rampart was one of the coveted assignments because of the cosmopolitan nature of the community.

Rampart was the home of the 18th Street Gang, Silver Lake, East Hollywood, Wilshire Boulevard, gated communities like Fremont Place, Hancock Park, Larchmont, and Mara Salvatrucha's beginnings or the now most powerful and vicious of the gangs; the MS-13. Quite the conundrum.

To quote the famous Dragnet series,...this is the City, Los Angeles, California. I was working the day watch on a quiet Sunday mid-morning. I was relegated to working on an old dyno tape machine to create names for a magnetic board. We received a batch of new officers from the Academy, and new names had to be created to blend the new and those veterans who were responsible for their training.

"Hey, Sarge," the senior desk officer growled. Something must have interrupted his reading of the Sunday paper. "Yeah, Gary, don't bother me now. I am trying to do your job and make this damn machine work." He came in with a 'keep it down' motion. "There is a guy here in a fancy suit that is asking for a ride-along. Did the Captain OK anybody for today? I don't have it on my sheet." "Let me look in a few minutes and see if it's in my watch commander's time book."

I decided to walk out to the lobby to greet our visitor. Sunday mornings were either busy or quiet as an empty church. This was a church day.

I reached out my hand to introduce myself and was startled to see a familiar face. Who was this, I asked myself? I know this guy from somewhere. "Hello, Sergeant," he said in a very mild manner that belied his command presence. "I thought my office cleared the ride-along with someone here, but I guess something went wrong. Sorry to bother you." He stood there hoping I would say something, but I was dumbfounded. "My name is Ozzie Nelson, and I just wanted to spend a few hours riding around with you guys."

It was Mr. Ozzie Nelson with an impeccable dark suit, blue plain tie, perfectly tied with a Windsor knot, a white shirt, and what looked like spit-shined shoes.

I asked him to come into the watch commander's office to sign a waiver. I called in a field Sergeant to take him out for a few hours.

It was a relatively uneventful day by our standards, but he had an enormous grin on his face when he came back in. "That was incredible, Sergeant. Thank you very much. If there is anything I can ever do for you guys, don't hesitate to call me."

He handed me a business card with just his name and a phone number. It did not say prominent bandleader, television star, father of David and Rick Nelson, or husband of Harriet Nelson. Just 'Ozzie Nelson.'

In June of that same year, I was reading a newspaper at home and saw an obituary. It was for Ozzie Nelson. I just stared at the article, not reading it but knowing what it said; and what it did not say. It said a lot about his accomplishments, his family, and television shows. But only a few of us knew about what was on Ozzie Nelson's bucket list. A ride-along in a black and white police car, patrolling the streets of Los Angeles, one last time.

Twenty-Three Minutes is a ride-along with Howard Hamilton. Many people dream of being in the front seat of a police car, looking at the streets, the people, the activity. They are talking with someone who explains every movement of a vehicle, the furtive movements of pedestrians when they see a police car, and the garbling of a police radio that only makes sense to those who know how to listen. So, let's ride along with Howard Hamilton, off-duty and on-duty, going to and from work and figuring out what to do on his days off with his family.

What's on your bucket list?

INTRODUCTION

Everyone loves a Detective novel. But how do you become a detective who has the wisdom and knowledge, plus street savvy? One starts by being a good Patrol Officer. And that is Howard Hamilton of Orchard Hill PD, or as his police friends refer to him, HH. His parents gave him that nickname because of their affinity with 'Old HH' Hunter Hancock, a 1950's radio DJ.

Officer Hamilton grew up watching reruns of 'Adam 12', a 1970's television show about uniformed cops Reed and Malloy. He was interrupted by a stint in the Marine Corps and a brief career in the grocery industry before settling, to some chagrin by his family, to a career at Orchard Hill PD.

Since getting off his probationary period of one year, he opted for the PM or night shift at OHPD and has hidden in plain sight for over six years. He loves the street, particularly after dark. He developed an affinity for spotting people with guns they shouldn't have and, working with one of his best friends, Donny Simpkins, who had an affinity for locating stolen cars. They made quite the team.

OHPD went on a hiring binge, and Simpkins opted to become a training officer. Hamilton went back to a one-man unit on PM'S. But his job, or career, was not his first love. Nor was it his second. His wife Clare was first and tied for second were Geoff and Marcia, his two kids. He shuns overtime, wants to get off on time, and thrives on his days off and vacations.

He prides himself in not going up to the third floor of the police administration building for over two years. He drives into the lot, going to his locker and briefing, which were all on the first floor, getting his assignment, and hitting the streets of Orchard Hill.

He occasionally visits the detectives on the second floor, but as you rise in the building to the third floor and Administration with the Chief of Police, his Captains, and staff, the air gets a little too thin.

With almost seven years now in patrol, he found himself in the middle of a homicide investigation that lured him into a working frenzy. He was loaned to detectives, solved the horrendous satanic ritual killing of a local reclusive, Ginny Karsdon, and raced back to patrol for some sanity.

Everyone says that Patrol is the backbone of police work. So why is there not more written about this adventurous piece of law enforcement? As we will see with Howard Hamilton, the handling of radio calls and observing what goes on in the streets gives you about a twenty-three-minute window of what goes on in other people's lives.

A Patrol Officer may conduct a preliminary investigation that results in a report taken. It is then shipped to detectives for follow-up, but rarely does that same officer have any idea what happens after. He may handle a domestic violence case, counsel, or make a report but not be there when the violence returns and mushrooms into an assault or homicide.

The eyes of a patrol officer view things in a thin reality that takes them to perhaps eight to ten different events in each shift. Many are never totally resolved. The opportunity to revisit a radio call from a previous shift is not always available. Add to the fact many officers are removed from their employed city on their days off because they live anywhere from ten minutes to two hours away. Ownership for a piece of turf is only for a specific period of work time.

Officer Howard Hamilton, however, lives in Orchard Hill and, if he misses a green light, is home in eight minutes. He can go home for lunch but chooses not to. His family interacts at the schools he polices, goes to church in the same community that requires his services, and shops at local stores and restaurants that know who he is.

He possesses a servant's mentality with a solid drive to protect his streets and never relinquish them. They are his and no one else's.

Is he a warrior? Is he a guardian?

DEDICATION

Officer Howard Hamilton of Orchard Hill PD is a composite of what we all see in our communities patrolling to keep us safe. We want all our officers in blue to be strongly principled, always make the right decisions, and shoot straight. But because we recruit from the human race, we will never know unless they are placed in extraordinary circumstances and tested. Really tested.

Not every police officer experiences harrowing, life-threatening encounters each day. Even the safest of communities are safe because of the undying efforts of the men and women who put on a bulletproof vest, a Sam Browne equipped with more items than a carpenter's belt, and seatbelt themselves into a powerfully built black & white patrol car equipped with technology that would challenge even the most avid video gamer.

The policing of a city today is complex and filled with influences and challenges that must be met with a level of professionalism, personal and physical strength, extraordinary decision-making, and the calm of a sequestered monk. Some are the guardians of our communities that ensure only minimal disruption in our daily lives. In contrast, others are the warriors that ensure the thin blue line stands between utter anarchy and safety behind closed doors.

Large metropolitan areas generate the daily news, but those communities that keep the peace and allow our cities to flourish and grow also need policing. The generation of law enforcement professionals that preceded you provide the only guidance possible; it is your turn!

It is to all, the warriors and the guardians of our cities, that this book is dedicated.

CHAPTER 1

IIIIIIIIIIIIIIIIIIIIIIIIIIIIIIIIIIIIIIIIIIIIIIIIII

NORMAL

Howard Hamilton thought he was just going to a simple yoga class with his wife, Clare. The necessity to concentrate on each move was his way of relieving stress from his patrol duties. Now he found himself looking down the darkest hole he had yet to encounter. Was there a train coming? Was it a rain cloud forming? It had a tail like some spermatozoa. There was a slight ant-like movement in the darkness. He followed his instincts and pulled back to see more light. The brown color was getting lighter and lighter.

HH, as his friends called him, was confused and curious at the same time. What was he seeing? Inkblots that was a psychological test of his perceptions? His creativity? He thought briefly of the psyche test he was given when he joined OHPD. The doctor had advised him that he was borderline in terms of his emotional functions. He saw things in the inkblots he should not see. He passed him, anyway.

Clare's and his hobby, model home snooping – more for decorating items than buying something new to move into – came to mind.

He remembered seeing the artwork on the walls of a model home that resembled the famous inkblots.

They worked well in interior design styles from modern to transitional because they appeared as mirror images and had balance and symmetry.

"They could add depth to the small den area, Howard," Clare told him. "It'll give a sense of intrigue, and it's perfect to just look at like a painting."

"Good grief," he had responded, "are we are going to analyze ourselves, our guests, or just have a fun conversation?"

Those moody patterns of people standing on their heads or having sex were just patterns that didn't matter, except to decorate a room.

Those thought processes kept him from thinking of the tensions of the job, the street, and officer safety demands. Not to mention standing on one leg. The pattern and hole he was concentrating on with a sharp focus were bothering him. He didn't see a train, people standing on their heads, or a sex position. Nor did he understand why, as he moved his concentration further away from the center, the circumference was lightening from black to brown to almost a blond.

Then came the sound of order, he was not anticipating.

"And release."

Maru, his yoga instructor, ordered the class out of the traditional triangle pose. This was a standing pose with legs spread apart, one hand on a block next to his left foot and the other straight up to the ceiling. The body then formed, or should, if done correctly, a triangle. She was gentle, but it was clear now where he was and what he was doing. He had been concentrating on the patterns embedded in the wood flooring of the room.

After what seemed like an eternity, she had the class concentrate on a spot on the hardwood floor. He had to release the pain he felt and relax, breathe, and concentrate on one spot. For what seemed like forever! The tunnel he was seeing went from black to brown to tan. It was merely the discoloration in the blond hardwood that formed a knot on the wooden floor.

The following command he was more than willing to do.

"Legs up the wall or shoulder stand on blocks, yogi's choice for savasana." It was not sleeping but a pose of relaxation to top off a strenuous yoga practice and release those endorphins. It could not have come too soon.

He immediately felt his muscles relax and his body cool down. He reached to his left and clutched Clare's hand as they got lost in the darkness of what was almost an orgasmic, semi-comatose euphoria.

The next voice he hears is almost a whisper, "gently bring your legs down from the wall, or remove the blocks from your sacrum. Bring your legs into your chest and rock side to side. Now, gently, and slowly, roll to your right, come up, and be seated in the lotus position."

CHAPTER 2

||||||||||||||||||||||||||||||||||||||||||||||

EAVESDROPPING

It had been a very unsettling six months for HH. After working on the Ginny Karsdon homicide, the three-week vacation away from the department was his only time without any turmoil. There seemed to be a lot of drama throughout this medium-sized Department that had been lauded for its policing.

Orchard Hill was an active community but a safe one. Most of the police work was preventative. His time on the night shift had been spent protecting and guarding while the residents slept, and the many businesses were closed.

Picking out who would cause trouble was easy. You looked for "fit." If the car didn't 'fit,' you merely followed it to its intended destination or watched as it left the City boundaries.

The same for "peds" or pedestrians. Those on a walk or those looking for trouble. It didn't matter the race or ethnicity. What mattered was the behavior or the 'look.' He knew a resident who jogged or walked, and he knew a stranger who could be looking for an advantage. He saw his job as not just policing the City but knowing the good guys from the bad and guarding the 'pie crust,' a term the Chief got in trouble with the press for.

The Chief had described Orchard Hill in an interview as having borders like a pie crust. Orchard Hill was connected or surrounded by LA City, LA County, and four other South Bay cities. Protect the pie crust, and the interior would be safe. Somehow, the press viewed it as profiling. But it wasn't. It was just good policing.

3

Profiling to most of the law enforcement community was a term made up by the frenzied media. He barely knew who he was pulling over, a man or a woman. With tinted windows and headrests, it was nearly impossible to tell an individual's race, age, or sex until the dangerous but necessary approach to the car's driver's side.

Hamilton, and all the OHPD, reacted *to things, body language, movement, furtive actions, hands, a plethora of traffic violations,* and a sixth sense one gets after a few years on the streets. He has stopped as many grandmas and middle-aged white people in business as he did anyone with protected status.

The crime was not rampant in 'The Hill," but it took an effort to keep it that way. While the County and City of LA were out of control with shootings, robberies, and car thefts, as well as a myriad of gang and drug problems, The Hill was somewhat immune to the epidemic of crime. There were a small number of robberies, some home burglaries, and a few auto thefts because of the large Mall, but all was under control.

His time on the day shift with the 'day watch maggots' was much more complex and didn't compare to the night or PM shift's 'real police work.' The maggots reflected the ugly kind of work involved during the day, not the people. Well, most of the time, not the people. HH felt like he took more shit from inside the Department than from those he connected with on the streets of Orchard Hill.

Arriving back from a well-deserved vacation, he wanted to do everything to return to the night shift. The problem was he had an Internal Affairs investigation pending for hitting a suspect with his fist after the fatal shooting of A.J. Johnson, a rookie officer. That effort was also 'well-deserved.' But not everyone felt that way.

He had been called into the Chief's Office the first day back from his time off. With a two o'clock appointment, he could engineer an end-of-watcher if he moved it to two-thirty. He called Janet, the Chief's secretary, and got it changed.

She'll never know or understand why. But that's okay.

He arrived at the appointed time, but Janet was not in her usual chair. She was probably doing whatever Chief's secretaries, or Administrative

Assistants, as they are now called, do. He took a seat in one of his clean uniforms. They were all clean because, with vacation, he was prepared to look the best he could. The Chief's door was closed.

As he sat in a very comfortable chair reading an out-of-date Sports Illustrated, he could hear loud voices coming from inside the Chief's Office. He could tell it was Captain Markham and the Chief mixing it up.

He heard Markham say in a rather disrespectful manner, "I gave you my recommendation to sustain the excessive use of force against Hamilton, and you're going to overrule it? Are you crazy?"

"No, I am not, Thom, and I prefer that you not raise your voice in this office," the Chief said calmly. "In my opinion, it was necessary to restrain the suspect. Hamilton didn't know if he was confronting an armed man, knowing he had more than likely been the one to have killed Johnson. There was a citizen in the garage, other officers, and one of our dogs. He didn't want to put them in jeopardy. I find it was what any reasonable officer, in that situation, with his level of training and experience, would have done."

The Chief's voice was calm and relaxed, but the tension between them was evident, even through the walls.

"With all due respect, sir," and Markham paused for what seemed like an eternity on the word, *sir*, "you guys from LA always seem to rationalize your use of force away. Here, we confront any use of force and discourage them from using any, and I mean any!" Markham was shouting now.

There was a long silence coming from the Chief's office before he heard the following comment. "I would ask for your support on this, Thom, but I'll leave it up to you. I have an appointment with Hamilton, and I'm going to advise him there was a disagreement, and this is my decision." Again, the Chief said it with conviction but without the emotion that Markham delivered.

The meeting appeared to be over, but Markham got in the last shot. "You know, Chief, you're sitting in my chair. My fucking chair. I came on this job wanting to be Chief here, had the opportunity until you came along from LAPD. This was my job, and you took it."

Hamilton could hear the other exit door open and close as Markham chose to avoid Janet's office as the choice of exit.

Hamilton took a deep breath and sat back to savor what he heard.

When he looked up, he was startled to see Janet behind her desk. She had walked in while he was concentrating on the eavesdropped conversation. He wasn't sure how long she had been there, and he was embarrassed to be caught flat-footed.

Janet smiled. Without communicating one word regarding what just happened, her next order was, "The Chief will see you now, Officer Hamilton."

Hamilton already knew what the Chief was going to tell him, but he would never let on.

CHAPTER 3

||||||||||||||||||||||||||||||||||||||||||||||

SPRINTER

It was coming down in torrents, but John Bresani didn't give a shit. The rain was beating on top of his motorhome like 30 caliber machine gunfire. Better yet, it was like New Year's Eve celebrations where stupid people shoot their guns in the air, only to have the lead come raining down on the hood of someone else's car or in the middle of their fucking skull. It became a constant rat-a-tat, rat-a-tat.

It was the rain that was so desperately needed in Southern California, but at the same time, it made rain gutters useless. *It was the same rain, the fuckin weather people couldn't predict or forecast. How many other professions would survive when they only get it right fifty fuckin percent of the time?* His thoughts were said aloud to no one.

"I am so lucky, so fuckin lucky," Bresani told no one in particular. The rain continued to pelt the roof of his new Mercedes Sprinter motorhome, but former police officer Johnny "B Goode" Bresani was not thinking about the weather. He was reflecting on what happened to him in the last six months.

He had been a member of Orchard Hill PD's finest, working the "hype" car and providing narcotics intelligence to those investigators that marveled at his contacts in the drug community. He had the uncanny ability to know when and where "things were happening."

He embedded himself in the drug world and became a part of it. Stupidly, he got greedy and shaved a kilo of coke, thinking his contacts wouldn't notice. They did! Their efforts and his carelessness put him in the hospital with injuries so bad he missed work. That asshole Lieutenant, Rikelman, found him in the hospital, figured out that his story was bullshit, took him back to the station, and turned him over to those fucking Narcs from the LA Deuce Task Force.

They tried to tie one of his only friends, Howard Hamilton, in with him because he used HH to unknowingly pick up a kilo he had stashed in his locker; at the police station!

How stupid. I almost got the only real friend I had on the Orchard Hill Police Department in trouble.

He corrected the record with Rikelman and the task force dicks, giving them information on his connections. But he showed them. The entire process, the internal affairs investigation, submitting the case to the District Attorney to file on his ass, took over six months. Because of his AB 301 rights, as outlined in the Peace Officers Bill of Rights, he continued to draw his paycheck until the matter was resolved. And, of course, they wouldn't let him work under those conditions.

He repeated it, "I am so fuckin lucky." After the investigation was completed, his attorney, Sylvia Landsman, struck a deal to resign from the Department rather than be terminated. The Chief had accepted the deal, thinking the District Attorney would file possession charges. As a former D.A. herself, Landsman was now in private practice defending cops and protecting their rights. She also knew the case against Bresani would not stand up, contrary to what the Department thought.

She was correct; of course, the D.A. didn't file charges. The search conducted by Rikelman and his cronies proved to be questionable, and the likelihood of conviction left them no alternative. Bresani resigned, and the matter was closed from everyone's perspective who cared. He didn't give a shit about Rikelman or the Department. He got what he needed from both and, they could all go fuck themselves. He beat them all.

The rain continued its tat-tat-tat on his new Sprinter commercial van. It was best-in-class with a two-stage turbo diesel, a seven-foot standing ceiling, and of course, it was a Mercedes. He opted for the Blue TEC clean diesel technology with a super high roof and plenty of cargo space. The 2018 model had all the bells and whistles. He got every one of them.

If he was going to be in the drug trade, he wanted the best, the most inconspicuous, and a richness that said; I've made it. He ordered removable seats, blackened windows, and a sightline from the interior. You could see everything, and no one could see you. Perfect.

He ordered a special stowage box package with heavy-duty leaded lining. He didn't want to stand out, even if it was a Mercedes, so he opted for Graphite Grey Metallic. Not white because that's what plumbers and contractors picked, according to his salesperson, Nicole. He declined the Jet Black because it would be only a matter of time before the ghetto drug dealers would choose their transportation of choice after their Escalades became too conspicuous. No, he settled for the Grey Metallic. It was the perfect compromise.

He got the Sprinter with all the upgrades, and, after he figured out Nicole was a weekend cokehead who chipped on the side, he let her know of his connections. He could supply her all day long. A head job from Nicole closed the sale.

And, after bringing one of his druggie buddies in for a new van, he fucked Nicole in the pullout bed. Hey, it came with the deal.

CHAPTER 4

||||||||||||||||||||||||||||||||||||||||||||||

THE CARD

Bresani kept repeating his latest mantra. "I am so fuckin lucky." He rationalized that he never wanted to be a police officer. Ever. His brother-in-law, or now ex-brother-in-law, Charlie "Gabby" Hayes, talked him into it. Now that Charlie was dead from his ongoing heart problems, there was no pressure to remain in a profession he would never have chosen on his own. He knew too much about other businesses to miss this one. But - and it was a big but - he made his time on the job pay off.

Bresani could not attend the funeral services for Gabby. Too many uniforms and detectives that knew his "situation." He developed relationships on both sides of the fence. And he knew he owed HH a big favor. Unknowingly, Hamilton had provided a shield that resulted in the D.A. not filing charges on him.

When the previous Chief of Police left under a dark cloud over falsifying a DMV form regarding purchasing an exotic car, a new Chief from LAPD had come in. In his zeal to change things for the better, the Chief designed a new ID card but didn't change the badge. The Department quickly changed the ID card with the new Chiefs' signature block and an entirely new scheme.

During the chaos that followed the changes between Chiefs, Bresani had been on vacation. When he returned, all old ID cards had been recalled and the new ones issued. He merely went to Human Resources and got the new one, indicating that he had turned his old one in before vacation, and someone screwed up the records.

When he separated from the OHPD for good, he turned in his badge, the new ID card, his uniforms (except the one in the cleaners), proprietary keys to doors to the station, his coveted locker key, and a few odds and ends. His name was erased from all computer databases, and he was blocked from access to any police records or dispatch information. Forever.

But he managed to keep the old ID card 'as a keepsake.' With his old police identification and one uniform he could hold back, he looked at his passports to a new life and new career.

They are so fuckin stupid. They didn't even figure any of this out, did they?

The rain continued throughout the night, but he didn't care. He was going nowhere anyway.

Almost a year ago, he'd obtained a storage unit at Orchard Hill Storage, on the City and the county's border. He was renting a condo in Irvine, just 40 miles south of Orchard Hill, off the 405 freeway. He and Nicole took up residence in Orange County to be out of the Orchard Hill area as much as possible. When he needed to be in the South Bay, he would park his new Sprinter at the storage lot. The manager, who thought he was still with the PD, let him park it behind the gates in the rear of the facility in one of the open spaces for free. Another gratuity.

With his personalized license plate and magnetic placards to place on the sides, he'd convinced the storage manager that it was an undercover surveillance vehicle so that it couldn't be parked at the police station. Placards proclaimed businesses for mobile grooming services for pets, dry cleaning services, and restaurant delivery vans for high-end caterers.

He was all set to do business. But now, he needed an excellent strategic business plan.

CHAPTER 5

||||||||||||||||||||||||||||||||||||||||||||||||||

DOLPHINS

As the Chief confided to Hamilton in the past, personnel matters were the department's most significant issue. Upon his return from vacation, he found the sexual harassment bug had bitten the Department. Though no great loss, one of the department's long-time supervisors, Sergeant Biddle, was no longer around. He was charged with sexual harassment.

Now, everyone had to take those ridiculous classes that told you not to be stupid. For some reason, Hamilton thought the problem was directed to training officers because they broke in the new breed. That included people like the latest female recruit, direct from the police academy, Mel Flowers. She was a knockout recruit who just graduated from the Police Academy, recruited by Hamilton, and was currently on the graveyard shift.

Donny Simpkins, HHs' best friend on the job, was already wrapped up with 'the Wolf,' Pat, don't call me Patricia, Woford. Still, there were plenty of T/O's or training officers trying to take advantage of some of the boot probationary officers that just 'happened to be female.' But in his estimation, that would be idiotic. You were opening yourself up to a lawsuit, divorce, or worse.

Jesus, everybody involved carried guns!

Howard wouldn't think of crossing that line. Clare was his anchor. No one got him excited like Clare. And never would. Nonetheless, the dolphins were running on the graveyard shift. Rumors would fly regarding who would be the first victim of a complaint about an unwelcome sexual advance or a "so you want to make probation, huh?" offer.

It was hard enough to stay awake at three or four o'clock in the morning. Working with an absolute ten like Flowers would have the entire watch, at least the males, including the Sergeants, walking around with a perpetual erection. And no one on that shift took Viagra.

Now, because of Biddle, everyone was on pins and needles. It seems that he had the Records Manager, Shirley Allegan, in the weight room one late Tuesday night. She had been filling in for one of her supervisors on the night shift. Somehow, he coaxed her to the weight room where he "allegedly" requested sexual favors of some sort. Someone caught Biddle trying to take his uniform off. At least below the waist. Shirley immediately screamed and ran to the person who had interrupted Biddle and shouted, "thank you for coming! He was trying to rape me!"

At least that's what the dolphins were saying.

Dolphins gossip among themselves and seem to get pleasure from it. They identify themselves with a unique pattern of whistles and clicks. Years ago, one of the guys vacationing in San Diego at Sea World heard a lecture on the gossip habits of dolphins. The scientists at Sea World proved that when dolphins communicate, it's not uncommon for them to use the name of a third dolphin when the third one is not present. Therefore, as it was told, dolphins gossip about each other. So do coppers.

Biddle had been harassing her for a while, being the station sergeant for the last year or so. She had no idea why he wanted her to go to the workout room but found out quickly, at least according to the dolphins.

Biddle had been in a real estate partnership with Lieutenant Steve Hospian, the Detective Commanding Officer. He had enough time to retire, so rather than fight it or wait until the investigation was done, he submitted his papers for retirement. The Chief approved it, and the investigation was closed.

But not the lawsuit. Shirley Allegan immediately filed a civil suit against the City, saying they should have controlled this monster as several of her record clerks had also been victimized by the lecherous Biddle.

As was mentioned in the classes that everyone attended, Biddle was technically over the Records Unit when he was on duty, and Shirley was subordinate to him. She indicated in the lawsuit that the sexual advances were unwelcome, and she did absolutely nothing to warrant such an outrageous attack.

The real culprit here was the City. The Chief and command staff, managers, and everyone else under the sun, including the city manager and city attorney. All were to blame. This insidious act established a climate of passive acceptance of sexual harassment.

The City Council merely wanted the whole thing to go away. It seemed like everyone was at fault for Biddle's actions but him. In an Executive session, where all major decisions are made away from the public eye and categorized as 'personnel matters,' the City Attorney convinced the City Council to use their insurance to settle the matter.

The matronly Shirley Allegan, Records Manager of OHPD, was so distraught that she left her employment after obtaining a recommendation for future hire. She could not return to the vile workplace that was OHPD.

According to the dolphins, she walked away with over $300,000, tax-free.

CHAPTER 6

||||||||||||||||||||||||||||||||||||||||||||||||

THE LIST

The minute HH returned to work from vacation, Lt. Rikelman was all over him. Ib Rikelman was an enigma at OHPD. He exemplified the position of 'asshole Lieutenant,' which was an oxymoron. He walked with a corn cob stuck up his ass, was a bit arrogant, but the best tactician in the Department. He had garnered the nickname of Norman Bates because, like the character in the Hitchcock movie, "Psycho' he flexed and showed he was in charge. He was OHPD's version of Ollie North. Even looked like him.

Rikelman didn't talk to you; he summoned you. He not only intimidated his officers and supervisors, but many of the Captains had a fear of him. He could be almost insubordinate when dealing with them. There would be no arguing or even discussion. It was his way or the highway.

But today, it was like he wanted to mentor or prod Hamilton to do bigger things. He just about ordered him to apply to be a T/O or training officer. Being a T/O had its privileges, but it also had its responsibilities. HH was more of a loner and wanted to just be in a black and white by himself on the night shift.

Right now, he was stuck on days, with the day watch maggots. Rikelman promised him his old watch back, along with his desired beat, if he would apply for T/O and get it. The underlying premise was that the Chief was putting pressure on Rikelman to get Hamilton to apply. With the new crop of academy graduates just released for training, the

Department needed good T/O's. Other hires were in the pipeline, so the Chief went to the City Council and obtained a few more budgeted positions for training. Rikelman figured the Chief not only liked Hamilton but, more importantly, that HH had what it takes.

After a conversation and *permission* from Clare, he would apply for the position. The oral interview would be easy. He would make it all about officer safety and babysit or train the new kids, male or female.

Officer safety was one of his strong points. He read a book many years back, written by an LAPD Captain who became Chief of Police in Lakewood, Colorado. His name was Pierce Brooks, and the book *"Officer Down, Code Three"* was not a best seller but became mandatory reading in most police academies across the country. It was filled with tragic examples of how officers go down a path to injury or death and how they should and could avoid that fate. He knew the deadly errors and rattled them off like a shopping list.

His closing remarks would be along the lines of, "and I will instill those principles in my trainees each day until they are as ingrained in them as they are in me." Of course, he would get the job.

For the most part, he and his trainee would try to agree on the same days off. It would be easier with the hybrid shift schedules at OHPD. It was not the lousy 5 ½ percent pay increase that mattered. It was the responsibility to get into a kid's head and preach Pierce Brooks' principles. He could do that because he lived in officer safety and had stories to match.

One of the first lessons for any Officer is maintaining proficiency and care of your weapon, vehicle, and equipment. After a briefing, this becomes critical to starting your shift.

"Your black and white is your office and your Glock, your best friend. Keep both clean and operating at the max." He would tell the stories about how bad the LAPD cars were. He saw an LAPD car blow up after a high-speed pursuit because the brakes caught fire.

"Take your long rifle, or shotgun, whichever you're more comfortable with, and check it out, make sure you have backup ammo, your chambers are clear, and no dirty guns."

He would ask what the most common way an officer could get hurt. He would get an answer that would be wrong most of the time.

"Shootings are third on the list. No, good guess, but improper searches, no search, or improper use of handcuffs can get you killed."

He had his own story to drive the point home. Two unnamed officers from OHPD brought in a homicide suspect. After HH interrogated him, the suspect pulled a wooden flute out of his boot and began to play it in the interview room. It was examples and stories such as reminding rookies to "forget what you see on television or in the movies, we don't do wall searches, nor do we handcuff people in the front. And, always, always check the backseat of your black and white—more than once a shift. You never know what you'll find. And, make them take off their boots!"

He would also deliver with passion his mantra of coming to work ready to go. "Get plenty of sleep, especially with 10- and 12-hour shifts. Don't go the 'Disco Dan' route and party hardy. And don't let your guard down, even for a moment. The things they teach you in the Academy matter."

There is never a routine call. One never knows what's happening at the other end after they hang up from the 911 operator. And, always watch the hands—male, female, juvenile, or senior. The hands tell all! Listen and watch for those verbal's and body language cues. They'll tell you what you need to know.

He had rehearsed his set of principles until they rolled off his tongue.

Use a cover that works and never give up the tactical advantage. Rose bushes do not provide cover. Walls and cars do. Your sixth sense matters. If something doesn't feel right, go with your instincts. Call and wait for backup, whether it's a domestic violence situation, an open door, or a car full of characters. Don't have 'tombstone courage.'

Police work is 80% boring and 20% pucker—no apathy, no relaxing, and for sure, no injury or worse, a toe tag. Go home with a clean uniform and no medical treatment.

HH lived it, and if you had the luxury of being his boot out of the academy before you got in the black and white, he would say all this before you even left the station.

CHAPTER 7

||||||||||||||||||||||||||||||||||||||||||||||

THE BOOT

HH reported to the Training Officer Committee meeting on Wednesday of his first week back after vacation. Seven Officers, Sgt. Ron McGinty and Lt. Steve Hobson were in attendance. Lt. Hobson chaired the meeting and went over the essential elements of being a T/O.

In the next six months, HH would be assigned to the Peace Officers Standards and Training (POST) Field Training Officers program. In the meantime, he would be teamed up with a recruit who was currently at the Academy and scheduled to graduate in the next thirty days.

So, I do the job and then get sent to training?

Sgt. McGinty went over the schedule and how the program was going to work. HH would get in touch with his assigned recruit while still in the final phase of academy training and act as a mentor, orient him to OHPD and make him feel at home.

McGinty spoke in his best tactical voice. "The problem with the old T/O program was we were washing people out and not training them. We lost several over the past few years that went to other agencies and were successful. OHPD was getting a bad rap. We revamped the program to give you more latitude with these people and, not just watch them fail, but teach them how to be good officers."

He then handed out the new training manual. "You're expected to read it and know its contents. Use it, and make sure your trainees are proficient in it and do all the required paperwork. Lt. Hobson and I are available for any questions. Anytime. We'll meet once a quarter or if we feel a need to call a meeting. Any questions so far?"

The union president, Greg "the squint" Meacham, posed his typical attorney-type question. "Lieutenant, "he cleared his throat to make sure he could be heard, "how are we going to be assigned these boots? I already have Flowers as a trainee."

"Good question, Meacham," Lt. Hobson responded, feeling it was directed at him. "You'll not receive a new boot until we rotate Flowers to another training officer. She's yours until she completes Phase Two of her training. Then you get another one."

"I figured that, Lt," he said a bit sarcastically, like *don't try to insult my intelligence.* "What about the other T/O's?"

"We'll randomly assign them as we see fit. Any <u>other</u> questions, Meacham?"

HH turned to Hunter McDaniel, or "Tab," as he was called, and muttered, "Why does every Lt. have to be an asshole?" He didn't want or need a reply, but he did get a nod of agreement.

They spent the next hour going through the manual and impressing everyone on the need to do daily, weekly and monthly evaluations. The paperwork was overwhelming. Teaching techniques were discussed of what worked and what did not. McDaniel shared a funny story about a trainee he was assigned a year back that could barely speak English.

"His Spanish was great, but he couldn't put three words together in the English language!'

"How did he get through backgrounds and the Academy?" HH asked incredulously.

"Beats me," McDaniel quipped, "but I think he made Lieutenant!" No one laughed.

McGinty jumped in. "The police academy of today is different than when we went through," waving his arms to include everyone in the room. "While I disagree with it, the Sheriff's Academy doesn't de-select for outside agencies. Their view is to get them through if they pass the academics and physical parts. They let the T/O's sort it out at their agency, and that's you guys."

"When do we get a female T/O, Sarge?" Meacham asked.

"Soon, Meacham, soon. Any <u>other</u> questions?" There were no other questions.

Lt. Hobson then stood up and strolled to each T/O with a packet. "Here are your assigned recruits, boots, probationers, trainees, or whatever you want to call them. The packet contains a copy of their original job application and a progress report from the Orange County Sheriff's academy staff."

HH looked over his papers and saw his first assignment, "Michael Alcazar, a male Hispanic, 24 years old, bilingual and living in Wilmington."

"Well, now I better brush up on my Spanish," HH laughed, looking at McDaniel.

"You may not have to, HH. Your new boot just might be your teacher! But you may have to teach him English."

Elapsed time: 69 minutes

CHAPTER 8

IIIIIIIIIIIIIIIIIIIIIIIIIIIIIIIIIIIIIIIIIIIIIII

OUCH!

HH decided to stay on the "day watch maggot" shift at the request of his family, at least for a little while. It was not his choice.

The last five months had been relatively uneventful, absent the adjudication of his use of force involving the killer of A.J Johnson. It was Thursday, his last shift of the week, and he was ready for briefing, knowing that soon he would have a trainee. He had Alcazar's phone number and would contact him this weekend.

He strolled into briefing five minutes early and went to his reserved seat in the back row. There was a buzz in the room, and he couldn't figure out what it was all about. Had someone else died, been fired, or picked up for a DUI?

Lt. Steve Hospian, the commanding officer of Detectives, and the day watch commander, Sgt. Kip Bennett was in the hallway in a rather animated discussion. Huddles were all around, but on what topic, HH didn't have a clue.

Kip read off-the-beat assignments and looked over the top of their heads to make sure everyone dressed appropriately. It was his way of doing an inspection. He immediately turned it over to Lt. Hospian.

"Jeez, this is early, you guys, but we need to snuff out some rumors here." He unbuttoned the top button of his hundred and fifty-dollar dress shirt and loosened his seventy-five-dollar tie, trying to make a point that some essential shit was coming.

"I received a letter from the District Attorney in charge of our courthouse next door that he was not going to file any cases of ours without some video to go with it."

"What the fu....!" Was the first response. "We don't even have any cameras. Does that mean they won't file any of our cases?" It was Tab Hunter with the outburst that they all would have said.

"Hold on, you guys, hold on!" Hospian was getting a bit exasperated. As he always does, Kip stepped in to calm the waters.

"Relax and listen to what the Lieutenant has to say." Kip had a way about him that whatever he said should be taken seriously. The room went quiet.

"Thanks, Kip. I know we don't even have cameras yet," and he paused for effect, "but they're coming, and soon."

Hospian should have just kept talking, but he paused just long enough for Jimmy "the Greek" Bowen, with his best command baritone voice say, "They may be comin', but I ain't wearin'."

"We'll talk about that later," Hospian said, now becoming frustrated. "Right now, I'm here to tell you the Chief and I have been able to put that D.A. Notice on hold for the time being. Hermosa and Redondo already have cameras, but we've made sure the order is null and void for the South Bay. It didn't come from downtown. It was just our local D.A." He finally had arrived at the point where he could take a breath.

"What he's saying," Kip interpreted, "is that if you talk to your friends from other South Bay agencies, no matter what the local D.A. said, the idea of having the film for every arrest is *NOT* going to be a criterion for filing a case. At least right now. Did I say that right, Lieutenant?" Kip had a way of expressing the rank he was addressing in almost a condescending manner. Many thought he could intimidate the Pope.

"Yeah, that's right, Kip. But what this has also done is give the Chief ammunition to go to the City Council ASAP to get the funds advanced, so we can at least start experimenting with those damn body cameras. So just a word of caution, guys, they are coming, so get ready."

Lt. Hospian took a deep breath and excused himself with a "later" comment.

HH raised his hand as if he was in a classroom and not a roll call briefing. "Sgt. Bennett, sir, is somebody working out all of the gory details on this so that the Greek here won't get fired for refusing to wear a damn body camera?"

Kip looked directly at HH, and with his final comment, silenced the room as only Kip can, "I don't know Hamilton, why don't you ask the Chief? You seem to have a good relationship with him?"

There was no "oooooh, or ahhhhh," just silence as he softly muttered the word, "GTA." Only a few in the briefing knew what that meant.

Elapsed time: 23 minutes

CHAPTER 9

||||||||||||||||||||||||||||||||||||||||||

COMMITTEE

Both of Sgt. Bennett's last few words at briefing resonated with Hamilton. The 'GTA' meant that today if one of his 'favorite officers" picked up a 'rollin stolen,' that is a stolen car with a body in it, instead of a sitting duck, he could impound the car, book the suspect, do the paperwork and then go home. No matter how much time he had left on the shift. The 'duck' was just a stolen car left on the street by some joyrider or crook who was done with it. That didn't count.

Orchard Hill had several 'dump spots.' Kids would steal a car to get from point A to point B and leave it parked for the police to pick up. Kip would get the Community Service Officer meter maids to impound them and get the car returned to the rightful owner. For the coppers, he wanted an arrestee in the car that detectives could work with. Why? Anyone who was a car thief was also involved in other crimes as well. It was always a good arrest, and returning a vehicle to its rightful owner was something to take pride in.

Simpkins was a master at locating GTA's or Grand Theft Auto on the street. HH had a thing for sniffing out guns, so today, he would be the one to find a stolen car and go home early. There was no Donny Simpkins working today, so HH stood a good chance of finding that stolen car and getting off early to go home. But the first comment from Kip bugged him.

"Why would he say I had a good relationship with the Chief? Was it that obvious? That would not bode well with everyone else," he thought. *"Our last Chief was here his entire career, as well as mine, but I said hello to him, maybe*

three times. This guy from LA has been here just over one year, and it seemed like we were friends. But how did Kip know?"

Bennett's unmistaken voice bellowed, "Hamilton, see me before you hit the streets." HH knew it was not a suggestion.

"Reporting as ordered, Sgt. Bennett," he said with a smile after getting his equipment and black and white ready for the day.

"I didn't mean to catch you off guard with that comment, HH but, here, read this." He handed him a memo from the Chief. "Please notify the following Officers they have been assigned to sit on a working committee to select the best body cameras and assist in writing the policies for their use. This matter is of utmost importance and should be considered as a primary duty assignment. Overtime is authorized." The names of others were on it, with 'Howard Hamilton' in the middle of an alphabetized list.

"That's what I was referring to about your relationship with the new Chief. You must have made an impression on him," Kip said. "Looks like this is becoming a major priority with every Department today. Nobody trusts us anymore. Too bad."

HH wasn't thinking about the committee. He thought Kip's comment was related to his use of force case and wondered how anyone, even Sgt. Bennett would know about it so soon. He was relieved that it was a committee assignment and not about the Chief overruling Captain Markham on his case.

"Hey," Bennett said, almost apologizing. "I'll clear up my comment at the briefing tomorrow. Oh, wait, we're off after today. I'll do it next week. Don't want to give our shift the idea we have a snitch here," he smiled, but HH knew what he meant. That was as close to an apology you would get from him.

Time to hit the streets and find that 'rollin stolen' or whatever is out there, he said to no one.

Elapsed time: 23 minutes

CHAPTER 10

||||||||||||||||||||||||||||||||||||||||||

CRAFTSMAN

After satisfying himself that all was right with the world, or at least with Bennett, he jumped in his favorite black and white, unit 885, and hit the streets. He tapped the 'clear' button on his mobile digital terminal, or MDT, letting dispatch know he was available for calls.

While most of the shift went to Starbucks almost immediately, or two at a time, as the Department Manual dictated, he was off to *his* spot, Peet's. The only OHPD people he might run into were John "Red" Walker or Mel Flowers. Flowers was on the graveyard shift, but it wouldn't be long before she found her way to the day watch. He would do whatever he could *not* to be her training officer. He recruited her, so someone else can train her, he thought.

He was just pulling into the Peet's parking lot when the dispatcher broke his train of thought. "L75, L75, monitor your screen for details. See the woman at 949 Kensington Rd, a welfare check." He hit the ACK/INR or acknowledge and in-route button, ran in to get his au lait and the multigrain scone. Sophia, his personal 'barista,' saw him coming, and his regular order was waiting.

He quickly paid with his pre-paid Peet's debit card, only losing thirty seconds in the response time. He had it down to a science!

He knew exactly where he was going. Then it hit him! The last welfare check he did on Kensington was at the behest of Sgt. Biddle. He found Ginny Karsdon, the sister of the Orchard Hill car mogul David Karsdon, savagely killed in a ritualistic, occult murder by her gardener, plumber, and electrician. Was this to be a rerun of that case?

The Karsdon case was in the 400 block of Kensington, a street lined with old Victorian homes. The 900 block was utterly different. As he pulled to the curb, he recalled these were more of the Craftsman style of homes. Large porches, old wooden floors; not as much character as a Victorian, but still very recognizable. The style had been perfected for California and made famous in the 1930s and '40s.

He could see the low-pitched roof with multiple intersecting gables and the exposed rafter tails that were the Craftsman style's hallmark.

How many homes today have real, honest to goodness porches like these? he asked himself.

The exterior was a typical shadow grey with a stone retaining wall surrounding the front yard and more stonework climbing up the exterior fireplace to the chimney. The entrance was a cobbled walkway right out of Avignon, France. The steps led to an elevated entrance.

As was his habit, he parked one door down from the home and checked the neighborhood. He hit the *'at scene'* button, saw a few people in front of their homes but no reporting person or RP. As he alighted from his car, he noticed the door of a Ford F-150 open, directly across the street. A lady dressed in shorts and a light-colored blouse who appeared to be in her early forties waved and approached him.

"Did you call?" he asked as the first order of business.

"I did," was her response. "My dad lives here, and I've left phone messages and knocked on the door, and there's no answer. I'm concerned because he's almost eighty and...well, you know."

"What's your name, Ma'am?" HH asked.

"Terry Coyle, but my friends call me Tac. It's my initials."

"When was the last time you saw or spoke to him?" While he asked that question, he was thinking of the Ginny Karsdon case. *Oh, no, not another one*, he told himself. *Why does this happen to me?*

"Do you have a key to the house?" he asked.

"No, but maybe there's one in a planter or something."

"Let's go knock a bit louder," he offered, walking to the front door.

It was a two-story home, well maintained, with two identical pots of arborvitae with alyssum and ivy cascading over the sides greeting you.

There was a built-in bench on the right side of the porch. He checked the mailbox and noted no mail, which was a good thing. He hammered on the door with his trusty baton but to no avail.

"Stay here in the front. I'm going to the backyard." He walked around the house and found the back door. It was a simply maintained backyard with grass, more flower pots, and a small covered patio.

Even though it was daylight, he brought his MAG flashlight, just in case, remembering the Karsdon case. He tried the back door.

Bingo, it was unlocked! Now the fun was to begin.

CHAPTER 11

||||||||||||||||||||||||||||||||||||||||||||||||||

GUY

HH paused for a few minutes to collect his thoughts. This was bringing back the memory of Ginny and discovering her dead body. Should he call for backup? There was no sign of danger or foul play.

What's the worst thing that could happen? He would find Mr. Coyle either injured or dead, right? He can handle this.

Better yet, he would call the RP and go in with her. Again, there was no reason to think that he or Tac was in harm's way as she asked to be called. He backed off the back steps of the house and called down the side of the house.

"Tac, can you come to the backyard?"

She immediately responded, and he advised her of the open door.

"I guess I should have checked the back door, Officer. Thanks," she said, somewhat embarrassed.

"I'll just stick around until you see if your Dad is okay if you don't mind."

"Not a bit," she said as she stepped into the house with a, "Hey Dad, are you in there?"

There was no answer. Hamilton followed her lead. Craftsman floor plans are generally laid out very simply. They have few hallways, with rooms flowing one into another. The high level of detail is designed for the functional living that it accommodates. With many built-in pieces, from cabinetry to benches and seating areas, there was little furniture. What was there was all in place and not disturbed.

"Mr. Coyle was, I mean is, a bit of a neat freak," he said to Tac.

"Oh, yes, that's my Dad. He was a cop too, you know."

"Oh?" HH responded, a bit surprised. He didn't know why he was taken aback, but he was.

As they started to climb the wide, steep, creaking stairs, he felt like they could give way. HH heard a door open down the hallway of the top flight.

HH and Tac both looked down the hall as they reached the top stair step and were met with, "Terry, is that you? And who's that with you?"

What a relief, HH said to himself. *He's alive!*

"Dad, don't be mad, but I've been ringing the doorbell and knocking forever. I called the house, and there was no answer. I thought maybe…" she paused just enough to give her father a chance to complete the sentence.

"You thought maybe I was dead?"

"Well, no… just maybe injured and couldn't get up or answer the phone."

"Well, young lady, I didn't want to be bothered, so I turned on the answering machine and shut the door to my little office space. Couldn't hear a darn thing."

If truth is known, Dad, you can't hear when we stand next to you," Tac said in a rather loving manner, not trying to be harsh. After all, he was alive!

"Well, if you must know, I've started to write my memoirs. I've been locking myself in for four hours every morning and getting started. Need to concentrate, you know. Not as easy as it used to be."

"I am so sorry, Officer Hamilton, we were so wrapped up with this I didn't introduce myself. I'm Guy Coyle, retired LAPD."

"Officer Howard Hamilton, sir, but how did you know *my* name?"

"Ha, it's on your breast pocket, big as life!"

HH was red in the face at this apparent faux pa.

Guy Coyle was laughing way too hard for the circumstances. "I'm not laughing at you, Officer Hamilton. I'm laughing with you. For most of my time on the streets, we never had nameplates. We were anonymous out there. That's just one of the many things that have changed over the years."

CHAPTER 12

||||||||||||||||||||||||||||||||||||||||||

COFFEE

After more small talk, HH and Coyle said their good bye's. Tac thanked him for helping resolve her 'uncomfortable' feeling. Heading back to his black and white, he was surprised to find that Coyle followed him to the curb without his daughter.

He talked in a low voice so as not to be overheard. "Tac's my oldest, Officer, so I hope you don't mind if she gets worried."

HH quickly countered. "Not at all, sir. I understand. When did you retire?" he asked to change the subject.

"December of 2000. A long time ago."

"Have you lived here since then?"

"Nope. Been here about five years now. After my last divorce." There was a silence on both sides for that statement. "Hazards of the job, I guess."

"I hope not," HH said rather clumsily. "If I could ask, what rank were you when you left or retired?"

"Oh, I retired alright. Almost forty years. Was a lieutenant two. We have two ranks of Lieutenant, and I was a two."

HH had to ask, out of his total ignorance, "is that higher or lower than a one?"

"Higher. 5 ½% higher."

"Got it. Sorry, I had to ask, we only have one rank of Lieutenant," *and most of them are assholes. Was Coyle an asshole?*

"The reason I moved here was because of your City's reputation for catching the bad guys. Even Orchard Hill has them, but OHPD seems to be very good at it. I read the papers, and it seems your city and your Chief, who I knew as a young pup in LA, are getting great press. Better than we ever could."

"We get lucky, I guess," HH said with a sense of shyness.

"Take the luck! And thanks again. Drop by for a cup sometime. I would love to talk police work with you. I do miss it. It'd be good for me."

"Do you drink Peet's coffee, Lieutenant Coyle?"

"Officer Hamilton, may I call you Howard? If I can, you can call me Guy."

"Yes, you can call me Howard, but I may have some difficulty calling you Guy. But I'll work on it, sir."

"And yes, I drink Peet's coffee. If you have time, I have a quick story to tell you about that."

"Dad, Dad," Tac shouted with evident frustration from the Craftsman porch, "let Officer Hamilton go! He's got better things to do than chat with you!"

Guy Coyle immediately apologized for taking up Hamilton's time and excused himself. As he backed away from the black and white that for years he called home, he whispered:

"Come by for coffee. Just make sure you don't see her car here." He smiled and walked away.

He agreed to stop by. As he typed in the 'welfare check' disposition on his computer, he noticed a message on the screen. *"Sometime today, drop by Human Resources and see Sgt. Rydell"*.

"Wonder what HR wants with me?" No calls were pending, so before he got too busy, he decided to return to the station to see Sgt. Rydell.

No time like the present!

Time elapsed; 23 minutes.

CHAPTER 13

|||||||||||||||||||||||||||||||||||||||||||||||||

SPECTOR

Sgt. Blair Rydell's nickname was 'Golden" for several reasons. He was being fast-tracked to be the next Lieutenant, Captain, or who knows what. He was also a 'golden boy' because of his last name. The fifties and early sixties performer, Bobby Rydell, was now teamed up with two other fifties performers, Fabian and Frankie Avalon. The three were dubbed the "Golden Boys," so his nickname was a 'twofer.'

Sgt. Rydell was head of background investigations for new hires. Working out of HR, his office was down the hall from the Chief. For almost two years, Hamilton had prided himself on not even going to the third floor. A bad habit! Now he was making it a habit.

"Need to chat, HH." Rydell's demeanor was as smooth as his silk tie.

Must get his clothes the same place Hospian does, HH mused.

"How's Patrol?"

"Good! I love it, but this day stuff is killing me."

Blair Rydell and HH had worked together briefly on a few projects. They had never worked in a radio car together, but HH liked him. Not because he was just a co-worker. Rydell had been a good street cop and, even though he had this 'cushy' job, had not let it go to his head.

Regular guy. Had not changed…yet. Maybe when he's a Lieutenant, he will. They all do.

"Sorry to bring you off the street, but this is kind of important." Rydell motioned for HH to sit and casually closed his office door.

Oh, Oh, he thought, what's going on here?

"HH, what I have to talk to you about is strictly confidential. No one else, other than the Chief and I, and now you, know this. Well, I had to tell Captain Pierson, but that's who I work for. So, I guess there's the four of us. Probably too many, but others will eventually find out, so we need to ensure at least the four of us have all the facts."

What could be so crucial as to cloak all of this in such a hushed-up manner?

"You were just assigned a new hire who's still in the Academy. Michael Alcazar, right?"

"Yeah, I was going to chat with him this weekend. I figured he was busy during the week. Should I have made the connection earlier? What's goin' on, Sarge?"

"Well, I'll try to give you the short version, so bear with me. I did his background and had some real concerns. Hey, this is confidential shit here, Hamilton." Rydell looked around like the room could be bugged.

"I got it!" Hamilton said, sitting up just a little straighter in his chair.

"We," and he raised his hands, "really like this kid," obviously referring to the Department and those in the know.

"That's good. We only take the good ones, I hope."

"Yeah, we do get to be a bit picky, but Alcazar has a little; how can I say it? Baggage."

"Well, I guess we all have a little baggage coming into this job," HH agreed.

"Alcazar went to Banning High in Wilmington. Grew up there with his brother and mother. No father in the picture."

"Lot of gangs in Wilmington," HH added.

"Yeah, but did you know that Banning's best-known graduate was Vince Ferragamo, quarterback for the L. A. Rams? He took them to the Super Bowl back in 1980. His brother, Chris, was their football coach later. I know because they kicked our ass. I went to Pedro High. Oh, well, they got beat by the Steelers, who had Terry Bradshaw. Anyway, where was I?"

"You were, I mean, I mentioned that there are a lot of gangs in Wilmington."

"And that's where I'm going with this, HH."

"Is he, or was he a gang member? I thought we didn't hire bangers?"

"We don't. Have you ever heard of the street name 'Spector'?"

"Sounds familiar."

"Spector was killed last year. I'll go into that later. He was a member of the Will/Ord street gang. And a leader. Will/Ord is a Wilmington…"

"I know about Will/Ord, Sarge. They're a third-generation gang in the Wilmington/Long Beach area and pretty active. Go on."

"Active isn't the word for it. Every year they battle the Harb Boys. The Harb Boys are…"

I know the Harb Boys too, Sarge. They're an LA City/ LA County gang along the strip and border Orchard Hill."

"Ok, yeah, I know you know, but I got to tell you all this, Ok?"

"Got it."

"Well, for the last five years, those two gangs were trading off killing a member of each other's gang, on the anniversary of the first execution in 2012. You don't need to know the particulars, but they seem to celebrate every year, and last year it was Will/Ord's turn in the barrel. We're coming up on it being the Harb Boys turn."

HH was getting lost in the storyline, so he stopped Rydell, holding up his hand. "OK, what does all of this have to do with me and this recruit, Michael Alcazar? I guess I can ask that question, can't I?"

"Sure can, but first, 'Spector' got his nickname from some guy Phil Spector who was a crazy lunatic that always waved a gun around and killed for the fun of it. I don't know what his hero was all about, but this guy did the same."

HH smiled to himself because he knew who Phil Spector was, even if he didn't know this 'Spector. "Phil Spector was a Hollywood record producer who was a bit of a druggy and is currently doing time for killing a girl at his house in Alhambra."

Oh," Rydell said. "You seem to know more about this than I do."

"Oh, no, Sarge. I just knew who he was. I don't know what you know. What do you know?"

"Well, I know that our Spector's real name is, or was, Manuel Alcazar. Michael's younger brother. Your Michael Alcazar, and now, our Michael Alcazar!"

CHAPTER 14

||||||||||||||||||||||||||||||||||||||||||||||||||||

ULTIMATE

"Our most important concern about Alcazar," Sgt. Rydell said, "is the way Spector was killed. Well, I hate to use the term but rather spectacularly."

"What do you mean?" HH queried.

He sighed, "Well, each year, the homicide exchange seemed to escalate in intensity and drama. Let me show you." Rydell opened another folder on his desk with photos. "I obtained copies of these from LAPD's homicide unit that works the Harbor Area. Here's a 'before' picture of Manuel."

HH studied a series of pre-booking photos from what was presumed to be one of his arrests. He wore a wife-beater tank top to show his muscles and tattoos and 'a fuck the world' facial expression. At the same time, he did resemble Michael.

"You can see that he had tat ropes on his neck, sleeves of dragons and shit, and one teardrop on the right side of the face, just below the eye. "You know what that means, don't you, HH?"

"Unfortunately, I do." Was his reply.

"He also had a large tat across his chest that said, 'Wilm/Ord,' in fancy script."

"Not surprising," HH said.

"Well, here's another photo of Alcazar, this one not so pleasant." Rydell pulled an eight by ten from the folder and turned it so that HH could get the full effect.

The photo depicted Alcazar on his back, near a tree trunk in freshly planted grass, at what appeared to be a park area. As if a car had driven over the grass, there were mud tracks, spun its wheels, and dug up everything surrounding the body. Across Alcazar's chest were muddy tire tracks directly over the "Wilm/Ord" tattoo. There was a single bullet hole on the side of the ear, with dried blood that oozed out onto the muddy grass.

"The ultimate 'fuck you,' HH said rather quietly.

"To Alcazar, the gang, and his family," Rydell added for emphasis. "And I guess to the community and us as well. Like saying catch us if you can. Pretty vicious."

"Looks like some good trace evidence with the tire tracks and all," HH commented.

"Yeah, LA guys thought so too, but it was a Long Beach stolen that was recovered in Pedro. Burned beyond recognition down at the docks."

"When did this happen?" he asked and caught himself. "Oh, I see the date on the photo. Just about six months ago. If they make the killings annually, it means we only have six months to prevent the next one."

"HH, you are an eternal optimist," Rydell said very straightforward. "I tell you all of this so that you can go in with your eyes wide open with Michael. You need to know what you're getting into."

"What's the rest of his family like?"

Well, he's twenty-four and lives with his mother in Wilmington. No other family that we know of. As I said, no dad in the picture, but I'll let him tell you the rest of the story." Rydell folded his notebook, collected the photos, signaling the meeting was over.

"Any more surprises, Sarge?" HH asked, hoping for a negative reply.

"Sure! Get this. Lillie, his Mom, is a volunteer at the police station in the Harbor. She also has a small bakery in downtown Wilmington and bakes wedding cakes."

"Ok, and…," HH queried.

"Well, she always knew about the weddings, wakes, and birthday celebrations in the community and kept the Harbor Gang Unit up-to-date. When it came to the gang events, the unit was always deployed around the area, and that kept the shootings down."

"Incredible!" was all HH could muster.

"Oh, yes, but from the seat here in HR, there is a surprise every day. You couldn't believe what we see and hear. The type of applicants we get," waving his hand across the desk, "could write a book. They used to say that, hey, we're just recruiting from the human race, but lately, I'm not so sure. All that said, Michael is a good one, so train him well, Hamilton, train him well!"

"Will do my best, sir, if my best is good enough." *Yes, I do. But I have my doubts.*

Elapsed time: 23 minutes.

CHAPTER 15

||||||||||||||||||||||||||||||||||||||||||||||||

TRAFFIC

Hamilton took the weekend to sort out how he was going to deal with Alcazar. He had to think about being upfront and at the same time not insult him or show any bias for his family situation.

Not everybody grew up in idyllic Orchard Hill, he knew, but this would require a more direct approach. After all, this was police work. He had to be confident this guy could be a warrior and not against the department.

He was good at compartmentalizing the issues he faced. Alcazar was this weekend. His shift and getting through today were utmost on his mind. But he was thinking about those damn body cameras. He knew that many agencies had adopted them as a partial solution, but he'd also heard the horror stories. Stupid policies like requiring video to file a case were just typical.

"Not going to happen at OHPD," he mused. Just something else to think about other than family and fun.

"L75, L75, a traffic collision, auto versus Ped, 19th Street School. Ambulance en route. See the Principal."

"L75 Roger, but no traffic units available?"

"L75, no, they're all on a training day," was the reply.

"Great," He muttered. He hated traffic calls. They take too much time away from real police work.

He placed himself 'in route' and was there in less than three minutes. 19th Street Elementary was where Geoff and Marcia had gone a few years back. He wondered if that same old sour-faced Principal, Mr. Sledge was still there.

He arrived in front of the school just as the ambulance left the scene with the victim. The new Principal introduced herself. Ms. Goffney was an attractive, light-skinned black lady, late 30's and dressed to the nines.

The school was in mid-semester, so they had settled into how they conducted business, trained the students, and, more importantly, trained the parents. But apparently, not all were on board with the plan.

"The driver of the car," she said, pointing to a white Escalade, "...that hit Owen is in my office. She's shaken up, Officer...Hamilton," reading his nametag.

"Can we talk before we go to my office and see Mrs. Kendall?"

"Sure," Hamilton nodded and followed her to a lunch table in the yard.

She looked at him very seriously for a moment. "I want to assure you we want to cooperate in this investigation, but you need to know what's been going on here."

So far, he only said one word, and another was forthcoming now.

"Okay."

"First, my brother Kyle is an LAPD Officer, so I know a bit of what goes on. I was transferred here from Estates Elementary on the Hill. I was VP, oh, I'm sorry, Vice Principal. I didn't mean to talk teacher talk, but I figured you would know, right?"

HH smiled but let her continue. Then his radio interrupted.

"L75, your victim has been transported to South Bay Emergency. ER number there is...." Dispatch gave him the direct line to get an update on the victim.

He copied down the number but almost knew it by heart anyway. "L75, Roger, will contact them ASAP."

Another one-word conversation opener, "Sorry."

"No problem," Ms. Goffney said, even though he could tell she did not like to be interrupted.

"You have an Officer Dean Harris, right?"

"Yes."

"Well, I can tell you that the teachers, and the parents, are highly upset with him. I was going to go down to the station to complain. I just have not found the time to do it yet. I guess I'll take it out on you. Can I file a complaint with you?"

"Well, Sergeants usually handle the complaints but, what seems to be the problem?"

"Oh, and you're not a sergeant? What are those stripes on your arm?"

"A sergeant has three stripes, Ms. Goffney. I just have two. I'm a training officer."

"I see," she muttered. "Ok, well, back to your Officer Harris. He rides a motorcycle and has been ticketing my parents every morning. Then they come in to complain, but no one will go downtown to talk to someone. They think I'll handle it." She looked more exasperated than relieved she got it off her chest.

"What were they cited for? If you know."

"Double parking. They stop on the street in front of the school and run around the car's passenger side to walk their child to the school's front. Then run back after dropping them off with a teacher's aide. In the meantime, Officer Harris writes them up for double parking!" Goffney was now a little more relaxed after explaining her frustration.

"Ms. Goffney..."

"Call me Amanda, please," she interrupted.

"Maybe later," he said, but thinking, maybe not.

"Let me call the hospital and get some vital information and an update on our victim."

"Oh, I'm so sorry," Amanda said sincerely. "I was interrupting your work, Officer Hamilton. I'll be in my office with Mrs. Kendall."

Hamilton placed the call and found the parents had arrived at the hospital. Owen Browning was not in critical condition but did have several broken bones, including a leg, arm, and jaw. Nothing that wouldn't heal.

He walked into the Principal's Office, this time as an officer and not a parent. A sturdy, dark wood desk with a cushioned chair and two smaller chairs for those with business to conduct. The position and symbols of authority are always there.

Funny how time changes our positions, our intentions, and our perspective. The thought amused him as he took the only other small chair left.

He was introduced to Dawn Kendall. One look told him everything.

Mrs. Kendall was the dreaded soccer Mom extraordinaire! Blond ponytail, running shoes, and black speckled yoga pants with a light mint green sweatshirt. And an attitude.

CHAPTER 16

||||||||||||||||||||||||||||||||||||||||||||||||

ADMISSION

Dawn Kendall was the coach of one of the soccer teams that competed against Marcia's team. Hamilton didn't know her but heard enough through Clare and the soccer mom's grapevine. She was foul-mouthed, aggressive, and very strong-willed. And, those were her good qualities.

He didn't know whether she recognized him or not. He did not indicate that he knew her or even knew of her. The introductions were cordial, and Ms. Goffney excused herself, realizing that some interview or interrogation would occur.

"Mrs. Kendall, I'm Officer Howard Hamilton, and I'm investigating this incident. All I need from you is a driver's license, insurance card, and your current registration."

She provided all three documents in silence.

"I want you to feel as comfortable as possible, Mrs. Kendall," referring to her in the most formal of manners to impress upon her the seriousness of the situation.

"Am I, like, under arrest?" she stuttered.

"No, Ma'am. I just need a statement as to what happened. This isn't a criminal investigation. It's merely to gather the facts for a report that will eventually end up with your insurance company."

"How's the boy?"

"He'll live, Ms. Kendall, but has several broken bones." She started to cry uncontrollably. Hamilton waited a moment and went to the door.

"Mrs. Goffney, can you bring us some water?"

She drank the glass as if she had been surviving in the desert for a week.

"Can I have another?"

"Sure," and Hamilton made the request again.

"I was on my way to the gym after dropping off my boy and was really in a hurry."

"Ok." Hamilton was back to the one-word interrogation technique. He felt like Carl Jung, the psychiatrist. Dr. Jung never said much but elicited emotion after emotion from his patients.

"Tell me what happened, Ms. Kendall, in your own words," as he turned on his pocket recorder.

"As I said, I was driving my son to school and couldn't find a damn parking space. I hadn't seen that damn motor cop yet. Oh, sorry," She said it, realizing it was too late not to offend.

"I thought he might be harassing - I mean ticketing - somebody else." She was getting a little flustered as she tried to choose her words more selectively.

"I couldn't find a parking place in front, so I stopped my car, ran around to get Aiden, my son, and went to the back of the car to get his books. I walked him to the front of the school and turned him over to the teacher's aide."

She was talking faster than her brain could engage. "I was coming back to my SUV when I saw my car rolling down the street. I screamed, but there was so much going on, I don't think anybody heard it. I don't think anyone could have done anything anyway." She stopped to collect her thoughts one more time and take another sip of water.

"Well, it wouldn't have mattered, I guess, because it just rolled into the street, hit that boy, and ran up the curb and into a tree. My husband is going to kill me!"

After realizing what she said, she tried to correct herself with, "are you sure I'm not under arrest, Officer? Is the boy going to be alright?"

Hamilton read his notes back to her for review. "Did you set the parking brake?"

"I don't know."

"Did you turn on your hazard lights? Your blinkers? Use the emergency brake?"

"I don't think so."

"But you do remember putting it into park, right?"

"Oh, yes, Officer, I put it in park. I always put it in park."

"What happened that the car moved if you put it in park?"

"It must have slipped out of park. By accident," she resigned herself, knowing she didn't secure the gear shift or put the emergency brake on or activate her hazard lights.

With her statement, the ambulance taking Owen to the hospital, and the parents waiting for him to arrive, he was done. He obtained a few more witness statements, including a classmate of Owens' and another teacher. Same story.

After he took a few photos, the Auto Club towed her car. He had checked the gearshift, hazard lights, and emergency brake. All were working as expected. "Just being thorough," he said to no one.

As he was getting into his black and white to head to the hospital, Dawn Kendall approached him on the driver's side of the car.

"Your Marcia's dad, right?"

"Yes, Ma'am. I'm Marcia's dad."

"She's an excellent soccer player. You should be proud. I tried to get her on my team, but...." Kendall realized she had gone one step too far.

"I hope the boy is going to be okay. Will you give that message to his parents?"

"Of course, Mrs. Kendall, of course," putting Shop 885 in drive and slowly pulled from the curb.

CHAPTER 17

||||||||||||||||||||||||||||||||||||||||||||

HOUND

Before heading to the hospital to meet the Brownings and complete his report, he took a tour around the school's streets. He had driven past many times before, but not in an official capacity if there was such a thing. He saw kids playing basketball and kicking a soccer ball around and handball games being played. Cars were parked in the lot, on the street, and into the surrounding neighborhoods.

He headed to the hospital, thinking about the germination of an idea. He needed to talk to Harris, the motor cop, who was pissing off all the moms and probably many of the teachers as well.

Dean Harris had joined the Department about a year after Hamilton. He was on bike patrol right off probation and then applied for motors, got on the list, and overcame a very grueling motor school to pass up guys with more seniority. The word was out that all he wanted to do was ride a motor from the time he got out of the academy. No one was upset, not because he was a good rider, but for who his father was - or is.

Wally Harris was a slick, good-looking Ronald Coleman type detective. Coleman had been a forties movie star with chiseled looks, a pencil-thin mustache that looked painted on, and dressed like he was a fashion model. Wally Harris had been on the Department for twenty-five years and was currently in charge of the Burglary detail at OHPD. Dean was his oldest son.

It was well known that Wally was a playboy, or in the police world, a 'cock hound.' He would tap anything he could and still plead innocent. If you held a snake, well...

Rumor had it years ago he was caught by the City Manager getting a head job in the City Hall parking lot late one night. Nothing was done because the person he was with was the Chief's young secretary, administrative assistant, Janet. It all went quietly away, but the City Manager and Janet had come to an understanding.

Janet had been looking for a husband within the Department, but Wally was looking for a blow job. Janet found a husband about a year later. The timing was perfect because the day Wally told everyone that he was getting a divorce, Janet announced she was engaged to the Department's Juvenile Diversion psychologist/counselor, Theodore 'Ted' Rankin. Rankin's nickname was appropriate 'Teddy Bear.' And not just for the song, but for the stuffed animals in the kiddy room next to his office.

At the time of Wally's divorce, his son was fifteen years old, so that would have been over fifteen years ago, Hamilton thought, way before he came on the job.

Almost immediately, Wally Harris married again. This time he did it right, marrying a young, wealthy widow from the Hill that had been the victim of a burglary. She quickly had a baby boy that grew up around the OHPD detective squad room and now was in the Academy, slated to graduate in a few months.

Hamilton had heard that James, don't call me 'Jimmy' - Harris, was even a better kid than Dean and more motivated. Regardless, everybody knew that Wally didn't have to work but loved the job so much that he chose to work, even though his wife had inherited a lot of money.

So, why the long story about Harris's? Everyone, even the newspapers, thought that having three Harris boys in the same Department was unique. The most exciting part was that the two boys were stepbrothers from two different mothers. It made for jokes of large proportions over the years, even when James had not been a member of the Department.

At OHPD, there are all sorts of things to amuse ourselves, Hamilton thought, as he pulled into the parking lot at South Bay Emergency.

Elapsed time; 46 minutes.

CHAPTER 18

IIIIIIIIIIIIIIIIIIIIIIIIIIIIIIIIIIIIIIIIIIIIIIII

STALLIONS

Second-grader Owen Browning was resting comfortably in the emergency room. Both loving parents were hovering and speaking words of encouragement. Hamilton obtained the information he needed, talked to the station nurse. She advised him that Owen would have surgery in a few hours and would probably be hospitalized for three or four days.

The diagnosis was no head injury, just a broken femur, arm, and jaw, all to be reset. The road rash would be more painful. He'd be fine and able to return to school in about a month.

He thanked the parents and advised them that a report would be available in a few days, but they would probably hear from Kendall's insurance company, the Auto Club. He also gave them the message from Mrs. Kendall she was sorry. Hamilton took one last look at Owen and reflected on how he would feel if this had been Geoff or Marcia.

Devastated, he thought, just devastated. He reminded himself to give them each a special hug and kiss tonight—just a little tighter and a little longer.

He requested and received approval for Code 7, lunch, and went to his favorite spot, In-and-Out, for a protein burger, two patties, cheese, animal style. He took it to go and decided to go to Kensington Park, a place of solitude that was hardly used to its fullest potential. At least during the week.

Orchard Hill parks were famous for their landscaping and deep, dense settings. Much of the park was maintained by residents through an agreement with the City. The grounds took one back to a simpler time, as one could envision horse-drawn carriages pulled by magnificent stallions that pranced rather than trot.

Hamilton took the time to think about those damn video cameras and the impact on the Department and the public. To hell with the suspects and arrestees, he thought. It would only be to their detriment. But the public outcry for the wearing of body video cameras was deafening.

It will be a game-changer, he thought, just like when they put radios in patrol cars. There were body-worn radios, shotguns, long rifles, ballistic vests, PR 24's or batons, and TASERS all over the past decades. Body-worn cameras would not solve everything or be the 'silver bullet' like the media and police activists think. Like any new tool or piece of technology, the key will be the developed policies and training.

With a vanilla shake washing down the protein two-by-two burger, it struck him that, more than the video, it was the audio that was going to be the key.

What if the camera angle isn't right? The sounds and conversation will get picked up to aid the viewer in painting a picture of what happened. The audio picks up the sounds of the incident, including the officer's words, suspect, and perhaps even witnesses. It'll pick up sounds of a baton or TASER being deployed. The number of shots fired. The sound will give you emotion, the out-of-breath foot pursuit, or the tenseness of a situation. It could even portray an attitude on either side of a conversation.

Hamilton had already resolved that he was probably pro body camera or dashcam. Some guys didn't want to be filmed, but the times and police work were changing, and OHPD needed to change with them. The cameras could be used successfully in civil cases, particularly for 'he said, she said' complaints or other false complaints that have no basis of fact.

He hoped the Chief put things together so that everybody else will buy into it. Otherwise, the OHPOA will eat him up. Hamilton took a notepad and made a list of his questions:

Was it going to be mandatory, just like we do our vests?

What are the penalties for NOT having it on?

What is the best field of vision the cameras on the market have? Does it match human vision?

What is the quality of the lenses? Are they HD?

How do we settle the enormous conflict when human perception and memory become dramatically different than what is recorded on camera?

Is the video public or evidentiary and only subject to a formal discovery?

Easy turn-on-turn-off or voice-activated?

How about a casual conversation with my partner, trainee, a cell phone call to my wife, or even hallway conversations.

Does the Chief wear one when in uniform?

What if I accidentally delete something?

What if another officer is taping me? Do they have to tell me?

Who stores this video? Is it digital? On thumb drives? How long does the Department keep them?

If one malfunction while in the field, do I come in and get another?

How do we handle things where it only recorded partial events, like when I forget to turn it on in an incident I thought was routine, but it then escalated before I could activate it? Kind of like Rodney King.

If the scene is video recorded, can I say in my report, "see the video?"

Are there mounting options? Add another pound to our uniform belt or chest?

Will they hold up in inclement weather?

How are they for nighttime use? Do we carry floodlights too?

What's the battery life? Do they stand up for an entire ten-hour shift? Can it draw power from my car, like a cell phone?

Hamilton laughed at the list he developed while on his forty-five-minute C-7.

"I'm ready for the meeting!" he quipped. "Bring it on."

CHAPTER 19

||||||||||||||||||||||||||||||||||||||||||||

FRIDAY

Hamilton always looked forward to his days off. After four ten-hour days in a row in uniform, it was time for blue jeans, a tee-shirt, and casual shoes. And family.

Friday was the wind-down day with Clare while the kids were in school. Yoga, coffee in the morning, and honey do's were always looked forward to. Saturday was soccer for Marcia and Geoff, shopping as a family, and yard work. He opted not to talk about Dawn Kendall and the traffic accident. It was not his story to tell.

He was planning to call Michael Alcazar, just to introduce himself. As he was getting ready for a yoga class with Clare, his cell phone rang. He looked at the screen and saw the prefix numbers were from the station, but he didn't recognize the extension number. Against his better judgment, he answered.

"This is Howard," was his standard greeting.

"Officer Hamilton, Sgt. Rydell here."

"Hey, Sarge, to what do I owe this pleasure? On a day off?"

"I think you may have wanted me to give you a call after you hear what I have to say."

"Okay, shoot."

"I just received a call from the Orange County Sheriff's Academy. They forgot to notify us they're releasing the cadets next week for a ride-along with their agency. As you know, they have their recruit trainees, and they handle them. The outside agencies weren't notified until today. The bottom line is you'll have Alcazar riding with you starting on Monday for four days."

Hamilton let some silence pass as he thought about it.

"Was I right? Would you have wanted me to let you know?" Rydell asked rather innocently.

"Yeah, I guess so, Sarge. I was going to call him this weekend anyway to introduce myself. Now it's even more important."

Rydell added, "I'll handle the paperwork and let your Captain know because we have two other training officers to notify. They're getting their cadets too. We get these kinds of screw-ups occasionally, so no big deal."

"No big deal for you, but my next week will surely be different. Was not planning on it this quick. Better brush up on my training skills," Hamilton responded.

"You'll be fine, Howard. You're one of our best. See you on Monday." Rydell quickly signed off and left Hamilton staring at his cell phone.

Hamilton knew that being a training officer was one of the most important parts of police work. He wanted his stamp on this kid. It was going to be a challenge, but he could handle it. His job was to transition Alcazar from the academic setting of the Academy to street duty. Just because he may graduate doesn't necessarily mean he will be a good street cop. Alcazar's updates on the law were better than his because he had the most recent information. But Howard knew the streets and how to do the job.

The ball was going to be in his court, the Training Officers Committee and Sgt. Rydell's, to make sure a gang banger did not infiltrate the OHPD. It will be up to him to determine if this guy will be acceptable and eventually become a solo patrol officer for OHPD.

The Department had done its job. They tested him with a written exam, he passed the physical fitness and psychological test, was more than likely medically fit, and Rydell did his background. The Academy was almost ready to have him graduate. Now, it would be HH's responsibility.

Was he ready for it?

CHAPTER 20

||||||||||||||||||||||||||||||||||||||||||||

WARRIOR

His day was already starting different than expected. But it was time for yoga with Clare, their yogi friends, and Maru, their instructor. They walked into Yoga Bungalow with their mats in hand, greeting everyone and selecting their favorite spot to place their mats, towels, and belts. Her belt was grey with stripes of magenta. His was solid black and longer to accommodate his larger frame.

Maru prepared for the class by distributing two blocks and a blanket to each class member. There was the usual number of students, perhaps ten to twelve, but Hamilton never paid much attention to who was and was not there.

Clare was engaged in quiet conversation with several of her friends while he warmed up by laying on his back and holding his knees, rolling back and forth to loosen the stress on his lower back muscles. Clare returned to her mat and gave Howard the silent stare that said, "You're in trouble."

What now?. But his mind was on yoga and Maru's instructions. He would find out in an agonizing ninety minutes.

Each movement in yoga is sequential. Muscles are stretched in various positions, with belts used to push the limits of the various poses. Maru was very artistic in her methods, and if one ignored her directions and what movements were necessary, one would be out of sync with the rest of the class.

He took the time to look around to make sure he was not the only guy in the class. Two others were brave enough to attend with their wives. He saw they were struggling, just like he was. There were holding poses, and there were holding poses – for over a minute. He held the 'Warrior Two' for what seemed like an eternity. His feet were spread as far apart as his groin could bear, with his right foot pointed straight to the center of the room and his left at an angle to ensure his little toe and heel were flat on the ground. His arms were parallel to the ground with the palms up, and the head followed the right hand to the center of the room.

After an agonizing time, with only the guys grunting and moaning, 'Reverse Warrior' was finally the next instruction. It was not more manageable. It was only different and permitted the relaxation of some muscles and the tensing of others.

There was nothing he could do but take a deep breath and move into the position. It required moving his right hand down the side of his leg, resting it on his lower calf. His left hand was stretched past his left ear, pointing upward to the ceiling.

"Place your gaze either on the ceiling," Maru softly commanded, "or, yogi's choice, look down to your left foot. Better, yet, alternate if you can."

He had not looked at Clare because it was all he could do to concentrate on Maru's commands, waiting patiently to be released from 'Reverse Warrior.'

After what seemed like forever, "and release" was finally instructed.

Before he knew it, the session was over. Savasana was on your back with legs up the wall, draining the blood against gravity to support the heart. The only problem was that this resting pose was not held for nearly the time that warrior one or two had been. Could there be a nap in his future?

He rolled his mat and helped Clare with hers, taking both blankets and four blocks back to their station. Casual goodbyes were made with 'good class, good class, good class,' accolades to Maru. Clare spent about a minute in close conversation with Maru.

He was walking to the car when Clare asked the question, "well, warrior, or Howard, when were you going to tell me about Dawn Kendall?"

CHAPTER 21

||||||||||||||||||||||||||||||||||||||||||||

DENIABILITY

They walked to the Explorer in silence. Parking at the entrance to the Bungalow was more advantageous than he had planned. They sat in complete silence, with the only sound being the injection of the key into the ignition of the Explorer and a quiet start of the engine. It was as if everything would then be in order. Howard pierced the moment with, "Coffee?"

"Sure!"

As he backed up, looking for cars, yet not wanting to make eye contact with Clare, he said, "I didn't tell you about Kendall because it was not my place. I didn't want it to get back to her I spread information around regarding what happened."

"Howard," she said rather sharply, "I don't do that! I don't talk about things to those ladies! I can keep a secret."

"Clare," he said almost apologetically, "I know, but I didn't want to take any chances of anything coming from our side of the case. I'm not going to be the one who files charges if they are to be filed. Our Traffic Follow-up Unit will do that, but I'll probably get blamed anyway."

"Well, Howie," she quietly sat back in her seat, "I guess the word will get out that I knew nothing about it because I found out from Emily, who had talked to Dawn."

"That's the way it should have happened. To me, it was routine. I vow I will not get caught up in the soccer Mom drama in this place."

Howard was feeling a bit more in control now. "Look at it this way. I saw the shocked look on your face when the girls told you whatever they told you. It was natural, genuine, and I think they saw that too."

"So?" was the one-word response. It was evident that Clare didn't see where he was going with this.

Howard had figured out how to get out of the dog house but needed to press the point. "The look on your face told them I hadn't told you anything about the accident. They could see that. My not telling you gave you the innocence of plausible deniability. You denied knowing, and they could see you weren't faking. You didn't know anything about it."

"Well…" Clare drug out the word, but there was nothing more to be said. He had made his point.

To redirect the conversation a bit, HH quickly responded with, "and the kid, Owen Browning, has a bunch of broken bones and road rash, but those are all orthopedic, so he'll be fine." Do you know the Browning's'?"

"They're new to the school. What a welcome, huh?" Clare leaned back in the passenger seat, feeling better but not completely satisfied with his explanation. It would have to do; for the time being.

She rested her left hand on his right hand, patted it with the unspoken message that closed the issue for now.

CHAPTER 22

|||||||||||||||||||||||||||||||||||||||||||||||

MADRE

Saturday mornings at the Hamilton house were the best. A quick breakfast and chores were assigned to everyone. Everyone except Clare. All to be done after early morning soccer games. Marcia was to work on her room to get it better organized and make a list of books needed at the library. It was unspoken in the household that homework was not to be done via Google or Wikipedia.

Both Geoff and Marcia were to educate themselves on the library system at the Orchard Hill public library. This included the Dewey decimal system and where all books could generally be located. If the internet was to be used to get information, prior approval was needed. It was just a house rule, and all knew it. Up to six books could be checked out, but videos or DVDs had to be cleared through one of the parents.

Unlike Marcia, Geoff was a self-starter. He was almost compulsive in his obsessive orderliness, cleanliness, and attention to detail. While not yet OCD, he set the trend for the Hamilton kids. Marcia didn't get that trait. He worked from lists kept in his room and didn't have to be told twice. He was uncanny. Just when Clare or Howard would bring a task up, he would comment, "already on my list."

HH kept his list in his head. Probably not a good thing, he would lament, but it worked for him.

Other than what Clare had on her list for him, HH had one work-related task to do. Get in touch with Michael Alcazar and advise him he would be his training officer next week. He thought he should meet before Monday, his official first day to ride along.

At ten o'clock, he looked at the three-one-zero area code given in the file folder by Sgt. Rydell. Interesting, he thought, it was also his area code in Orchard Hill, but Wilmington seemed like such a long-distance away. In more ways than one.

"Hello," was the salutation after picking up on the second ring. It was not a male voice.

"Hi," HH said rather quietly. "This is Officer Hamilton of the Orchard Hill Police Department. Is Michael Alcazar there?"

There was a short pause, then, "Uno momento, por favor."

HH could hear her lay the phone down. It sounded like an echo chamber or empty hall, as the female voice called out, "mejo, it's the police. Are you in trouble?"

He could hear a male voice in the distance. "Who is it, Mama?"

"An Officer Hamilton, I think his name is. Quien Sabe?'"

"I'll get it in my room," was the male voice response. "Hang up when I pick up."

"This is Michael."

"Hi, Michael, this is Howard Hamilton from Orchard Hill PD. How are you?"

"Great," was the very enthusiastic response.

"I'm going to be your T/O for your ride-a-long next week and the first few months. I thought we should talk before Monday. Are you free this weekend to meet for coffee or something?"

"Yes, sir." Was the quick reply.

"Oh, please. Don't call me, sir. It's Officer Hamilton or HH. That's my nickname."

"No, sir, the Academy staff told us to address our T/O's as either Sir or Officer. See, we're not officers yet. They want us to start on the right foot. Ok, Officer Hamilton?"

"If you and they insist, but I'll call you Michael or partner for a while."

"Partner? Wow, I like it." Alcazar's enthusiasm was transported over the telephone as if he was standing next to his caller.

"Could you meet, say, tomorrow, Sunday, about ten?" HH inquired.

"Well, it could be a problem. I'm taking mi Su Madre, sorry, my Mother, to nine o'clock Mass at Our Lady of Lourdes here in Wilmington."

They settled on one o'clock after agreeing to meet at Peet's in Orchard Hill. HH and Michael exchanged a few pleasantries regarding the job. Both ends of the phone call left a strong, positive impact on the other.

Wow, HH said to no one special after hanging up, *"this guy reminds me of me when I first started. But I think he could be better, much better."* He then cautioned himself. *Gang member for a brother? Lives at home with his mother?*

CHAPTER 23

||||||||||||||||||||||||||||||||||||||||||||||

SIR

The Hamilton family went to church at St. Elizabeth's in Orchard Hill. Their service of choice was the Saturday night, five-thirty Mass, so Sunday was all theirs.

Filling Clare in on his one o'clock appointment, HH left out the details. "Just meeting my new trainee to go over a few things before Monday. Won't be but an hour or so."

The staff at Peet's was entirely different than during the week. His barista must have been on a day off. He was early and took his favorite seat, the one he and Clare shared. Coincidentally, it was the same one he sat with Mel Flowers, coaching her on her oral board interview for OHPD. He was such a victim of habits, most of them good.

HH spotted Alcazar as he parked his car, an older, grey Honda Prelude. Clean, but not immaculate, like his cars. His clean sidewall Academy haircut told everyone he was either in the military or getting ready for high school football camp. He looked that young.

Alcazar walked into the coffee shop and headed directly for HH. Just over six feet, lean but not buffed out, Alcazar walked with a sense of purpose. Their eye contact gave the signal they were easy prey to identify. Michael and HH were dressed almost identical. Blue jeans, an untucked colored T-shirt to hide the off-duty weapon, and running shoes. The non-descript baseball cap with "UCLA" in gold was the only out-of-uniform attire. Was he a Bruin?

"Michael." HH stood and reached out to shake his hand.

"Officer Hamilton, great to meet you, Recruit Michael Alcazar reporting, sir." A nervous but firm introductory statement had HH a bit uneasy.

They talked about the Academy training program, the instructors, and a few of his classmates. HH reminisced about his Academy training and how things had changed, and some things remained the same.

"You're set to graduate in about a month, huh?" HH asked.

"Yes, sir, December 16th. I'm very excited and more excited about working for, I mean with, you."

"What did I say about calling me, sir?"

I know, it's hard not to call everyone 'sir' that's involved with all this training and stuff."

"Well, assuming you graduate, and there's no reason why not, you'll be calling me HH by the time you get to phase four of your training. But we have plenty of time to talk about it. Tell me a little about you."

Michael filled him in on growing up in Wilmington, attending Banning High, and working at the local Boys and Girls Club in Harbor City. He had been an average but eager-to-learn student with great mentor teachers. He boasted about learning leadership skills at the Boys and Girls Club.

"Mr. Hernandez at the Club was my best mentor and kind of steered me to LAPD. I applied at OHPD at the same time. You guys offered me a job first, so I put my app on hold in LA." HH was impressed with how sincere and articulate Michael was in explaining his dilemma.

"I'm not sure LAPD would have been a good fit, though, because of my brother. Sgt. Rydell told me he told you, right?"

"Yeah, he told me." Nothing other than an acknowledgment was warranted at this point.

"You're okay with that, aren't you? I mean, it's my brother or was my brother, and I'm not him. No way, Officer Hamilton, no way." They both looked out the window at a family getting out of the car.

The silence was like walking into an empty room. It needed to be filled by someone.

"I see that Michael, I do," HH replied in a soft tone to soothe what appeared to be a defensive, but controlled, Alcazar.

"Tell me something, Michael, if I may ask, why do you still live at home?"

CHAPTER 24

||||||||||||||||||||||||||||||||||||||||||

LILLIE

The question was pushed out there like a boomerang hoping that it would be caught and returned as quickly as intended.

"I've lived in Wilmington my whole life, Officer Hamilton. I don't know any other place. Mi Madre is old. She had us late in life, and now it's just her and me."

"It just struck me that at your age, you would be out and about, I guess."

"I date a little. Mostly, I just worked at the Club and took care of her. My Mom volunteers at LAPD Harbor, at the police station, and knows many guys and girls there. She likes doing whatever she does there."

"Was she still working there when your brother..." like a twig thrown into a moving stream, it drifted off, wishing he could retrieve it?

"She wasn't there at the station, if that's what you mean, but, yeah, she was still doing work there. I had just been accepted at OHPD when it all happened."

"Gosh, one son getting ready for the Police Academy and one...." HH's words drifted away again.

"Yeah, one of us going to be a cop, or officer, sorry,"

Was he struggling because he viewed cop as too much slang or because of his family situation? Howard was not sure.

"And one a gang banger that had a hit out on him, yeah, I know what you mean."

"How did she take it? His, your brother's, death?" HH now wished he had not gone down this road.

"As to be expected. She was a wreck. Didn't want me to be a police officer and be killed in the line of duty, then she would have no sons."

"I could see that," was all he could say.

Michael kept right on talking. He wanted to get it all out now. "She had a bigger issue to deal with almost immediately."

"You mean finding his killer?"

"No, she knew that more than likely that wouldn't happen, but something else happened that she needed to deal with. About a month after...," he paused to compose himself and take a bite of his pumpkin scone and drink some coffee.

"One of her buddies at Harbor, Detective Ira Coleman, took my brother's photo, the one from the Murder Book, and started showing it at community meetings to demonstrate the perils of gang behavior. Have you seen that photo?"

"I have." Was HH's tart reply.

"Well, I haven't, and I don't want to. He was going to die someway; somehow, I knew it. Seeing his photo wouldn't have mattered to me. But the fact Detective Coleman was showing it in the community bothered her. And, she was at one of the meetings where he showed it. Jeez, how fuckin' stupid. Oh, sorry, sir."

"I could see where it would, Michael. HH chose to ignore the profanity. What did she do about it?"

"Well..." Alcazar paused again. "She didn't want to go to his captain, the guy at Harbor, so she asked to meet with Detective Coleman. My Mom, Lillie, is a straightforward person, Officer Hamilton. Very direct."

"Sounds it." HH wanted to keep Alcazar talking. This was good for him, he thought. Maybe he needs to get it off his chest.

"She met with Coleman privately and told him she was still grieving over the loss of my brother, her son, I mean. She asked him if he would stop showing her dead son's picture around the community."

"What did Detective Coleman say?"

CHAPTER 25

||||||||||||||||||||||||||||||||||||||||||||||||

BATHTUB

"You have to know, Officer Hamilton, Lillie was revered at Harbor Division. They loved her. She was everybody's mother there." It was clear to HH Michael was wrapped up in his mother's grief.

"Well, Coleman got defensive at first but came around quickly. He tried to rationalize it as a *Scared Straight* type of thing to shock their conscience about the perils of gang life. She didn't buy it."

"Did he finally agree?"

"Yeah. He did ask if he could contact her in a year and have her reconsider. I think he thought she might go over his head if he disagreed." Michael chuckled at his mother's tenacity. "She was a pistol to deal with outside the house, sir. Whether at church, the market, playground, or even at the station, she viewed everybody as her sons and daughters. Right now, though, I'm her favorite."

HH laughed, "I hope so."

"Well, it wasn't always that way. She and Manuel were close. He told her everything. I mean everything."

"Even about his gang escapades?" Now he had HH's attention.

"Just what he wanted her to know, sir. He wasn't stupid, but he also knew she would be talking to the Gang Detail at Harbor. She would feed them information she got from him regarding gang activity. He only gave up info that would benefit Wilm/Ord, but that was enough to the Gang Unit."

They sat in silence for a moment before HH could not resist asking, "Did your brother ever give her any information of value?"

"Sure, but he would test it out to see if she was giving them his information."

"How?"

"Well, he would tell her this incident was going to go down, you know, between gangs. He would say when and where and who the players were if it wasn't Wilm/Ord. Sure enough, the Gang Detail would stake it out, and bingo, they would bust some of his rival gang members. He knew that he was the only one with the info about a meet, so when he told Lillie, she called Harbor right away."

"Did your brother ever let on that he knew what she was doing?"

"No, and to this day, Lillie thinks she had something to do with reducing gang violence in our part of the City by what she did. Her wedding and birthday cake business gave her access to a lot of info about events in our town."

"Was he ever afraid that the other gangs, Harb Boys or whomever, would do a drive-by at your house in Wilmington?"

"Oh, they have, sir. We live on a cul-de-sac, so there's only one way in and one way out. They come by, turn around and blast the house. You can see the bullet holes on the front side of the place."

"Isn't your Mother afraid? For you and her?" HH was caught in the drama now.

Her bedroom and bath are in the back of the house, as is mine. But she's okay."

"Stupid question, but why don't you both move?"

"She wouldn't hear of it. Are you kidding? Move from her beloved Wilmington? You would have a fight on your hands."

"Whoops, sorry for asking," HH said, holding his hands up in defense.

"No, I ask her all the time," he said in an exasperating manner. "She always says no, I want to die in this house. Anyway, she has her tub."

"Her tub?"

Yeah, in her bathroom, she has one of those five feet long, claw foot cast iron freestanding old-fashioned slipper tubs."

"Ok? Doesn't everybody? But..."

"Well, that's where she sleeps. She has a small mattress set in it with

65

pillows and sheets. Gets her night's rest there. It's shaped like a slipper and fits her perfectly. If there's a drive-by, she figures that the bullets will only get to the living room, and her tub is bulletproof anyway. I think it's solid cast iron. And weighs a ton. Go figure."

CHAPTER 26

||||||||||||||||||||||||||||||||||||||||||||

0530

They spent over two hours talking shop. Alcazar talked freely about his experience in the Academy and how the academics were challenging. He loved physical training or PT. He was set to graduate as an expert with the Glock, and if he could knuckle down for the final exam, he stood a shot at graduating in the top ten percent of his class.

"Wow, that's great, Michael. I was in the top twenty, so I know how hard you gotta' work. Maybe I could help with some of your studying when you get to the final."

"I could use the help," Alcazar quickly responded.

The conversation had reached a lull. "Anything else you want to know about me, Officer Hamilton?"

"I think you've told me quite a bit already," Hamilton responded. "Are you ready for Monday? Uniform? Bookbag? If you meet me early, I can go over some of our reports. We don't use the Orange County Sheriff forms. Most of our stuff is on the computer."

Alcazar took no time to respond. "What time?"

"How about five-thirty? That'll give us some time before the briefing."

"I'll be there."

"Hey, Michael. Can I ask one more thing?"

"Sure."

"Do you have a girlfriend?"

Alcazar laughed out loud. "Not yet. Had one in high school, but nothing serious. Been taking care of Lillie and working. Why do you ask?"

"Well, Clare, my wife, will be asking. Do I have to say more?"

"I'm going to wait until after I make probation for any kind of a relationship, Officer Hamilton. I got enough on my plate."

"You do, Michael. You surely do."

Hamilton got a refill of coffee and sat in his SUV to reflect on the conversation and observations of one Michael Alcazar.

He liked him, really liked him. Then he caught himself. His first impression of Michael was very positive. But that was just a first impression.

You don't need a friend, Hamilton. You have plenty of those. You need a partner. Someone who responds to your direction watches your back and has the same work ethic as you. Somebody the other guys at OHPD can count on. First things first, Hamilton, and then maybe, just maybe, he can also be a friend.

Was today Sunday? A day off?

CHAPTER 27

||||||||||||||||||||||||||||||||||||||||||||||

KARL

He called Clare and found out she and the kids were at the Mall and expected to be home in a few hours.

He had an idea. He went back into Peet's, ordered two cups of coffee, now paying with his iPhone app. The world was changing.

He headed to the 900 block of Kensington Road and the home of Guy Coyle. He pulled to the curb and took both cups with him to the front door of the Craftsman home. If he were on duty, this would be the worst officer-safety tactic he could imagine. Both hands are full and vulnerable as hell!

He rang the doorbell and waited. He rang it again and heard footsteps. Coyle opened the door, and Hamilton offered, "Coffee?"

"Officer Hamilton, this is a surprise. Is this another welfare check?"

"No, sir, it's not." Hamilton replied, "And, it's Howard, sir."

"This will be the last cup of the day, but do come in."

"Thought I'd drop by, you know, just to chat," he said a bit shyly.

"Great. I needed a break from writing anyway."

They exchanged pleasantries about Coyle's family, chatted about the department, then Hamilton sobered.

"Well," he said, fumbling for the proper voice expression, "I guess the reason I stopped by was...I wanted to hear about the old days of LAPD. I never wanted to be an LAPD officer and didn't know any of them well, but the police work and the incredible level of activity there always interested me. I enjoy patrolling my City but what we deal with here is just routine, you know?"

Coyle motioned him to sit on the couch as they both sipped their coffee. "I have to laugh, Howard. I saw you standing in the doorway holding two cups of coffee. Your guard was down, so I guess you do handle routine things," putting air quotes around the word 'routine.'

"I thought the same thing," he laughed. "But a guy has to be off-duty sometime."

"What I was smiling about was, I remember when I was working the graveyard shift and patrolling the LA freeways before the CHP took them over, I think it was about 68', and we needed coffee to stay awake. Remind me to tell you about it someday."

"Those are the stories I love to hear about," Hamilton said, hoping to cheer him on.

"Did you ever meet Joe Wambaugh?"

"Oh, yes," he chuckled. "Joe and I worked together for about a month, actually the month after the first Watts riots in 65. September of 1965."

"What was he like?"

"Well, Joe was just a regular guy. Good Cop. He had a Master's degree in English and never mentioned anything about writing books. He quit, not retired, but quit, after only fourteen years to write full time. Have you read *The Onion Field*?"

"I have, and Pierce Brooks' book as well."

"Every police officer should read both of those, Howard. I'm sure you know then, Ian Campbell, the officer executed in Bakersfield, played the bagpipes as a hobby. They played the pipes at his funeral, and from that moment on, bagpipes are played at just about every law enforcement funeral."

Howard sat back on the couch. "I never knew where that tradition came from. Wow."

"I briefly met his partner, the survivor, Karl Hettinger. He was never the same since the incident. Their kidnapping is still the subject of a lot of attention in officer-survival classes. He carried a lot of guilt, that guy. But if he didn't do what he did by running when he had the chance, those assholes would have executed him as well."

"We always talk about not giving up our guns, but until you're placed in that situation for real, I don't know. I don't know what I would do." The silence between Coyle and Howard told it all.

"You know," Coyle broke the quiet with, "Karl ended up becoming a member of the Kern County Board of Supervisors. Can you believe it? A damn politician. I think he died in 93 or 94."

"But he was never back on the street after, was he?" Howard knew the answer to that question, posing it anyway.

"No. Chief Parker took him under his wing as his driver/bodyguard for a few months, but that didn't work either."

"Hey, where does the time go, sir? It's been good to see you again, but I've got to get home."

"Don't call me sir."

They parted company with an agreement to get together occasionally. Finally, Howard thought, someone to talk to about real police work.

Elapsed time: 23 minutes

CHAPTER 28

||||||||||||||||||||||||||||||||||||||||||||||

BULLET

HH got used to the day-watch maggot shift with weekends off and worked Monday through Thursday for ten hours a day. But it still wasn't his favorite. He was itching to get back to the PM or night shift for his version of real police work.

The conversation with Guy Coyle would stay with him for the rest of the weekend. Past his time with Geoff and Marcia, or dinner as a family. For the rest of the day, he went with the flow. He felt he was sitting on Guy's couch, listening to his stories all over again.

When he wasn't thinking about *The Onion Field,* he thought about Monday morning and how he would go about his first day as a training officer. There was so much to cover. How could he tell Michael everything he wanted him to know in those first few hours? It would be impossible. What did the kid know about being on the street in a uniform?

He was reviewing his mental checklist of instructions when Clare challenged him. "What are you thinking now, Howie? Is it about us, your family? I don't think so. I can tell when you're not here with us, you know."

"Sorry, just thinking about work,' was his cautious reply. "What's goin' on?"

"You don't remember, do you, Howard? We're going to your Mom's house for an early dinner. It's her birthday, for crying out loud. If you can forget about work for a while."

"I knew that," he fibbed, "but what else tonight, anything?"

"We'll just come home and have a nice Sunday evening. You know how your Mom overdoes her early dinners. Are you okay with that?"

"Sure, may be able to work on the garage as well." Did he dodge a bullet on that one? Not too sure.

Monday could not come soon enough. He was to meet Alcazar at the PD at 0530, and he was not going to be late. He went to bed early, at least for him, and set the alarm for 0430. He was showered and out the door, quietly, by 0500.

Arriving at the station in plenty of time, he found his favorite parking space available next to the locker room door. He wore the typical off-duty uniform of an untucked, no logo t-shirt. With his weapon stuck under his belted blue jeans and running shoes, he quietly unlocked the back door of the locker room.

CHAPTER 29

||||||||||||||||||||||||||||||||||||||||||

NERVOUS

He had expected that, at this hour, he would be the only one there for day watch. Not so. There were Sgt. McGinty and Tab McDaniel already getting dressed for the street.

"You guys are in early today," HH commented.

"Big day, HH," McGinty said rather casually. "Two boots from the Academy are scheduled for ride-along for the next four days. You and McDaniel here are going to start these kids out on the right foot, and I'm here to make sure you do."

"I told my boot to meet me at 0530 to give us some time before the briefing."

"Oh, you did, did you?" McGinty laughed. "So now you're authorizing overtime for him?"

"No, sir, just thought we could get a jump start on our first day. Didn't think about the OT."

"That's why we have sergeants, HH." He laughed at both he and McDaniel. "Not an issue as they don't get OT anyway, so are you going to put in for it?"

"Hadn't thought about it," HH and McDaniel said almost at the same time.

"Good," was McGinty's one-word response.

He dressed quietly, making sure he had his cleanest, short-sleeved uniform available. It was still warm for a fall day, and he wanted to make sure he was comfortable for what was going to be an exciting shift.

He walked by the coffee/lunch room on his way to the briefing room when he noticed some activity by the dispensing machines. There in full uniform and looking like the boot that he was, was Michael Alcazar! He was dropping coins into the coffee vending machine, one by one.

"You don't want that shit," HH said in his most vital command voice.

Alcazar jumped and dropped the remaining coins on the floor. "Oh, sorry, sir," was all he could say. HH laughed and bent over to help him retrieve his money.

"I came in the front door, all dressed and ready to go, and someone escorted me back here. Is it okay to be here?" Michael said rather shyly.

"Hey, you're almost one of us, so I guess so, Michael. How long have you been here?"

"Since yesterday, I think. No, just since about 0445. I'm used to getting up early, and this is much closer than the Academy in Orange County."

"We'll get some better coffee after we hit the streets. Let me show you around," HH said in a much more relaxed manner.

Hamilton gave him a station tour, starting at the front desk and the watch commander's office. "I only saw this from the front lobby side. It sure looks different from this end," referring to the shotgun behind the counter and the array of report forms and computer screens.

They walked through the Records Unit, and HH provided instruction on where essential files were maintained and how to get the clerks to do their bidding. He introduced Alcazar to several graveyard clerks and advised that the day shift would be in by 0700.

Next was the dispatch center. "This is where all the 911 and other non-emergency calls come in. They don't like you wandering in here distracting the operators, so stay clear unless you have a business to conduct. Generally, your best bet is to go through their supervisors."

He pointed to the bay of computers mounted on the walls and then turned to face Alcazar. "And no dating any of them! At least not until you're off probation! Got it?" HH said with a bit of humor, but it came out as an order.

Showing Alcazar the detective area was going to take some time, so he planned for that right after the briefing. "Let's get back down to roll call, and I'll get to the detectives and Admin later."

They walked into the briefing/roll call room, and both Michael and HH were immediately caught off guard.

CHAPTER 30

||||||||||||||||||||||||||||||||||||||||||||||

SHOTGUN

HH and Alcazar entered briefing from the back door. HH looked at rows of tables and saw that his spot in the back row was still empty. He looked up to see Lt. Hobson and the Chief standing on the riser of the watch commander's desk. *What was going on here?*

He directed Alcazar to sit in the front row without telling him that the boots sat there until they were off probation. Alcazar followed his lead. HH looked at the clock, and it was three minutes before the briefing, so at least they weren't late. There was no Lieutenant watch commander or even a Sgt. Bennett to be found.

With one minute to spare, HH heard the familiar slow walk of Bennett. Kip did his usual flick of HH's ear as he walked by carrying the briefing lineup and who knows what else. It looked like everyone working that day was there, bright-eyed and bushy-tailed, as the saying went.

The Chief started. "Well, good morning, everyone. I'll try not to take up too much of your valuable briefing time, but I wanted to take a few minutes to introduce two of our newest Officers. They're here for a ride-along before they graduate next month." He pointed to the apparent new kids on the block in the front row.

"This is Michael Alcazar, and this is Roland Tenery." Both Officers stood up and acknowledged the Chief and turned to face the ten Officers present for the briefing. "We're currently hiring a lot of new people, so get ready to see more new faces. We're starting three in the next Academy class in Orange County, but in two months, we'll have three more graduating from the LA Sheriff's Academy as well. We have enough T/O's, I think, but they're all going to be very busy."

There was a bit of silence in the room. Everybody knew that the training officer program had been under scrutiny because they washed out too many people in the past.

Lt. Hobson cut the silence with," We want to welcome these two fine officers to OHPD and let them know we're looking forward to them being a part of our family."

It was evident to HH and the more seasoned veterans in the room what was happening. These two and the others on the way will make their probation and get through training and be a part of our family.

Washing any of them out is probably not going to be an option unless they are a vegetable, HH said only to himself.

He knew Michael would not be a problem if he had anything to say about it. McDaniel must see about Tenery.

The Chief and Lieutenant Hobson turned the briefing back over to Sgt. Bennett and the remaining session went as planned. About fifteen minutes before they had to be on the street to relieve the previous watch, Hamilton took Alcazar around the basement floor and showed him the Kit Room with all equipment, from black and white keys to shotguns, portable radios, and Z-Pac drug testing equipment to be signed out. It will not be long before Body-Worn Cameras, or BWC's would also be issued out of the Kit Room.

Alcazar was shown the Officers Report Room and the locker room, showers, and workout room.

"You'll get a locker the day after graduation," HH said. "And, you'll be able to work out after graduation as well. You won't have to wait until you're off probation like I did when I was a boot. Different policies now."

Alcazar just nodded, taking it all in.

"Looks like we'll have to do the upstairs detectives and Admin tomorrow," Hamilton added.

Hamilton checked out the equipment needed for the day, signed all the documents required, and took two sets of keys to Shop 885. He handed one set to Alcazar and told him, "whatever you do, don't lose them. If I'm incapacitated, and you need the car, you won't have to fish around for my set of keys, got that?"

"Yes, sir," was the instant reply.

They arrived at Shop 885. It had been used on the previous shift but was otherwise clean and gassed.

"Always check the gas gauge, Michael. The ones who drove it last must give the next shift a full tank. If they don't…well, no excuse. They need to fill it."

"Yes, sir," was the repeated reply.

"Check the back seat and the trunk. Put your bookbag in the back seat or the trunk. Your call. But before you do, make sure the back seat doesn't have anything in it that it shouldn't."

"Like what?" Alcazar innocently asked.

"Like contraband dropped by an arrestee the previous shift booked. Coffee cups, In-and-Out wrappers, anything. They're built-in hard plastic bench seats, so make sure the seat is clean."

"Yes, sir."

HH broke down the shotgun and showed Alcazar what he was doing. "I know that much," Michael assured Hamilton. "You follow the BEEFS acronym. Check the barrel, extractors, ejectors, and then the firing pin and safety. Been on every test since almost day one." Alcazar reassembled the shotgun, loaded it, and did not chamber a round. "No round in the chamber, sir," he announced.

"They probably haven't trained you in long rifles anyway. I don't check them out. I like the shotgun. If I need a long rifle, I'll call a sergeant." HH turned to the car. "Check the mileage and log us on. Do you know how to put us in service?"

"No, sir, they said that every agency does it differently, and you would show us when we got here. I can do the generic one we used in role-playing."

Hamilton showed Alcazar the primary use of the in-car computer. "Remember, this is just a ride-along. I don't want you to take any action unless it's life-threatening. If we get in a pickle and I need you to do something, I'll call you a name other than partner, Michael or Alcazar, got it? Don't know what name, maybe Fred or John, but only if we're in deep trouble, got it?"

"Got it."

"OK, looks like we're ready to roll. Got bullets in that gun of yours?" The silence was deafening.

CHAPTER 31

||||||||||||||||||||||||||||||||||||||||||||

GOTCHA

"Well, sir, it's like this." They had been sitting in the station's parking lot, and it looked like they were the last unit to show themselves clear for calls. "We don't wear a loaded gun while at the Academy. Just the weapon itself, sir." Hamilton could see that Alcazar was embarrassed but decided to push it anyway.

"So, your gun is not loaded?"

"No, sir."

"Do you think Tenery loaded his weapon?"

"I don't know, sir. They're out of the station already. I didn't think about it with him, and it's my screw-up, sir. Am I fired? You going to write me up?"

"No, Michael, you're not fired. Do you have any ammo?"

"Yes, Sir, in my bag."

"OK. Get it and load it. Use that barrel over there," pointing to a fifty-five-gallon drum tilted at a forty-five-degree angle on wooden stakes and half-filled with sand. It was designed explicitly for safely loading or unloading weapons. "Put one in the chamber and make sure you have at least three full magazines, got it?"

He received the response that was now wearing thin.

Hamilton had an idea. He grabbed the mic and asked the dispatcher, "A75, we are clear, is A77 in service yet?"

Dispatch responded, "Yes, A75, 77 is in service but assigned a call."

79

Dispatch gave the address via the mobile digital terminal. "Roger, show us backing them up."

"What are we doing backing 77 up? Do they need backup?" Alcazar innocently asked.

"We'll see," said HH. "We'll see."

They quickly arrived at the scene of 77's call. McDaniel and Tenery were handling a family dispute in the fifty-two hundred block of St. Augustine. Right behind St. Elizabeth's Church. Hamilton's church.

He pulled up and parked behind McDaniel's black and white and sat there.

"Let them handle the call. They know we're out here if they need us, but I've been here before, and they don't need us."

"OK, sir, but why are we here?"

"Just play along, Michael. And could you just call me partner or Officer Hamilton? That sir thing is getting to me?"

"Yes, sir, I mean, okay, partner."

They watched Tenery and McDaniel walk off the porch and towards their car. Hamilton opened his car door and called out to McDaniel, "Hey Tab, got a minute?"

"Sure," Tab said, responding to Hamilton and seeing his partner get out of the passenger's side.

"I'd like to meet your new trainee, Tenery, here. Didn't get a chance to meet him at the briefing."

They exchanged greetings, and Hamilton introduced Alcazar to McDaniel.

"My partner wanted to talk to Tenery as soon as possible. Is that okay?"

Alcazar looked at Hamilton quizzically. "I do?"

"You do." Hamilton stared rather coldly at Alcazar. "You do.' with a bit more emphasis.

"Oh, Oh, yes, I do," Alcazar finally realized what was going on.

Tenery and Alcazar stepped away, out of earshot.

McDaniel responded to Hamilton, "Hey, this guy Tenery is incredible! He was a Captain in the Marines, two tours in the Middle East, and has a degree. Kip will love this guy, both of them being black."

"Well, maybe, Tab. Maybe. You know Kip's harder on his race, but not sure I want to tackle with this guy. Pretty impressive, even if he doesn't know what we do yet."

They said their goodbyes and got back in their respective cars.

"Same thing?"

"Yes, Officer Hamilton, the same thing," Alcazar said with a smile, referencing the fact that Tenery had not loaded his weapon either.

McDaniel's and his partner pulled away from the curb.

"Watch this," Hamilton said with a smile.

McDaniel drove about fifty feet and then slammed on his brakes, leaving skid marks on the roadway.

"I love this job!" Hamilton said to the windshield and Alcazar. Tenery had told his T/O about his unloaded weapon.

Hamilton and Alcazar could not stop laughing.

CHAPTER 32

IIIIIIIIIIIIIIIIIIIIIIIIIIIIIIIIIIIIIIIIII

HANDS

During their first day, Hamilton covered every element of officer safety. He brought up the shooting of Officer Johnson as he tapped on Alcazar's vest under his uniform to make the point.

"In the Academy, they only talk about two things from OHPD," Alcazar commented. "Officer Johnson not wearing his vest and a search done by an Officer that resulted in him getting pricked by a syringe when he reached into a suspect's pocket," he responded. "They had a picture of Johnson's vest draped over the passenger seat. It made quite a statement. Do you know why he wasn't wearing it?"

"I do," Hamilton explained about Johnson's tryout with the NFL, pumping iron and the fact his shirt was too tight. "He was working a report unit and felt that he could do without it for four hours. Then the pursuit, the…well, you know the rest."

He told him about arriving on the scene within seconds, the suspect's search and capture, and his charged with excessive force. "I was also involved in the syringe caper. Guess I'm just a regular shit magnet. I wonder how the Academy found out about the syringe incident?"

"They check with all the agencies they train for real officer safety issues. I guess it hits home if the scenarios are based on real events."

"Ok," Hamilton chagrined, "Let's talk about other things. How about probable cause to stop someone?"

"Well, I've read up on the law, but now it looks so much different from this end," Michael said.

Hamilton pointed to the car in front of them. It was an older Honda with a faded paint job and tinted windows. "What do you see?"

"An older car needs to be washed. He isn't speeding, and I didn't see him run a red light. What did I miss?"

"Two things. Look at the license plate. California, right?"

"Yeah, should I run the plate?"

"Sure, he probably has warrants."

"How do you know?"

"Two things here, Michael, actually three."

"Three?"

"Yeah, first, he has no brake lights, second, his license tag is expired by six months, and third…." Hamilton paused for just enough time to make his point. "How do we know it is a 'He'? With the windows tinted - and that isn't good enough to make the stop by itself - we don't know if it's a male or female, young or old, black, Hispanic, Asian, or white. So, we get the registration information and see if anything matches up."

Hamilton flicked the red lights on and motioned for the driver to pull over. The car slowly moved to the right and then turned on a side street from the busier commuter street of Workman Avenue.

He parked the black and white offset to block any traffic behind him that may try to use the same lane. This was necessary to protect him while he talked to the driver. It also gave him a better view of the vehicle. He explained his rationale to Alcazar. They both unbuckled their seat belts simultaneously.

"Stay right where you are, Michael. Let's assess what we have here. How many in the car can you see?"

"I think one, just the driver, but I really can't see much. The headrests are in the way."

"Why do you think the driver pulled over onto the side street?"

"Possibly to be out of the traffic flow?"

"Or to get us on a more secluded street. Where are the driver's hands?"

"Can't see them."

Hamilton never looked at Michael, keeping his eyes on the driver's headrest for any movement. "Don't take your eyes off the occupant, Michael. Not just yet."

"Any return on the DMV info?"

"Not on file, it says."

"Ok, this isn't a felony stop, so we won't get them out at gunpoint—more reason to be extra careful. Let dispatch know we're Code Six, out for investigation, on this license plate. And give them the location, even though they know where we are with the auto locator on their screen. I'll take the driver. You walk to the right rear of the car, just like they taught you in the Academy. Check the back seat. Ready?"

They both approached the Honda. Alcazar stopped at the right rear with his right hand on his holstered gun butt and left just touching the car's right rear quarter panel. Hamilton slowly walked to the driver's side. He could see his reflection in the side-view mirror, so he knew the driver could see him approaching. The window slowly came down.

"Good morning, sir. May I see your driver's license, insurance, and registration?" Hamilton requested.

CHAPTER 33

||||||||||||||||||||||||||||||||||||||||||||||

CITE

The driver turned out to be an elderly black gentleman on his way to an early doctor's appointment. He lived in the Orchard Hill Senior Housing unit for independent seniors. The units were designed to have the tenants take care of themselves, but with some staff oversight, if needed. Homer Broome did not require assisted living, but he was getting there.

Hamilton brought back a handful of paper provided by Broome and showed it to Alcazar.

"Here's the deal. He's been going round and round with DMV. Primarily over smog issues. He had no clue his brake lights were out as he doesn't drive much except to go to the doctor. He says he paid his fee but never received a sticker updating his registration. He has insurance, but I'm not certain he should even be driving at this point. What should we do, partner?" HH stressed the word partner and carried it out like p… ard…ner.

"Jeez, sir, I mean Officer Hamilton, I don't know. I guess we write him up for all of this and let DMV solve it. We need the cite, don't we?"

"No, we don't need the cite—no pressure for tickets in OHPD. Our goal here is to solve the problem. We get very little revenue as a city from tickets. State gets most of it, so who cares. Here's what we're going to do." Hamilton paused to look at the driver still sitting in his car, wondering how he got in this mess. There was no doubt he was worried about making his doctor's appointment.

"I took his DL info down. We'll send him on his way but let him know

85

we'll be in touch. We'll go to the Senior Center, talk to someone in charge, explain the situation, and advise them to assist Mr. Broome in resolving the problem and get his brake lights fixed. I'll fill out a DMV form asking them to re-evaluate his driving ability. He'll be eighty next month, and we need to make sure he can still function."

"Makes a lot of sense, Officer Hamilton. And it should solve the problem. I see that now."

HH advised the driver and sent him on his way.

"Okay, what did we learn here?" HH said as he turned off the emergency lights and pulled to the curb.

"Well, I learned that you don't have to write every ticket you see. And I didn't even see it."

What else?"

"I never saw his hands before we approached the car. I couldn't tell if it was a man or woman or what race he was. Nothing. Only you knew when you walked up to the driver's side. It was only after I walked up on the right side did I see there were no passengers."

"Anything else?"

"Not everybody keeps their cars up to speed, maintenance wise or clean."

"Anything else?"

DMV is pretty fucked up!"

"You got it!"

Elapsed time: 23 minutes

CHAPTER 34

||||||||||||||||||||||||||||||||||||||||||||

ESCORT

The remainder of the day went rather quickly. There were routine calls, a few traffic stops, and more discussions of officer safety.

"It's something that you have to think about every day," HH said. "Your days off are yours, but when you come to work, it's time to put the game face on. After you graduate, get two books, Pierce Brooks' *Officer Down-Code Three* and Wambaugh's s book, *The Onion Field*. Much to learn from both. Stay in shape, and you know what the most important thing is?" HH put it in the form of a big question.

"Clean your gun every day?"

"No, Michael, it's even simpler! "Just pick a good woman! One that shares your views and your values. One that understands your job and will support you in your career. Don't pick somebody cause she's a good lay. Think of her politics, views on human nature, and her overall outlook on life and kids."

"Does that mean I should pick another cop?"

"Fuck no! Don't go that far. That could be a recipe for disaster. Remember, you both carry guns."

They were interrupted by a tone on their terminal.

"A75, meet Mary 85 on Wardlow, just south of 19th Street School."

Alcazar hit the acknowledge button and showed them en route.

"Who's that?" Alcazar asked.

"I think it's Dean Harris, a motor cop that has this side of town. Let's see what he wants."

They arrived within a few minutes. Dean Harris had a year or two less on the job than HH and more than a few pounds over his Academy weight.

"What's up?" HH asked, getting out of the car.

"Hey, Howard, good to see you. Who's the new kid?" They exchanged introductions and a brief explanation of Alcazar's status.

"Heard my name came up in conversation last week with a couple of parents at 19th Street."

"Yeah, and it wasn't good. You're writing the shit out of the moms, and they don't like it."

"Do you blame me? Look what happened to the kid. The stupid mother left the car running and...."

"I know, I know, I took the report because you guys were feeding your face at a training day," HH responded, trying to get his goat a little.

"Next thing you know, I'm the bad guy for trying to corral these mothers to do things right. But I have an idea, HH. Maybe you could help, and we can keep the peace here. I don't want to write these ladies tickets. I want to fix the problem." Harris was starting to get serious.

"School won't be out for a while, so can we go over to the parking lot and talk about this?" HH saw that he was already putting on his helmet and climbing back on the bike.

They drove to the parking lot.

"This is the faculty parking that's closest to the entrance to the school." HH decided to jump in and pointed to an area filled with Audi's, Honda's, a few BMW's, and Mercedes.

"And all of this never gets filled up," pointing to the west area of the parking lot with as many empty spaces. "Why can't we have the Moms drive in this lot and drop their kids off on school property and let the kids get out here?" Howard asked Dean.

"Exactly what I was thinking!" Harris said.

"Good idea, but then the kids would have to walk to their classes by themselves," HH responded.

"Better yet," Alcazar softly interjected, "If I could add a thing here, why not have the faculty parking moved over here and let the mothers pull right up to the front of the school inside the safety of the parking lot?"

"Good idea, Michael," HH acknowledged. "I was thinking that the school could select kids from the most senior class who earn the right to be designated as escorts to the kids being dropped off or picked up. They could get those bright yellow vests and take the kids to their class, with minimal supervision by the teachers or an aide."

All three stared in silence at the mental image of their plan.

"I see it coming together, I do," said Harris. "I can get some cones, or better yet, Mrs. Goffney could get them from the school district. We could make a funnel with the cones, so the mothers never have to get out of their cars to pick up or deliver little Johnny."

What do we call this magnificent plan?" HH just threw the question out there as they continued to stare at the faculty parking lot.

"How about the 19th Street Elementary School Student Escort Program?" Michael said sheepishly.

"Sounds good!" Harris and HH said almost in unison.

"Now, who's going to meet with Mrs. Goffney on this to get it started?" Harris posed.

Alcazar and Hamilton responded almost in unison with, "You."

They all laughed as if the joke was on somebody else. "You're the one on the dark side with the moms and the Principal. You be the hero, put it down on paper, and get one of the traffic sergeants or the Lieutenant to sign off on it. Take credit for solving the problem." Hamilton delivered the scenario almost as an order from on high.

"You guys don't mind?" Harris weakly asked.

"Hell," Hamilton joked, "this will get you back in everybody's graces, and you can go pick on some other unsuspecting souls. I don't care. Before we break up here, can I give you a word of advice?"

Hamilton now put his serious face on. "Whatever you do, if you stop a mother by the name of Dawn Kendall, go easy on her. She's the one whose car hit that kid last week. She could use a break."

"You got it, HH. I don't want those soccer moms on my tail. I got a kid of my own in that group, but they don't know who I am yet. I want to keep it that way."

"Hell hath no fury like a pissed-off soccer mom," HH said with a smile.

CHAPTER 35

||||||||||||||||||||||||||||||||||||||||||||

ROGER

Fourteen hours later, it was day two of Alcazar's ride-along. Hamilton was surprised at how at ease he and Michael were with each other. *It usually doesn't happen this fast*, he thought. *At least he didn't think it would.*

In five minutes, HH familiarized Alcazar with the training material in the briefing room, the electronic pin maps, OHPOA bulletins, and postings for training opportunities. The briefing was completed but not without a few BOLO's, a wanted suspect that some of the detectives were looking for, and a quick discussion about the evils of using your personal cell phone to take a picture related to a crime or arrest.

With the threat of rain again today, HH advised Alcazar to put his boots and rain gear in the trunk.

"What rain gear? What boots? We haven't been issued any of that stuff yet. Is this as bad as not having my gun loaded?"

"Not quite, but close," he laughed. "Oh well, you'll get wet. No worries. See, something else to consider. Every day is a training day Michael. You have to remember that a good cop doesn't get wet, go hungry or not get off on time."

"For a long time to come. I guess I have a lot to learn."

HH smiled, "Let's get a coffee and see what happens today."

They went through the checkout procedures, and already Alcazar was anticipating things and seemed to grasp the routine quickly.

Alcazar hit the 'A75 Clear' and available for calls button.

After a quick introduction to HH's personal barista, Sophia, they received a call as they returned from the coffee shop.

"A75, see the manager at the Storage Center, a barking dog. No further information," Was all the screen said. HH looked at the address and quickly grabbed the mic.

"Isn't that in the county area or LA?" he asked dispatch. "That doesn't seem to be in our City. I've been on that street."

"Negative A75. The odd numbers are ours, even is the County."

"Got it. But a barking dog?"

"10–4," was the frustrated reply with an undertone of 'just do it.'

"Roger," was his anti-ten code reply.

Three minutes later, they pulled up to the electronic gate of Orchard Hill Storage and Box Company. The buildings were the typical sand-colored stucco, with red trim and a marquee sign providing the name and address. HH could see an office off to the right as the gate slowly opened. As he crawled his black and white slowly over the raised entrance, he saw the office door open. A middle-aged Caucasian male, mildly overweight, with glasses and one of those metro beards everyone was wearing, walked in front of his bumper.

As they started to exit the patrol car, the assumed manager held his hand up. "Stay in the car, officers. The dog is in the back. I'll take my golf cart. Follow me."

Hamilton took his gun out and placed it under his right thigh. "Just watch for right now. Could be an ambush or some kind of setup." He motioned to Alcazar to do the same.

HH slowly crawled the patrol car behind the cart as the manager weaved around other customer's cars and trucks. Hamilton directed his new partner to look down each alcove on his right, and he would look to the left, announcing 'clear.'

It seemed to take forever, but they finally found themselves in the last row of storage compartments. The final set of buildings abutted a concrete brick wall.

To the left were parking spaces for unhitched trailers and recreation vehicles. Hamilton saw several parking spaces on the far side, but only one was taken up with a new Mercedes Sprinter Van. It was backed in, so the right side was up against the side of the storage building. He was too far away to see any plates as the manager directed him to a unit directly in the middle, Number 122.

He holstered his weapon and advised Alcazar to do the same. Both officers looked around, and aside from the barking dog, things were quiet.

"Hi Officers, my name is…" and he pointed to his name badge… "Evan, Evan Crowder. I'm the weekday manager here.' The dog was barking nonstop, so they stepped back a few paces to continue the discussion.

"Today is Tuesday, and yesterday I started noticing a dog barking but didn't think much of it. The weekend night manager didn't say anything or make any notations on his log, so I figured it would go away. I don't get back here much." Crowder was now sweating from his level of excitement and lack of physical stamina.

"Are these all rented?" HH asked.

"Yeah, they're all rented. That's why I don't come back here. People want their privacy. Well, you know."

"Yeah, guess we do," HH said, not sure what he agreed to. "Looks to be about fifteen in a row back here."

"Yes, fifteen in a row exactly. Good count."

"Which one is the dog in?" Alcazar asked rather timidly.

"Like I said, Number 122. But there's no lock on it, see?" Crowder pointed to the only rollup without a lock.

Both officers saw the mechanism to hold a lock was empty. All other storage lockers had either a combination or key access lock securing the door. HH moved towards the door and put his ear against the heavy corrugated metal door. The dog's bark let him listen for no more than three seconds.

"Can you show me what the inside of one of these looks like?" HH asked Crowder.

"Sure, look right here," as he walked across the asphalt pathway to an empty unit with no lock. Crowder pulled up on the rope handle that permitted an easy roll-up and walked in, flashlight in hand. "They're all about the same size, fourteen or ten by twelve. Number 122 is fourteen by twelve. This one is ten by twelve."

HH surveyed the empty storage locker. He saw in-door sprinklers overhead, a single thick four by six beam running laterally along the entire locker bay area. There were no overhead lights, but there were electrical outlets on the inside of the door jamb.

HH asked the manager if he could confer with his partner.

"Something isn't right here, Michael. It looks like somebody inside has blocked the door from sliding up on unit 122. It still could be a setup, but I'm thinking of something else. Let's try to push the door up from this side, Ok?"

"OK, partner, you're the boss."

HH smiled with a smirk that said, "Oh, shit. Don't I know it."

CHAPTER 36

||||||||||||||||||||||||||||||||||||||||||||

EXIGENT

HH motioned for Crowder to step aside and stay two doors away. Both officers then used their hands to push the door up using their brute strength. It only pissed the dog off even more.

Was this what they called exigent circumstances?

HH went back to the open storage area directly across 122 and pulled the door straight down while he was inside. He came back to where the dog was now yelping as if in pain.

"That does it!" HH said and kicked the left side of the corrugated door about waist high. Nothing. He then went to the right side and did the same. That's when he heard what he wanted to hear. A piece of wood fell onto the concrete floor.

"I think someone propped a block up against the corrugated door so that it blocked rolling the door up from the outside," he said to Alcazar. "Mr. Crowder, can we get the ownership information on this unit?" Crowder held it up to show he had anticipated the question.

Hamilton directed Alcazar. "Before we pull this up, do two things. Get on the horn and ask for a supervisor to come to this location and ask for Animal Regulation, got it?"

"Got it, sir." was the military reply.

As the manager provided Alcazar with the ownership card, Hamilton advised, "Mr. Crowder. We don't know what we're going to find here other than a very unhappy dog. I'd prefer you to stand away from the door, so my partner and I can go in prepared if you know what I mean. We have more than enough information to open this without a search warrant. I'll take the heat if there is any. but we may be faced with, well... I don't know what, so let us handle this."

Crowder was now hyperventilating. "Take some deep breaths, sir," HH said as Sgt. McGinty was asking for him in the earpiece. "And by the way, can you let my sergeant in the front gate?"

Crowder hit a button on his waistband to activate the front gate. HH advised McGinty of their location.

"Alcazar filled me in. We have enough exigent circumstances to open this thing. Particularly with the manager here," McGinty advised HH when he arrived. "Let's do it."

Alcazar and Hamilton got on each end of the door, with McGinty standing on the side, blocking the view of the now weak-kneed manager. They pushed up halfway as the black Labrador whimpered but stayed right where he was.

CHAPTER 37

||||||||||||||||||||||||||||||||||||||||||||

LAB

The metal door was now moving freely and was finally rolled entirely up. The black lab was whimpering softly but still didn't move from its position. The dog, Crowder, McGinty, and the two officers all were looking at the same thing.

About forty years of age, what appeared to be a male was hanging from a strap-like device. His hands were secured behind his back, and a step stool lay on its side about two feet from his right foot. A small pool of blood was directly under both feet. The dog's mouth and body were covered with blood.

"Mr. Crowder," HH said with the most authoritative voice he could muster," I think we take it from here. Can you close the entrance to the storage area from the public and escort out all those who are currently here? I'll get someone to get their names and information before they leave."

Hamilton looked to Sgt. McGinty and received confirmation. The supervisor walked away and made a notification to detectives of a possible homicide at their location. Alcazar located a rope from inside the storage room and leashed the dog away from the body.

"From all appearances, this looks like either homicide or suicide. Not sure yet." Hamilton commented to Alcazar. "Are you alright with this? Not making you sick or anything, is it?"

"No, I'm good."

"It's obvious that he's dead, so no need to cut him down. Detectives and the coroner will take care of that. Our job is to protect the scene until they get here."

"Got it." Michael acknowledged.

The body was hanging about one-third of the way into the twelve-foot-long locker. Behind it, a small partition separated the front of the locker with cardboard storage boxes stacked at least five high. An extension cord was plugged into the electrical box and led to a spotlight that still illuminated a makeshift desk created with other boxes.

Alcazar examined the body from about a foot away as if he was a surgeon preparing to dissect a cadaver. Being careful not to step in any small amounts of coagulated blood that pooled below each foot, he saw the apparent reason for the blood. The dog had eaten the victim's feet, toe by toe from the phalanges of the large toe to the heads of the metatarsal bones of the lesser toes on both feet.

The medial portion of the muscle on each foot was frayed, almost like an electronic wire whose individual lines had been ripped from its base. The dog made a meal of each foot but, due to the height of the foot off the floor, ran out of foot in the quest to eat his master and survive on its own. At some point, coagulation stopped the draining of the blood, but not until the dog had licked it.

It was also apparent that the venous network on the dorsal foot and the lateral and medial saphenous veins, located on the inner and outer portion of the foot, respectively, had been compromised, causing gravity to drain blood to the floor.

Alcazar tried to explain to HH his observations in layman's terms.

"How the hell do you know that?" HH said, looking at him quizzically.

"Just got my AA degree in anatomy, sir. But don't ask me too much. That's all I know about the foot. There are a lot of nerves there that affect the whole body. He didn't lose too much blood because the veins and vessels are too thin in the foot, and they gel quickly."

"It's a lot more than I know, Michael. Come over here and look at this." He motioned to the makeshift desk discovered behind a small partition. The spotlight still hovered with an LED bulb overhead hanging from a wire clothes hanger.

Hamilton used his flashlight to light up two scrapbooks opened on top of a large box. The photos depicted a basketball team in various staged poses and news clippings of players in action. "Looks to be at least college and maybe semi-pro level," Hamilton posed. "We're not touching anything. Put these on just in case," he motioned, handing Alcazar a pair of plastic gloves. "Can never be too prepared."

"Hamilton, Alcazar, come out of there! Don't touch anything. Detectives are on the way," McGinty advised.

"We had gloves, Sarge, no worries," Hamilton displayed the blue surgical gloves covering his hands.

"I don't care, Hamilton, we don't know what we have here, so keep out until the dicks get here," McGinty said, coming as a direct order.

"Sorry, sir." Both HH and Alcazar said almost in unison, realizing they just got scolded.

"Let's just hold this scene. Alcazar, can you go upfront and make sure the manager doesn't let anyone else in other than the dicks and CSI? Also, make sure any other customers are ushered out without any fuss," McGinty directed. "You can also direct the detectives back here when they show up."

"Yes, sir," was the response.

McGinty and Hamilton stared at the hanging corpse. Both saw it at the same time.

CHAPTER 38

IIIIIIIIIIIIIIIIIIIIIIIIIIIIIIIIIIIIIIIIIIIIIIIII

TALL

But it wasn't the visual picture of a hanging corpse that McGinty and Hamilton were looking at. The body was draped in a woman's black nightgown with thin lingerie swaying lightly in the breeze. The neck was stretched beyond its regular length, with gravity the only thing that mattered. The victim wore a black brassiere and panties, but the individual appeared to be male for all other purposes. Complete with genitals.

McGinty spoke first. "I think what we have here is a transgender or crossdresser, Hamilton."

"Well, that's a first for me," Hamilton said almost reverently in the presence of yet another corpse. "Before you got here, Sarge, I was looking at books he had laid out in the back, behind that partition," pointing to the area with two scrapbooks open. "Our victim had it open to some news clippings and basketball team photos. He looks tall but hard to say with that neck stretching as far as it does. Maybe he was a ballplayer."

Just then, a detective car and CSI van pulled up. McGinty waved them to where he and Hamilton were standing, just outside the view of the body. Two detectives got out of the car rather nonchalantly. Hamilton recognized the homicide supervisor, Dave Niemen, and Dieter Rollenhagen. Niemen had worked homicide since Hamilton had been on the job. Dieter, he knew, was new to the team. He was selected for the spot vacated by Sherman Oakes. Oakes had gone on vacation and never came back from someplace in bum-fuck Wyoming. Quick retirement. Rollenhagen had been on the waiting list for homicide and had worked the auto theft table for several years.

"What do we have?" Niemen announced to no one in particular.

McGinty spoke first. "Not sure if we have a homicide or suicide, Dave." He quickly recounted the events that led to the finding of the victim. "It also appears we're dealing with a crossdresser or some kind of transgender issue here."

Niemen finally acknowledged Hamilton as Alcazar returned from the storage manager's office.

"How are you doing, HH?" Niemen finally asked. "Who's your partner?"

Hamilton introduced Alcazar to both detectives and explained his training status, and he would be around all week.

Alcazar spoke up," Here's a copy of a contract from our victim for the storage. Here is the manager's information, including his home address and cell phone. Here's the list of cars parked here in the storage area. Some are vintage cars, and others are trailers and RV's."

"Impressive," Niemen said to Hamilton and McGinty.

Niemen had the personality of a pancake. Flat, no sense of humor, and man of few words. Everybody respected him as the best homicide detective in the Department, but he was not one you would invite over for a barbeque or have a beer with at Home Plate. He had the requisite cookie-cutter Hitler-styled mustache, wearing clean, starched short-sleeved white shirts. There was a complete set of ammo and cuffs on his belt, with his trusty Glock in tow. Right out of central casting, Hamilton thought.

Alcazar's cell phone rang.

CHAPTER 39

||||||||||||||||||||||||||||||||||||||||||

BELTS

Rollenhagan was following Niemen around like a puppy dog. That was how HH had been with Red Walker on the Ginny Karsdon case a few months back. Being new to homicide meant that you took your lead from the senior detective on the scene and waited to be told what to do. The initiative, at least in OHPD, was not encouraged. Just learn until it becomes your turn to lead.

Alcazar answered his cell and, after a few minutes, said, "I'll let you know. Hold on." He held his phone down to his side to silence the speaker. "The manager said the press is out front and demanding to be let in, sirs," he announced to everyone. To him, everyone on the scene was 'sirs.'

Niemen responded quickly, "McGinty, can you go out there and just let them know we're conducting a death investigation and have not identified the victim or cause of death. When we know, they'll know. That should hold them. Try not to answer any questions, then let me know who's out there. Print, radio, or TV, okay?"

McGinty bounced towards the entrance for his five minutes of fame. Everybody but Alcazar got the joke. "Some guys just love the camera," Hamilton whispered to Alcazar.

Niemen approached Hamilton. "You'll be working with us someday, HH, so I want you to see how we look at this as either a potential homicide or suicide. Watch how we direct the forensics people." Nieman paused just long enough to separate his thoughts as he stared at the hanging corpse. "I want to make sure you didn't call the coroner. You didn't, did you?"

"No, I learned from Red how that goes." Hamilton wasn't sure if he should call him sir or by his first name. Oh, what the hell, he figured.

"Dave, let me show you something." He walked Niemen back to the scrapbooks to show his discovery. Photos of a college basketball team, newspaper clippings alongside plaques and certificates honoring the team from the Mid-American Conference. All from the Ohio University Bobcats back in the 1990s. There were eleven team members, the coach and assistants, and what appeared to be a team manager. Almost half of the team was black, so it would narrow down to the five white players if the victim were one of the team members.

Rollenhagan called out. "Found some ID. His Cal Op looks like him. A Broderick Samuel Mason," waving a wallet found in a set of trousers folded on the floor.

Hamilton turned the page and saw the name listed on the team photo. He pointed, "There he is." Then he closed the cover and saw the gold lettering inscription on the bound leather yearbook, *"Broderick Mason Ohio University Bobcats 1993-1995."*

"Take a look at this," Niemen beckoned to both Dieter and HH. He showed the intricate strap or belt formations that led from the neck to the beam about ten feet off the cement floor. Two long belts, one green, and tied around the beam with the buckle end hooked into the end of a second, longer belt, brown. At the buckle end, it was looped over to form a smaller loop around the victim's neck. Each belt looked to be about ten feet in length and maybe an inch and one-half wide. The ends were machine-sewn to prevent fraying. The buckles appeared to be of durable metal, stitched into the belt. They could easily support the victim's weight.

Another belt was tied around his wrists and behind his back. "Could someone do this by himself, or did he have help?" Niemen asked as an overhead question to anyone within earshot.

Hamilton could see that the belt around the wrists was smaller in length but the same width. "I think he could," Hamilton opined. He's tall and skinny with very long arms and could have tied them in front. If he was agile enough, he could jump through and secure them after they were behind him."

"How nimble?" Rollenhagan asked in his faked German accent as Sergeant Schultz of *Hogan's Heroes* fame, a television show from the

1970s. Dieter's nickname had been *Schultz* since his Academy days, and he flourished in imitating the character at every opportunity.

Niemen saw where Hamilton was going. "Looks like he was a basketball player that stayed in pretty good shape. I'd said he was six feet four and two-hundred ten pounds. Maybe still played in some pickup league around here." Niemen responded.

Niemen then directed the CSI investigator to photo anything and everything just how it was, including the dog. "We can probably get some prints off the stair stool to see if they match the victim but nothing from the belts. Maybe DNA to see if there is any other than from our Vic." CSI Connie Washington, a one-year 'veteran,' responded to Niemen. "We need to go through the boxes. I would bet that the only ones we need to book for evidence will be those he had open."

"I think right now we book everything." Niemen cut no corners. "Sorry, Connie."

Hamilton approached Niemen off to the side. "I don't mean to be ignorant, but this is the first transgender person or crossdresser I've seen in my sheltered life!" he stumbled on a few of the words, trying to make himself seem halfway intelligent.

"Well, we don't get a lot of them here in Orchard Hill, but LA has more than their share. I went to a conference recently where this was touched on. It seems science and social science people in academics don't know much either. It's changing dramatically as people have problems with their gender. I'll have to bone up on it for this case," Niemen said.

"What's the difference between somebody who's transgender, transsexual, or a cross-dresser?" Hamilton asked.

"Not sure right now, Howard. Give me a day or two. Can I get back to you?" Niemen laughed at his question. "Now I'm reporting to you too? Anyway, we won't know much until the autopsy."

"No sir," he quickly said as Alcazar walked towards him again with the latest update.

CHAPTER 40

||||||||||||||||||||||||||||||||||||||||||||

CORONER

Alcazar updated Niemen and Hamilton about McGinty's meeting with the press. "It was just the Times and Wave," referring to the two print media newspapers for the area. "They heard the request for a homicide team on their scanners and beat feet over here. I think the Sarge did a great job of telling them nothing."

"Great," Hamilton said as he saw the Animal Shelter pickup van roll into their aisle.

He directed the handler to the black Lab, who had not moved from sentry duty by his master. The handler was a slightly overweight mid-forties black male who had no problem approaching the dog rather purposely. No fear, just a lot of sympathy for the circumstances and his bloody condition. He exchanged his leash for the piece of rope used to anchor the dog.

The handler looked at the tags and read off the name. "'*Lady* is the name, and there's a phone number on the tag. Bet it goes with this guy here," pointing to the victim still hanging there. He returned to his truck and brought back wet towels to clean the dog in place. As he did so, the Coroner's van, affectionately called, of course, the *meat wagon*, showed up.

Hamilton could tell the detectives and CSI had things well in hand. He obtained the okay from Niemen to go back in service, with the commitment that if they needed him, he would return. "I think we got it," Niemen said.

McGinty left, and Alcazar advised dispatch they were clear and available for calls. Driving slowly out of the aisle, Hamilton reached the end to turn right towards the exit of the storage center. He saw a few cars parked in stalls and asked Alcazar, "Did you get those plates for the dicks?"

"I did, yes," was the reply.

"Including that one?" Pointing to a new silver-grey Mercedes Sprinter with a personalized plate of *B GOODE.*

"Yes, sir."

Hamilton thought there was something about the van that bothered him. Just then, he heard a voice from behind call his name.

CHAPTER 41

||||||||||||||||||||||||||||||||||||||||||

BUSINESS CARD

"HH, is that you?"

Hamilton knew the voice and everything else just clicked in. John Bresani, or *Johnny B. Goode* as he was known when he was an OHPD cop, called to him.

"What's up?" Bresani asked, putting both hands on the open driver's window door jamb. He had a stale morning breath that also reflected his attire. A wrinkled shirt, jeans, a hoodie, a baseball cap with a Mercedes Benz logo, long hair, and a month's beard growth. He looked like the typical ex, with an emphasis on ex.

"How are you, John?" Hamilton paused, not wanting to know, then asked, "What the hell are you doing here?"

"I keep my van here," pointing to the Mercedes Sprinter parked next to the storage building. *Now the B GOODE personalized license plate made sense. How could he keep that name after his actions?* Hamilton wondered.

"Saw you doing your thing down there," again pointing to the aisle where the detectives were still working. "Who's working this one?"

"Niemen and Rollenhagan, why? Do you know anything?" Hamilton casually asked.

"Nope, keep to myself. I have seen the dog, though. Who's your partner?"

"This is Michael Alcazar. Michael, Jonny B," introducing both without attaching titles. "Michael will be graduating from the Academy next month and is out for a week's assignment."

Hamilton was now feeling very uncomfortable. "Got to go, John." *There would be no 'nice seeing you or let's get together sometime.' For sure, no' see you at Home Plate.'*

"HH, hold on a minute. Need two favors."

"Really? John, from me? Got a little fuckin' nerve there don't you think?" Hamilton was doing his best to remain civil.

"No, I know where you're comin' from, Howard. But these are simple things. First, can I get your cell number…just in case I get…" he paused again, "…something you could use?"

"What's the second thing?"

"How do I get the dog, the black Lab? It looked like the owner won't need it."

"Go down to the Animal Shelter, John. That's where it was headed. Could probably just adopt it." Howard wrote his cell number on his business card. Then he tore it up, reached for a blank piece of paper, and wrote it again.

"Here you go, John, but you know I don't want anything to do with all that shit."

"I know, but I still feel I owe you one. If something big comes down, you can at least pass it on, can't you?" Bresani looked for agreement but got none. "Hey, I'm not working around here, HH. Doing my thing taking care of the soccer Moms in South OC. All those gated communities, you know." Bresani was bragging about his business exploits.

"Don't want to know," Hamilton responded as he handed him the plain piece of paper with his cell number.

Bresani looked at him, eye to eye. "No card?"

"No card, John."

Elapsed time: 92 minutes

CHAPTER 42

||||||||||||||||||||||||||||||||||||||||||||

NEFARIOUS

Hamilton was struggling with what to tell Alcazar.

Probably the best thing to say is nothing. Then again, Michael needed to know how to deal with situations like this. Jeez, he grew up in Wilmington and is going to know some people who are on the shady side too.

"John used to be with the Department, Michael," taking a deep breath to adjust his approach.

"I figured," Alcazar responded without asking a follow-up.

Hamilton decided to add some information. "Bottom line is that he's into nefarious things and was fired. He accidentally hooked me into it and stupid me. I had no idea what was going on."

He explained that Bresani was roughed up by some cocaine dealers he was working with, that he was a narco expert and ran the hype car, had many connections in the industry, and saddled HH with a kilo of coke without his knowledge.

"Nice guy," Alcazar said.

"The idiot had no idea he was under investigation and had me deliver what I thought was CD's to him while he was recouping in the hospital. Thanks to Lieutenant Rikelman, It was all investigated, and I was exonerated. Still didn't sit well with me."

"So, that's why he says he owes you?"

"Yeah. Hey Michael, not to change the subject, but… you did a great job back there sorting out what needed to be done."

"Thanks, but I think I have a great T/O. It helps."

"Oh, bull shit. But I'll take it."

There was a message on the terminal. *Meet Mary 85 at 19th Street Elementary at eleven-hundred hours.*

"Wonder what that's about?" Alcazar queried.

"Harris can't do anything himself. He's a walking target at the school. Probably needs our smoother demeanor," HH smiled.

They arrived at the appointed hour and saw Dean Harris waiting patiently next to his bike.

"HH, Michael, good to see you. My supervisor, Sergeant Sherman, will be here any minute, but I wanted your assistance because it was all of our ideas that created the plan."

He laid out the *19th Street Elementary School Student Escort Program* almost precisely as they had discussed, showing them his administrative memo to the Chief. "He liked that you were involved in this HH. Helped my credibility. My Sergeant, Sherman, contacted the Principal, Mrs. Goffney, this morning, and she asked if we could meet today. The issue is a hot priority for her and the District."

Hamilton looked at Alcazar. "Put us Code Six out for investigation here."

Sherman rolled up on his motor, and the four of them exchanged pleasantries as they walked into the Principal's office together. "Haven't been in the Principal's office lately, have you, Michael?" Hamilton laughed.

"Well, if the truth is known…" he left it there as they all laughed at his expense.

The Administrative Assistant to the Principal escorted them into Mrs. Goffney's conference room.

Walking in the door to the conference room, not only were Dean Harris and Sergeant Sherman surprised, but so were Hamilton and Alcazar.

CHAPTER 43

IIIIIIIIIIIIIIIIIIIIIIIIIIIIIIIIIIIIIIIIIIIIII

KUMBAYA

Three women and one man occupied the room. Mrs. Goffney made introductions to Dawn Kendall, resident soccer Mom, Angie Roblat, PTA president, and Tom Bradshaw from the Orchard Hill School District.

It looked like Sgt. Sherman and Mrs. Goffney had met before, and everyone exchanged business cards, at least those who had them. Everyone took their seats, and Mrs. Goffney started by saying, "OK, Sgt. Sherman, what do you have for us?"

Sherman walked over to a computer with a PowerPoint projector, shoved in a thumb drive, and brought up a slideshow with 19th Street Elementary School Student Escort Program under Principal Amanda Goffney's Direction. He then went through about ten slides graphically presenting Harris, Hamilton, and Alcazar's concept.

It was a well-done presentation with Google Earth maps, satellite photos of the school parking lots, and entrance to the main building, all with added graphics text.

Sherman wrapped it up with…" and we have Officer Harris here to thank for coming up with this program."

Harris held his hand up." Well, Sarge, Officers Hamilton, and Alcazar helped with it too," pointing to them both. Hamilton added, "yeah, but this would not have happened without the unfortunate incident with Ms. Kendall. Her acknowledgment and description of the magnitude of the situation called for some unique problem-solving. I think Officer Harris did the right thing in putting us all together."

"There is a sense of urgency, Sgt. Sherman, so when do we start?" Mrs. Goffney said.

"How about next Monday?" Sherman threw out. "That'll give you time to get a blast email out to the parents regarding the program. I can download this presentation so that you can include the map. In the meantime, we'd also suggest that the school assign a teacher's aide to oversee the program and select the upper-class escorts based on their classroom performance."

Everyone was nodding in agreement. "That'll also give you time to get some reflector vests. If you have a problem there, we can loan you some from our Police Explorer Post until yours come in."

Harris added, "I'll get some cones from City Yard. But make sure you let the parents know they'll never lose sight of their child until the Escort leads them to their class. It'll be as if they were right there with them."

Everyone was in a kumbaya moment as the meeting was about to adjourn.

Mr. Bradshaw sat up in his chair to get everyone's attention. "I have a problem with this," he said somewhat cautiously.

Hamilton's jaw tightened. *Was he going to throw cold water on things right now?*

"Looks like we're all in agreement, but if you could hear me out." Everybody sat back in their chairs, waiting for the school board member to put a damper on the program.

"Well, I hate to make a fuss over one word…but I will. It's the use of the word *Escort*. Don't you think it could be taken wrong? I mean, what do you think of when you hear that word?"

"I don't know," Dawn Kendall said. "What do you think of?" There was an emphasis on the 'you.'

"I see what you're saying, Mr. Bradshaw." Surprisingly said by Sgt. Sherman. "I worked our Vice unit, and it certainly has a different connotation there."

The room chuckled but with a tentative understanding of his comment.

"We hadn't thought of that," Alcazar, who had been extremely quiet during the discussion, "we also discussed using the term, *Valet*. Would that work?" The room went quiet again.

"I like it, *19ᵗʰ Street Elementary School Student Valet Program.*" Mrs. Goffney said with a strong emphasis on the word valet.

"Easy to change at our end," said Sherman referring to the PowerPoint presentation.

A consensus had been reached. HH could not resist the temptation as he exclaimed, "I guess this means no more double-parking citations for the soccer Moms, right Harris?"

Dawn Kendall jumped on the statement with," I think I'm the only one he hasn't ticketed."

There was a brief silence, and then everybody had a good laugh at Harris' expense.

CHAPTER 44

||||||||||||||||||||||||||||||||||||||||||||||||||

ESCORT

"You wowed us with that PowerPoint presentation, Sarge," Hamilton told Sherman as they walked back to the parking lot.

"Easy to do. Harris had it all written up yesterday, and we just turned it into something more formal with some photos and graphics. Funny how Bradshaw zoomed in on that word, escort."

"Oh yeah,' said Hamilton. "I'll bet he knows a thing or two about escorts," putting his fingers in quote mode.

"Oh, you are bad," Harris laughed.

Let's see what happens next week," he said, saddling up on his bike. Harris thanked Hamilton and Michael for coming and said he had cleared it through the watch commander. "I'll give him an update when I get back to the station. Can you guys help set up next week?"

"I can, but I think Michael here will be a little preoccupied with the Academy still. We won't see him again for another month."

"Right, sirs, I go back on Monday, but I would love to see, or hear, how this thing comes out." Alcazar was drooling as he once again saw the big BMW 2015 R 1200 RT-P motorcycle equipped with every bell and whistle, including a Rear Protection Bar. "Wow, this is an incredible machine. What happened to Harley's and Kawasaki's? Thought everybody rode those?"

"Not anymore. BMWs are more popular than ever. Internationally, nothing touches them, but there are only about 225 PD's using them.

Particularly the big ones like us." You could tell that Harris was proud of his bike.

Hamilton and Alcazar made a 360-degree move around the machine. Harris pointed to all the options. "Alley lights and the headlight light up a violator. Even better than your black and white. LED lights which I'm still getting used to, but also a baton and flashlight holder. If I wanted to check out a shotgun, this is where I could put it," showing the left side of what was now becoming a real show and tell display.

"Where do you live?" Hamilton asked.

"Long Beach," Harris replied.

"Take it home?" he asked, referring to the bike.

"Yup. We have a home garaging agreement, so it gets the best spot in the garage, and I keep it immaculate. See..." he pointed to the undercarriage. "You can eat off that muffler intake system."

"I'd rather not!" Hamilton joked. "Hey, I'll meet you here next Monday to get this program going."

They agreed on the time and location and parted ways.

Hamilton and Alcazar walked back to their patrol car, jumped in, and belted up.

"That was pretty exciting, sir," Alcazar exclaimed. "I've never been in a meeting like that to kick off a program that we made up."

"Yeah, I suppose so, Michael," said Hamilton. "But you know what?"

"What?"

"That's not real police work. That's just... I don't know what it was," Hamilton responded. "What do you think?"

"I see it like what they were talking about in our classes. It's community policing. It's solving a problem, rather than just reacting." Alcazar turned in his seat. "I have a lot to share in class next week."

Hamilton sat there, taking Michael's statement in. *It's still not real police work*, he said only to himself.

Elapsed time: 46 minutes

CHAPTER 45

IIIIIIIIIIIIIIIIIIIIIIIIIIIIIIIIIIIIIIIIIIIII

DORSAL

For the next two days, Hamilton walked Alcazar through the various intricacies of the station, including detectives, interview rooms, the crime analysis unit, traffic, and the juvenile diversion program. He made sure to use the time he would have typically been in the station doing a report or conducting a follow-up with detectives on a matter.

The key for a patrol officer, Hamilton impressed, was always available for that 'hot shot' call, no matter what they were doing.

They spoke briefly with Dieter Rollenhagen about the death investigation at the storage unit. It was currently being handled as a suicide, pending the autopsy results. And, because it was a possible suicide, that report could be weeks away.

Rollenhagan stepped up on his mythical soapbox. "The autopsy will tell us if he's undergone any sex change. You picked up on it with the scrapbooks. He was a big-time basketball guy back in the 1990s and played in the Continental League right here in the South Bay. He majored in accounting but was pretty much a loner. Can't find too much about any long-term relationships."

"Any idea how long he hung there?" Hamilton asked.

"We think he'd been there since Friday night. That's what the check-in system said at the gate. That would account for the drainage of blood and the dog's hunger. Damn dog ate down to the metatarsal bones on each foot. He couldn't get any higher, so that's why he started barking.

The small vein on the dorsal of each foot was what drained the blood," Rollenhagan finally took a breath.

"Hey, about the dog. Is there any kind of hold on... what was her name, Lady?"

"We asked the Shelter to hold for the typical ten days, but after that, no. Why? You want her?"

"No," Hamilton responded a bit too quickly.

"Your partner?"

No, at least I don't think so, do you, Michael?"

Michael had been looking at the photos. "What? Wasn't listening."

"Would you want to adopt Lady, the dog?" pointing to a photo with the dog and deceased.

"Ah, er, I don't know. I would have to talk with my mother. I live with her."

So, you don't have one now, right?" Hamilton probed.

"No, but let me check. I'd love for her to have someone there when I'm not home," Alcazar said rather thoughtfully. "But what about your friend, sir? He said he wanted the dog?"

Hamilton stammered in front of Rollenhagan. "That was just some guy on the street, Rollie. No big thing. If Michael wants her, I'll keep in contact with the shelter. Just let me know if anything changes." Hamilton's jaws were tight. He didn't want anyone knowing about his contact with Bresani. He wished he had never brought it up.

It was the end of watch on Day Four, and Hamilton still had an evaluation to complete on Alcazar. They said their goodbyes, with Hamilton agreeing to see him at graduation.

"I'll also keep in touch regarding Lady," he promised.

He was mad at himself for being a bit short with Alcazar after he brought up Bresani. He completed the report, giving accolades to Alcazar's observation skills and knowledge of the law, as well as his overall tactics.

It was more than time to go home.

CHAPTER 46

||||||||||||||||||||||||||||||||||||||||||

LOCKER

He walked out of the station with a bit too much on his mind. The phone rang.

"I see you didn't change your cell number, Howard," the voice said.

"Who is this?" Hamilton asked, somewhat annoyed.

"Johnny B."

"We don't need to talk, John. Get rid of my number."

"Hold on, Howard. Let me run something by you. I guarantee it'll be something you're interested in." Johnny was getting more confident. At least Hamilton had not hung up on him yet.

Howard let silence be his admission to continue.

"There's a shipment coming into the South Bay, and I don't want to have anything to do with it. I can set things up for OHPD or that damn Task Force. Those assholes that got me."

"So, what? Why should I care? God damn it! This isn't New York, where an arrest gets you promoted. Lose my damn number! I don't give a shit, John," with an emphasis on the *don't*, he was getting pissed.

"Well, do it for the fuckin' department then. But I'll tell you. I'm only going to deal with you. None of those asshole Narcs."

"John, listen to me. I'm not interested. Bye," Hamilton said as he hit the red button on his iPhone.

On the short ride home, he talked to himself.

Leave it in the locker room. Leave it in the fucking locker room. I don't care about all that shit. I just want to do my job and go home to my family. I'm putting the garage together with all the right handyman tools.

I'm looking forward to yoga, church, and Sunday dinners with the family. Much more important than anything Bresani may have.

Some of his thoughts rambled on to block out what he had just heard.

CHAPTER 47

||||||||||||||||||||||||||||||||||||||||||

YOGA

He was already priming Clare for his move back to the night shift. They liked it before he went to days, and they'll like it once again. He had already put in his request for the shift change. He was assured that he would more than likely be accommodated due to the rotation of T/O's. Back to actual police work and away from those day watch maggots.

Hamilton didn't mind day watch, but it was those damnable maggots. The work did not seem like police work. Dealing with the people issues of the Department, things like the Student Valet program, or whatever they were going to call it.

He always looked forward to Friday mornings with Clare at yoga. He on one side of the room and her on the opposite. He could see her in her poses and know that he was the luckiest guy in the room and perhaps, the world. She was sure looking good in all those poses.

Maru arrived five minutes before the scheduled time and passed out the usual blocks and blankets. Everyone placed their mats in line and were in the process of warming up for the ninety-minute stretching and strength exercises to come.

She reached into her bag of tricks and pulled out about fifteen long webbed belts. They looked to be about eight to ten feet long with two metal buckles on one end. "We're going to try something new today," Maru said in her soft, feminine voice that caused the room to move to silence. "It will help us stretch our unused muscles and strengthen our hips and shoulders."

I was game for anything that would keep me flexible, reduce my stress and add to my body definition, and yoga was already doing that.

About halfway through the program, Maru introduced the belt and directed everyone to loop the unbuckled end into the buckle and secure it, so it was taut, with the open end firmly in a loop. Her instructions were to lie on your back and place it on the right foot, extending the leg straight and up over the hip. The left foot would be extended with the heel on the floor and toes pointed up.

Hamilton held the strap over his head with both hands and stretched the right leg and hip joint. He then extended the right foot to the right, holding the strap by only the right hand, then moving it across his body to the left and changing hands, stretching the hip flexors, thigh, and calf muscles.

What a workout. Guys at the station would love this. He rethought his comment and realized that perhaps it was not time to introduce yoga to guys like Donny and Red Walker.

As he moved into the final pose of the class, it was time to lie on his back and let the muscles and mind relax while he practiced doing absolutely nothing. That may have been the directive from Maru, but it was difficult to shut his brain down completely. The body, yes, the brain, not so sure.

He lay there, knowing the relaxing part of yoga would only last a few minutes. Then, like a lightning bolt electrifying his entire being, it hit him. Square in his mind's eye, his third eye, or whatever that yoga term was.

CHAPTER 48

||||||||||||||||||||||||||||||||||||||||||||

BELT

Hamilton had seen it before. It was at the scene of the Mason suicide. Mason had hung himself by yoga straps. It was the same mesh weave fabric, the same width belt, length, and buckle. Now Hamilton was lying there, visualizing Mason using the step ladder, attaching one belt to a beam, the other end to the buckle of another strap.

He envisioned Mason using a smaller belt, placing them on his wrists, the loop of the hanging strap around his neck, and then jump up on the chair after placing his hands under his feet. Because he was so athletic, he could kick the chair away while his hands went behind him, and the strap from the second loop was around his neck. Gravity then did its job.

All with yoga belts! And all while Lady, that beautiful black Lab, was watching. If correctly done, the tautness of the belt loops would be stronger than rope, better than wire, or anything else to assure success in his efforts.

As everyone acknowledged Maru as the best of the best, he was waiting to ask her some questions. He placed his mat in the carry bag and saw that Clare was engrossed in discussion with other classmates.

"Maru, can I talk with you a moment?" Hamilton asked. He had never had an honest discussion with her, aside from just listening to her soft, mellow instructions as everyone worked through the various poses.

"Absolutely, Howard, what's up?" she cheerfully smiled.

"Where are these belts for sale?"

"Well, generally only through a yoga instructor. We carry them at the

Bungalow, but I'm sure you can get them online. Why? Would you like to buy one?" she queried.

"Maybe…but for right now, can I borrow one until the next class?"

"Sure," she said, handing him one from her pouch. "Promise to give it back?"

"Of course," he laughed, "Would I steal a belt?"

"I hope not, Officer," she said with a chuckle.

"If I can ask, do they come in different colors and lengths?"

"They do. The belts come in brown, black, green like these, or multi-colored like Clare has. And they can be bought in eight- or ten-foot lengths. Why?" Maru was now getting a bit curious.

"I'm not sure why, but if I have any other questions, I'll let you know," Hamilton responded in a more somber tone.

The belts! The belts! What is it about these belts and Mason? I don't know. I don't know… yet.

He examined the belt on loan from Maru. There was a tag sewn into the buckled end. "Barefoot Yoga Co." Attached to that was another tag, '10' he presumed indicated the length.

But what does it all mean?

CHAPTER 49

||||||||||||||||||||||||||||||||||||||||||

VICTIM

He wasn't sure why he was interested in this case, but something just clicked with him. *It was starting to bug him that he was bringing this shit home. Hell, it's only a suicide. The case is closed.* He's going to have to start giving himself commands as he does to their golden retriever, Bentley, *"Leave it!" Leave it in the locker. Enjoy the weekend.*

The weekend was another blur as everyone in the Hamilton clan was doing something almost every waking hour of the day. After yoga, there was shopping, the library, and Saturday evening church at St. Elizabeth's. The service, while uplifting, was too long. Rex Holcomb was in his usual alternative uniform, being a Deacon instead of a cop.

It was barbeque burgers for the Hamilton's after church and reading time for those who wanted it. Television for those who desired to escape. Homework was done, the garage reorganized a bit with more to come, and the cars were clean, dog groomed, and the yard was where they both wanted it, for now. No English Garden just yet.

So why was he fidgety? Hamilton's mind couldn't get rid of the sight of Mason hanging from a beam with the now identified yoga straps used to end his life. Why would someone who was a college basketball star dress in woman's clothes and hang himself? Life was too good.

Was there a transgender population in Orchard Hill? They probably don't commit any crimes, but they could easily be victims of violent crime, could they not?

Was there a mismatch based on sexual orientation? Was Mason going through some sex change operation? Was he just a cross-dresser, or was he transgender? Again, why would someone commit suicide just because they were a cross-dresser? The coroner's report should tell a lot. It is a world he knows nothing about.

Is it Monday yet?

CHAPTER 50

||||||||||||||||||||||||||||||||||||||||||||

VICAP

His Sunday was passing quickly. There was no thought to what was ahead of him for the week. Clare made sure that family issues were at the forefront of their activities.

He would do some research on the latest updates for training officers. He clicked into OHPDs' proprietary website and reviewed the latest training bulletins and Department orders. He looked at the notes from the Field Training Officers meeting he had attended and sat back to think a bit more about Alcazar.

He didn't know why, but he searched for Joseph Wambaugh and Pierce Brooks, the two authors he most admired. Wambaugh's s website was very elaborate and featured his charitable activities and promoted his latest books. Brooks' did not have a website, but when he entered his name, the book "Officer Down, Code Three" came up.

But something else was there that intrigued him. Under the author's name was an acronym called ViCAP. It stood for the Violent Criminal Apprehension Program. It was a unit run by the FBI for the analysis of serial violent and sexual crimes. What drew his attention was that it was founded by the author of *Officer Down, Code Three,* Pierce Brooks. He was the first Director of the unit because it was his brainchild. The key was that a database could be developed to link serial homicides by their signature elements. Brooks had pushed to have the FBI take it over and place it at Quantico instead of his Lakewood, Colorado location, where he was Chief of Police. And that was way back in 1982.

He read further to find it was designed to track and correlate information on violent crime, especially murder. They tracked and compiled information on sexual assaults, solved and unsolved homicides, particularly those that involved a kidnapping, apparent motiveless cases, sexual issues, or some apparent randomness. Crimes were also entered that were suspected of being a part of a series, including missing persons, but mainly if foul play was suspected. But not suicides or apparent suicides. Hmmm.

The system was not available to all law enforcement agencies until 2008, when a secure internet link was established. Mason was transgender, which placed it in the sexual category. It wasn't tied to a serial homicide, but to his feeble mind, something bugged him about the case. He wondered if Rollenhagan even knew about ViCAP.

Hell, it wasn't his case. Why do you care, Hamilton? It's Rollenhagan's. Just get back to the night streets and let it go.

I really don't care.

CHAPTER 51

||||||||||||||||||||||||||||||||||||||||||||

GUARDIAN

Briefings on Mondays are filled with updates from the weekend crimes and other activities. It sounded to Hamilton like those who worked the three twelve-hour shifts on Friday, Saturday and Sunday had it easy. They were satisfied to play guardian of the city, keeping everything at bay for another safe weekend for the residents of Orchard Hill.

He was trying to figure out how to explain to Alcazar the difference between being a warrior like LAPD is and being a guardian of the community. That was more what was needed in Orchard Hill. He let his mind wander in briefing and took notes to ensure he could explain it adequately to Alcazar.

Howard Hamilton had always thought about it. Is he the warrior that Donny Simpkins is? Donny could smell a stolen car. He could find sitting ducks that a car thief had dumped on a side street after either a joy-ride or had been used in a crime. He could tell from the style of driving whether the driver was familiar with the car or was nervous beyond black and white fever.

There was no doubt Simpkins had the warrior mentality. Yet he had never even had to a use force incident, whether it was a felony stop, takedown, or worse. His tactics were so good that he never gave the subject an advantage. But always, the guardian. He protected the City from the scourges of crime. His motivation was focused, just like Hamilton's. He wanted to go home every night with a clean uniform. He was able to translate the basic skills learned in the Academy to work on the street.

Being a guardian requires constant vigilance to ensure that the community is safe. Protecting businesses and residents from break-ins or robberies means you have a sixth sense of knowing something is wrong before it is wrong. Prevention means stopping something before it happens.

It means interjecting yourself in a manner that ensures by your mere presence, nothing terrible will happen. But when things happen right in front of you, there must be a strategic warrior mentality that ensures you dare to take appropriate action.

Hamilton knows the streets of today are very complex. Not that Guy Coyle's streets of years past were not. Today's warrior is tomorrow's guardian if the streets do not turn into battlefields. But it's harder to be a guardian. You must sift through the good to get to the bad. It's not right out in front of you.

Being a warrior is thrust on you by the circumstances of the street. Hearing a crime broadcast with descriptions of suspects after a diligent 911 operator has been given information that may be sketchy at best yet providing as much detail as possible.

Responding to a help request from a citizen means that someone has been victimized. It also means there are suspects to be apprehended when they don't want to be. A warrior must push out further than a guardian when the circumstances require. They must thrive in an ambiguous environment, with reasonable suspicion, without the benefit of time to consult. Is there a danger to me or others? Does the person pose a threat? How much information do you need to act? To confront? To use force? To shoot?

Some of his biggest excitement was checking the crimes in his assigned areas the next day. If nothing happened, he viewed his shift as a success. He was there, being visible and deterring, just by his presence. It was weird, but he knew what it all meant. Or did he?

He was daydreaming when he realized the briefing was over. What did he miss, he wondered?

Guess I should pay closer attention, he thought.

Maybe an early coffee with Mr. Coyle would help.

It was bothering him that there was something else he had to do today, and he couldn't remember what it was. All this day watch bullshit may require him to get a pocket calendar or start recording his meetings on his phone. Good grief.

He didn't have to remind himself because Dean Harris stopped him in the hallway.

"See you at 19ᵗʰ St. School in a few minutes, HH."

CHAPTER 52

||||||||||||||||||||||||||||||||||||||||||||||||

CONES

He had forgotten! Thank goodness Harris was there to remind him.

"We need to get there before 0700, or the parents will have screwed it up," Harris commented.

"See you there," was all HH could muster.

Within five minutes, both officers were there to meet with Mrs. Goffney and her crew. Cones were laid out, and Harris was beaming at the prospect of seeing their plan come alive. Hamilton noted the faculty parking lot was moved to the side of the school campus, and several teacher's aides were lingering at the entrance. Harris approached them and introduced himself.

One of them stepped forward. "I'm Laura Seiler," extending a hand of greeting. "We all know who you are, Officer Harris, but who is your partner?"

Harris was taken aback, "how do you know who I am?" he asked.

"You've ticketed most of us! So, of course, we know you." The other mothers just stared through him with daggers piercing his bulletproof vest.

"Oh, well, I can assure you, with this program, I don't think we have to worry, at least I hope not." He was trying to deflect their animosity into some level of acceptance. "Oh, and this is Officer Howard Hamilton. We both came up with this idea together, so you have him to thank, also."

Harris quickly walked away to unnecessarily redo the lineup of the traffic cones into the newly designated stopping area. No need to linger.

Mrs. Goffney went back behind a closed door and immediately

returned with five students wearing reflective vests. She provided brief instructions and introduced Officers Harris and Hamilton. Everyone looked up to see the first line of SUVs, passenger cars, and pickup trucks head for the funnel created by the traffic cones.

It was 'ready, set, go' for the 19th Street Student Valet Program!

Elapsed time: 23 minutes

CHAPTER 53

||||||||||||||||||||||||||||||||||||||||||||||

DEUCE

With two black coffees in a tray, Hamilton walked up to the Craftsman house and rang the bell. He had completed the initial kickoff of the Student Valet Program with Harris, and they agreed to return to the school at 1400 hours for the pickup. Now it was time for a Guy Coyle fix.

Guy was dressed as if going on a date when he answered the door. And, it was only 0900 in the morning.

"Coffee?" he offered.

"Sure, what's one more this morning? Come on in, Howard." Coyle stepped aside, and they walked to the kitchen table.

"Thought I'd stop by for a few minutes in between radio calls," turning his radio volume lower and inserting an earpiece to monitor calls. He paused for what seemed like an eternity. "You had mentioned I could stop by, and when I was getting coffee, I remembered you said you had a coffee story. So, what is it?"

"Well, when I had about as much time on the street as you do, I was working the graveyard shift. There was no Starbucks or Peet's back then, but there was Winchell's Donuts. They closed at midnight, so the only thing open was a little shack right off the freeways called 'Coopers.' They were open 24-7-365 days a year, and the owners generally hired the homeless to work. Their only patrons were cops and drunks. Coopers kept their coffee at just below boiling, I think around two-hundred-ten degrees. It was terrible, but it was hot. Damn hot. The only decent donuts they had were glazed, and they sat right here," pointing to his stomach.

"All night long. At three or four in the morning, that was the best we could do. They're another one of those things that are not around any longer, thank God."

"Wow," Hamilton said, a bit underwhelmed.

"I worked the freeway cars before the CHP took them over, but only on the graveyard shift. We were guardians of the freeways from eleven o'clock at night to about six-thirty in the morning. We were five or six two-man units that covered all freeways in the City." Guy could tell he had Hamilton's attention.

"We didn't have any women in the unit. We had souped-up high-performance Old's 88's and a Plymouth Fury for the Pasadena Freeway. We had to check every corner of our beat, log every stalled vehicle, and make sure there were no accidents on our beat."

"That sounded like fun!" Howard exclaimed.

"It was, for the first couple of months. Graveyard shift is tough enough on the body, but we had to be harnessed in and wear riot helmets in the car. Drove me crazy."

"So, you mentioned that you were a guardian of the freeways. What do you mean by that?" Howard queried.

Just this morning, he was pondering the difference between a warrior and a guardian. How strange was this?

"Hey, it was our beat, our turf. Every inch of the freeway was ours during those hours. Nothing could happen on those lanes we didn't know about, or the sergeant would have our asses." He smiled when he said it. "No one could be stalled or broke down on the side of the road or run out of gas."

Guy stood up to continue his monologue. "Every car had to be checked. We had to have a curb to curb vision that made sure the lanes were always clear. We carried gas cans for those who ran out of gas. Would change a tire for a damsel in distress. The bottom line was that we were responsible for everything that happened during those hours. If we didn't do our job, we'd be off the assignment in a heartbeat. It was a coveted assignment, with a waiting list to work it."

Howard could see that Guy Coyle was reliving his past right before his very eyes. "Did you consider yourself a warrior?" he posed.

"If warrior meant that we were aggressive about protecting those freeways, yes. We chased after DUI's. We called them 502's back then because those lanes were ours, and a deuce could screw things up. Gosh, we got the term deuce from 502, which was the original driving under the influence section of the Vehicle Code.

I think it's changed now. Hell, the law back then required a .12% blood alcohol. Then it went to .10% and now it's.08%. Things change, I guess."

"They do, Mr. Coyle, they do."

CHAPTER 54

||||||||||||||||||||||||||||||||||||||||||||||

STREETS

The coffee was great, the company even better. It was quickly time to go. Hamilton was clear and available for calls. He monitored the radio for anything important through his earpiece, but he listened to Coyle as if he listened to a book on CD. Coyle narrated as if he were reliving his past career, one day at a time. There would be more days of regaling the past, but today he had to get back to the streets, his streets.

As HH returned to his car, his cell phone rang.

"HH, Red here, got a minute?" John 'Red' Walker, or 'shooter,' his partner on the Ginny Karsdon case, was calling.

"Sure. For you."

"I heard you were out on that suicide last week with your trainee," Walker said.

"Yep. Interesting case." Howard was very cryptic.

"Well, I don't like to be picky, but do you have any insights on it? I think Dieter's more than willing to clear that case as soon as the autopsy is back."

"What do you mean, Red, it's Rollenhagan's case?" Howard said with an emphasis on *his*. "He can do what he wants with it as long as Hospian signs off on it."

"I know, but...I haven't looked at everything, but there's something about it I don't like," Walker chided.

Howard paused just long enough for Red to get the reason for his silence.

"I knew it, asshole. I knew it. You think so too, don't you? Don't you?"

"Well…" Hamilton stopped to collect his thoughts. "I had some concerns regarding how he tied his hands behind his back and used all those yoga belts to hang himself."

"Yoga belts? What yoga belts?" Walker asked.

"The yoga belts he used to do the trick," Hamilton responded.

"How do you know they're yoga belts, Howard?"

"Take a look. They're in the evidence room. They have a tag that identifies them. I've seen belts just like it in my yoga class. Do you know if the guy, Mason, or whatever his name was, did he do yoga?"

"Rollenhagan's report doesn't mention a damn thing about yoga belts. It just says 'belts' like a guy's belt. He never identified them as yoga belts. I think that's somewhat important, don't you?"

"I guess it is if it's not a suicide, Red, but hey, it's not my case. Maybe you could mention something to him. Did he check ViCAP to see if there is anything in there?"

"Suicides aren't in ViCAP, HH. Anyway, it hasn't come back from the coroner yet. Damn, I knew you would have a different take on it."

"Hey," Hamilton said, trying to shine it on, "drop Dieter a note or just in conversation throw that out there and see if he bites."

"Ok, but you should have gotten that position, not him," referring to the open spot in homicide.

"Life isn't always fair, Red. It was his turn."

His turn, my ass, they both thought but never said aloud.

CHAPTER 55

||||||||||||||||||||||||||||||||||||||||

DOPE

Hamilton blanked the Mason case out of his mind for now. It wasn't his case, his problem, and it was almost a week ago, ions in the world of patrol. He handled a few routine calls involving an illegally parked car and a burglary from a motor vehicle that looked like they were after the goods in the back seat. After all, it was Christmas time. Then his phone rang again.

He didn't look at the number, just answered, thinking it could be Clare.

"Johnny B here, HH."

"What?" Hamilton said with exasperation to make the point he didn't want to talk to him.

"This thing is going to go next week, Howard. You need to take this over. I'm in the middle, and it'll save my ass."

"John, listen to me. I don't care about your ass. You screwed your life up, and I'm not about to help you."

Bresani persisted, "Howard, this is not about just me. It's about the shipment. It's going to your schools, all around the South Bay. These guys have everything set up with a network to break it all down into street level and push it out there as quickly as possible. You gotta take it to the guys workin' dope."

Hamilton fell silent, and Bresani seized his moment.

"Here's what I'll do. You take it to dope but stay in the room on all phone calls. I'll talk to you but let them listen in on a speakerphone. I want you to be there, even in the background, so they don't screw me. I don't think they will if they know you brought them this one."

Hamilton listened. Things were mulling over in his mind as he put 'coke,' kids' and schools in one sentence.

"I'll talk to Lt. Cartwright and get back to you, John. That's all I'll commit to right now."

"That's fair," Bresani said. Knowing he had won this round,

"Howard, one more thing. I got Lady, the black lab, from the storage area case. The shelter had her on the list to be euthanized, but I took her. I thought you should know. I mentioned your name. It all went well. I just thought I'd mention it."

Bresani was mumbling and repeating his words. There was no doubt in Hamilton's mind that he was indulging in his product.

It would be another masterful engineering job to make sure he got off on time. Go out to the station thirty minutes before the end of watch, advising that he had a meeting with the Narcotics Unit.

He walked into the Narcotics Unit, asked for Lt. Cartwright, and was directed to his office by Joanne, the administrative assistant for the Vice/Narcotics Unit of OHPD. He entered a short hallway and saw the Cartwright nameplate on the closed door and lightly knocked.

"Come in," was the response. He did and was surprised at what he encountered.

CHAPTER 56

||||||||||||||||||||||||||||||||||||||||||||

SIRS

There were papers, maps, and photos spread across the Lieutenant's desk and a small conference table in the corner. Hamilton expected something was up but was assured of it when he saw Cartwright and Lieutenant Rikelman looking at the same documents.

"Officer Hamilton, what can we do for you," they both chimed in at the same time.

"I didn't mean to interrupt anything, sirs. It looks like you're busy."

"We are, but forget what you see here. What can we, or Lt. Rikelman do for you?" Cartwright said. "Maybe I should explain. It's my last week, and Ib, Lt. Rikelman, is taking my spot as the Unit Officer in Charge. I'm finally retiring. We were just going over some current cases."

"Should I come back later?" Howard asked rather innocently.

"No, I'll be here all week," Rikelman said. "What's up?"

"Got a call from Bresani. You knew the DA didn't file on him, didn't you?"

"Yeah, they explained it to us, but we still weren't happy campers," Cartwright grumbled.

"He wants to turn a deal with us... with me, actually. He wants me involved because he doesn't trust anybody else."

"What kind of deal?"

"It's a big shipment of coke coming from south of the border somewhere, and its destination is right here in the South Bay and targeting our schools.

Their network is already in place, and delivery is set for some time next week."

"We know about a shipment but don't know who, when, or where. Does he?" Cartwright responded.

"I don't know what he knows, sir. He said he wanted me to be involved every step of the way, or he would just let it come in. He said to set up a conference call, me and the Unit here, and he'll provide the details. Honest, that's all I know."

"Officer Hamilton," Cartwright said in a solid military manner, "would you mind waiting outside while Lt. Rikelman and I discuss this matter?"

"Absolutely, sirs." Hamilton backed out the door feeling like he had been in an inquisition.

Minutes later, he was beckoned into the office again.

"Here's how it's going to go down Hamilton," Lt. Rikelman directed. "I'll be handling this anyway because Ben here will not be around after Friday. Okay?"

Was he asking my permission, Hamilton thought?

"Okay." Hamilton was only going to respond with one word at a time. It's their show, not his, and he knew it.

"Let's set up a meet, and we'll see what he has to say."

"I don't want to meet with him, and he doesn't want to meet with you…us." Hamilton tried to say it as politely as possible.

"How does he want to do it?" Rikelman asked with an annoying emphasis on *he.*

"On the phone, as I said. At least until we get closer to the deal." Hamilton tried to be a bit condescending without being insubordinate. "He doesn't trust anybody here."

"When can we get him on the phone?" Cartwright asked.

"Not sure," Hamilton said, "I can try for tomorrow afternoon."

"Tomorrow afternoon it is, then," Rikelman said in his typical abrupt manner.

As Hamilton started to take his leave, Rikelman called out. "Howard, I want to say one thing about this little item you brought us. He's not going to run it. We're going to run it. You make that clear to him. I don't want any of our guys hurt because he thought he was in charge. Make sure he knows that."

There was no doubt in the message.

"He will, Lieutenant. He will."

Hamilton was about to leave when a closing thought came to him.

"Lieutenant," he stressed the rank again to make sure his point was going to be made. "I don't like this at all. I don't like informants, and here I am bringing you one. I don't like Bresani, he set me up, as you remember, but I don't want those drugs in our schools. And, I don't ever want to meet with him in person, ever, without you or someone else from the Department with me."

He emphasized *ever*.

"Got it," Rikelman said, looking Hamilton in the eye with a look only Rikelman can give.

CHAPTER 57

||||||||||||||||||||||||||||||||||||||||||

COMMUNION

Hamilton had to give this whole thing some thought. Bresani needed to think everything was his idea, and Lt. Rikelman needed to oversee this operation. He could not confide in anyone but Rikelman, but he didn't want to appear uncertain about handling the situation.

Oh well, he had some time to strategize, he thought. *But how much time? What would Guy Coyle do?*

He walked through the station on the way back to his patrol car when he noticed a cartoon flyer posted on a hallway bulletin board.

"Retirement Party for Val and Harvey Stevens" Wow! That was the news. Both were wrapping it up. Wonder what that's about? he muttered to no one.

He had never been to a retirement dinner for anyone on the Department. It just was not something he did. If he was working the night shift, he might not have even noticed or cared about it.

Harvey Stevens, Sergeant Harvey Stevens, was a mainstay on the Department and one of the only solid supervisors with a little bit of street cop left in him. What were he and Val going to do? They're too young to hang it up.

The problem with retirement is that when you wake up, you're there. Howard had to find out more about their plans. Hell, they were almost like family. Maybe he and Clare should consider going to this one. *Damn, this day watch, with all its maggots!*

He was back on patrol when his cell phone rang.

"Howard, is that you?" He had not looked at the number to see who it was; again—*got to remind me not to answer these calls so quickly—too many surprises.*

"Yes."

"Rex Holcomb here. Do you have a minute?" Those were always fateful words around OHPD. 'You got a minute' meant somebody was going to dump something on you. He put it on speaker as he left the station parking lot. "Sure, Rex, what's up?"

"Let me run something by you. You know I'm still a Deacon at St. Elizabeth's, right?"

Of course, Howard knew. He sees him almost every time he and the family go to church. It seems like he's always there,

"Sure."

"Well, we - Father Art - is looking for a few more Eucharistic ministers to serve communion and handle some other duties around the church, and I thought of you," Rex said rather sheepishly.

"W-well," Hamilton stammered, "how much time does it take away from family and all?"

"You go to Mass anyway, so all it would mean is assigning you to a service that you would attend regularly. You would just leave your pew to either serve the host or the wine."

"That sounds too easy. What's the catch?" Howard knew there was more to it but was waiting for Rex to add something.

"Well, there are four classes you need to attend. About 90 minutes long. You may get asked to visit the sick at some nursing homes, but not much else." Rex was trying to make it as enticing as possible.

"Let me discuss it with Clare, and I'll get back to you. Is that okay? When do you need to know?"

"No rush, HH. I'll give you a week or so."

"Sounds good. Can I ask you a favor now?" Something came to Hamilton as he was listening to Rex and reflecting on their relationship and his expertise.

Hamilton went through the details of the Mason suicide and described the intricate use of yoga belts to complete the deed, the background of the victim as a possible transgender person, a college basketball player, and an accountant.

"It's more than likely a suicide, but there's something just not right with it."

"Are you in detectives and handling this case, HH?"

"No, I'm back in Patrol, but I did the preliminary investigation and called out detectives. Rollenhagan has the case, but I think he's more than willing to sign it off."

"Don't know too much about the world of yoga. It's certainly not connected to Satanism, the occult, or anything like that. Why don't you let my nose around here and see what I can find out?"

"I'd appreciate it, Rex, but call me back, don't go to Rollenhagan with anything."

"I understand, Howard. I'll get back to you. Soon."

"Oh, by the way," Howard said, "We already checked with ViCAP but couldn't find anything there."

"When did you check?" Rex queried.

"Last week, why? I also found out that ViCAP doesn't include suicides, so I don't know what I'm looking for."

"That makes two of us, Howard!" Rex chuckled. "I'll get back to you if you get back to me."

"Deal."

CHAPTER 58

||||||||||||||||||||||||||||||||||||||||||||||

DOPE

The next day Howard informed Sgt. Bennett of a meeting with Lt. Rikelman regarding a case sometime in the morning. He would put himself out to the station and advise when it was going to happen. Bennett looked at him with a smirk, "trying to get into dope?" he said.

"Nope, to dope," he said, laughing at his joke. "Just some unfinished business with the Lieutenants." *Bennett will eventually hear about it*, he thought, *but he didn't want it to be from him. Loose lips and all that.*

He called Bresani and set up a phone call with everyone for one o'clock. *How had he gotten himself into all of this?*

He was a few minutes early for the meeting with Rikelman.

"Here's the plan," Rikelman said. "We listen to what he has to say, make no comments, or very few, and tell him we'll get back to him. Is that clear, HH?"

"Yes, sir."

"We have to have time to at least verify his information. We can't just rely on what he has to say. We'll have a rep from the LA Deuce Task Force who'll just sit in the room with us, along with Barber from my unit. Bresani is not to know that, okay?" Rikelman was looking for acknowledgment at every step.

"Yes, sir."

"If he asks, it's just you and me in the room. He won't know the difference."

"Yes, sir." There was no need to interject his thoughts. It was time to make the call.

"Yeah," Bresani muttered on the other end.

"Hamilton here, John, with the Lieutenant. I want him listening, but this conversation is between you and me." Hamilton looked around the room to see Sgt. Sam Barber and the guy/girl team from LA Deuce that had initially busted Bresani.

"It's just us John, what's up?"

CHAPTER 59

||||||||||||||||||||||||||||||||||||||||||||

CONTROL

Regardless of how in control one must be in the world of police work, there is a time when silence and listening are your best tools. Those in the room knew that they didn't know enough about this situation to garner an opinion. For now, the control freaks had to merely listen.

The recorder was on, the yellow notepads and pens were poised and at the ready. If Bresani thought he was being recorded and six pens were waiting to take down his words, he probably would not even consider this operation. *What he doesn't know won't hurt him* was all Hamilton was thinking.

Howard decided to start the move forward. "So, John, what do you have for us? I mean for Lt. Rikelman. He's listening."

"I figured. How are you, Lieutenant?"

"Fine, John. What do you have? Let's get to it." There was a brief silence on both ends as thick, unspoken mutual animosity built.

"Well, here's the deal. The shipment is due to come in next week. Friday or Saturday. It's coming from Juarez and through San Diego. It's about a hundred kilos pure. Its first stop will be in Orange County, but just overnight, the product will stay intact. I don't know whether it's in a truck, SUV, or what right now. It's destined for a commercial building in the City of Irwindale. I think that's in LA County, right?"

Rikelman, in his typical staccato fashion, shot out, "Right. Do you have addresses?"

"Not yet, but I will. Here's the deal. I'd prefer you take them down on their way to the cut room in the warehouse once we pin it down. They have plans to set up a big factory operation to knock the pure down to street level there."

"Let's us decide, Bresani," Rikelman shot back. The silence pierced the room on both ends like the blade of a sword through boneless flesh.

After too long for everyone's benefit, Bresani responded. "See what I mean, Howard? You guys can't run this! I know what's goin' on here, and you don't."

It was a message that Hamilton knew both John and Rikelman were sending to each other. *Who is going to control this thing?*

"John, let me hear your entire scenario and let us get back to you with how we want to do this. I don't think we want to set up the entire operation today, or at least right now." Hamilton's tone was less militaristic and designed to buy everyone some breathing room.

"Ok, glad you see it my way." There was no way Bresani would direct the plan, and everyone on Hamilton's side of the phone knew it. They just had to keep him talking.

"The plan is to set up shop in the commercial district of the City and do the doctoring of the product there. They got some locals to help. It'll take a few days, and then the word will spread to the South Bay distributors to come down and get it. So, the plan is to have everything done by next week, and Friday and Saturday will be distribution days."

Notes were silently, but feverishly, being moved around the table between investigators. One finally reached Rikelman. Howard was oblivious to their actions as he concentrated on staring into the speaker/receiver and 'watching' Bresani.

"John?" Rikelman posed the name as if asking a question. "You do know what weekend that is, don't you?"

"I do, Lieutenant, I do. Why do you think we planned it that way?"

Hamilton was lost in this conversation. He showed it with his facial expression and raised his hands in a "what the fuck" manner.

Bresani could not resist. "It's Thanksgiving weekend, and everybody in the dope world knows the Narc's don't work on Thanksgiving, Christmas, or New Year's."

The smile on Bresani's face could be seen through the digital phone lines.

CHAPTER 60

||||||||||||||||||||||||||||||||||||||||||||||||

WEBS

Hamilton and Bresani agreed to stay in touch in the next few days as the plans progressed. When they disconnected the line, there was a moment of pause before Rikelman looked at the LA Deuce team and asked, "Did you get enough to move on this?"

"Not quite, Lieutenant. We're going to need some info from Officer Hamilton here and do some digging of our own."

Hamilton looked at Rikelman and then the two undercover narcs. "You know, I don't even know your names. We need to lay some ground rules here. I don't mind giving up this stuff because I don't want this shit in our schools. But John is adamant he only wants to deal with me on this. I kind of feel right in the middle of something I can't handle."

Rikelman held his hand up in front of the two undercovers and responded, "That's my fault, Howard. Let me introduce you to Detective Bonnie Carvin and Mike LaBonge. Bonnie is from Whittier PD and Mike from Glendale. They're both on long-term loan to the Task Force."

Once the introductions were finished, LaBonge spoke up. "We need to get an Ops plan started. I don't know if you have any of it or not, but I'm going to ask," LaBonge said. "We need everything you have on Bresani. Addresses, phone numbers, photos, what kind of cars he has access to. Do you know of any of his street associates? Who else was he tight with here at the PD? Any idea if this is a setup, or is he for real? When we took him down last time, he didn't appear to have access to much product. Why do we think he can turn this?" It was all delivered in a staccato fashion.

Rikelman looked at Hamilton, then to Bonnie and Mike as well as Sgt. Sam Barber. In typical Norman Bates style, he announced," Hamilton and Barber can I see you guys in the next room for a minute? Bonnie and Mike, we'll be right back."

Both Hamilton and Barber knew it was not a request but an order.

Rikelman closed the second interview room door, invited no one to sit, and started his lecture. "Here is how we are going to work. Barber will be your contact point, Hamilton. You do or say nothing without running it by him. Barber will be the go-between with the Deuce team. Our goal here is to build a wall between Howard and our Unit and the task force, got it, Sam?"

"Was going to suggest that Lieutenant," Barber chimed in. "Have done this before, so I know what Deuce is probably going to do."

"What's that?" Hamilton asked.

"Well, once we give them the info they asked for, they'll get a search warrant and put a GPS tracker on his car, and probably bug his phone and watch everything he does. Do we know where he's living?" Barber was showing his knowledge about how the planning was going to go.

Hamilton responded," I have his vehicle info, and we all have his phone, so I guess we can start with that. I think Admin still has his photo. You can go through his file here and give them whatever is in it. But he's changed his appearance a little. Beard and long, unkempt hair."

Rikelman quickly got them back on track. "Ok, let's go with what we have as long as we're all on the same page." He nodded to the door as he led them back to the Narcs.

Hamilton gave them the description of the Mercedes Sprinter and the personalized plate, 'B GOODE.'

"The only phone number I have is the one he called in on. He could have throwaways for all we know. He says he's living in Irvine someplace. Will try to get an address."

"Does he have another car other than the van?" Bonnie asked.

"Don't know, but I can probably find out," Rikelman said. "I know his ex-sister-in-law, Vivian."

Hamilton and Rikelman's eyes met with a knowing look. Vivian was Charley Hayes' widow, and Charlie's sister was John's ex-wife. And,

Hamilton knew something that only Rikelman and the Chief knew, and that was that Rikelman had been engaged to Vivian at one time.

"Oh, the webs we weave," Hamilton thought.

"Are you kidding me with this license plate, Hamilton?" LaBonge asked with a bit of a smirk.

"No, and it's a long story. Ever heard the song, 'Johnny B. Goode?'"

"No."

"Well, then you wouldn't get it anyway, Mike."

The nickname Bresani picked up while with OHPD appeared to have stayed with him. Even after his separation from the Department. Everyone, Sergeant and below on OHPD, picked up a nickname after they were off probation, and of course, 'Johnny B. Goode,' an ancient Chuck Berry song, went to John Bresani.

But these Deuce guys would never get it! Hamilton told himself. *Stiff, way too stiff.*

"If it's any help, I know where he keeps the van." Howard threw out as a tease.

"Where does he keep it, and how did you know?" LaBonge asked with an accusatory tone.

It was Barber's turn to chime in. "Hey, you trying to interrogate my Officer?"

"No, Sarge, but don't you think I need to know?" LaBonge was not backing down.

"Hey, it's okay, Sarge." Hamilton directed his conversation to LaBonge and told him about the Orchard Hill Storage lot.

"So, he keeps it there with the approval of the manager, huh? Then he must have another car."

"Must have," Howard said. "I guess that's where your investigative skills will have to take you."

Bonnie broke what started to become a frozen icicle in the room with, "Touche', Mike. He got you!"

They all had a good laugh, finally figuring out they just may be on the same team. Maybe.

Rikelman knew that big task forces, particularly those made up of LA Sheriff's detectives, LAPD, and the more significant county PD's, was always wary of the smaller outside agencies. There was a need to test their integrity as a department and individually.

On the other hand, Other law enforcement agencies never liked the more significant departments pushing them around or trying to play savior, or 'we're here to show you how it's done.' That mentality at the municipal and County level was generally reserved for the Federal three-letter agencies.

CHAPTER 61

|||||||||||||||||||||||||||||||||||||||||||||

ZETA

"Before we go too far here, we need to discuss something critical." LaBonge threw the topic out into a room as it was starting to warm up. Everyone could tell that he would not quickly establish a 'we are family' relationship, at least not yet.

"I don't think this is going to be an easy takedown. None of these are easy, but we're going to need a lot more resources than an average buy-bust." LaBonge took the time to look each person in the eye, moving stoically from Barber to Hamilton and finally to Rikelman.

He looked directly at Rikelman with an 'I do not want you to challenge me' stare that left everyone uneasy. Including Rikelman.

"With all due respect, Lieutenant, you're new to this unit and the world of dope, and we've never worked with you, Sam, or anybody else at this department, other than that last caper."

LaBonge was in lecture mode. "In the past, you guys stayed at home here and just passed on bits of information over the years. I checked our files, and yeah, you occasionally contribute a body to our task force, but you guys are a closed shop and like to do your own thing. Am I right?"

There was a tacit but silent agreement. Everyone in the room knew LaBonge was not done with his little speech, but no one, except Detective Carvin, knew where he was going.

"Thanks to you, Lieutenant, you saw the necessity to bring us in on this. And we appreciate it. Did anyone other than Bonnie hear the key piece of information that your CI threw out when he was describing what was going down?" LaBonge knew the answer to his question before the response.

"Let's not play games here, Mike. What're you getting at?" Rikelman added, "we're not going to get into twenty questions challenge, here are we?"

He was not going to be intimidated by this guy. Rikelman knew he was getting into territory that he was unfamiliar with and decided to keep the conversation moving. He was coaxing it out of LaBonge, but his body language was still dictating who was in charge.

"Your CI, Johnny whatever, casually mentioned that the shipment was coming from Juarez." Mike let his words hang out there in the room for an extra moment. "Anything from Juarez is a red flag to us, to our unit." He looked at Bonnie for agreement.

Rikelman could see Carvin's concern and approval of the direction her partner was going.

"Lieutenant, with all due respect, sir, have you been to the narco investigation courses for new investigators or managers of a unit like this?" LaBonge threw his hand around in a half-circle to demonstrate his reference to their surrounded offices.

"Next month," Was the rather timid reply.

"Well, in those classes, they talk about the current drug wars and who's who in the zoo. The real drug war is not being fought between law enforcement and the dealers. A lot of the politics out of D.C. would let you think that we're losing the drug war because of failed policies, but that's all political bullshit. Just think of what it would be like if we did absolutely nothing."

"The real 'war,'" LaBonge put a quote on the word, "is between the various Cartels in Mexico and Guatemala. You'll learn this in classes, but the Sinaloa's, *El Federacion*, Mexican Mafia or *La Familia,* and a few other criminal syndicates down there are fighting for the top spot with the latest new Cartel, the Zetas. They make the El Salvadorian gang, *Mara Salvatrucha* or MS-13, look like babysitters. And, most importantly, if you go by the body count, the Zetas are winning."

All Rikelman could say now was, "go on."

"The Zetas or 'Z' is the most vicious and are on their way to dominating the drug wars. They think nothing of executing our DEA or other federal agents, but they're even more demonstrative, if you will, with their own. These are some seriously demonized mother fuckers."

Bonnie didn't flinch at the term. "Describes them perfectly," she nodded.

LaBonge had a captive audience now. "To date, the drug wars down there have resulted in over fifteen thousand executions and counting. Fifteen thousand! They behead, they skin, they hang, they rape, they kill women and children. Nothing is sacred, and they seem to do it as a sport. They're raising a new generation of kids that kill for smartphones and cars. Their career goals have become to be the chief lookout and grow into being a dealer and another 'El Chapo.'" He took a much-needed breath.

"Many of the old guard gunmen that have been jailed over the years were convicted of lesser crimes than originally charged and cut deals to get shorter sentences. They're getting out now and grooming these young kids to kidnap, kill and mutilate their victims and then..." he paused for effect, "...get this, take selfies with the cutup bodies."

LaBonge now stood up with outstretched hands. "At fuckin age 16! That becomes their initiation into the new cartels. And then, they want somebody to write a song about them!"

LaBonge was almost hyperventilating as he stared at everyone in the room. "They've sent us, I mean our federal offices, our agents' heads in a box that sends the message don't fuck with us. And some of those guys were my academy classmates.'"

There was a stillness in the room, and LaBonge was going to use it for effect.

"This may be the start of the Zetas getting a stronger foothold into the U.S. and particularly California."

"Why do you say that?" Hamilton asked.

LaBonge went back into his lecture mode, "Coke is becoming passé for the Cartels because of our thirst for the cheaper drug, meth, and fentanyl. They're manufacturing it in tons down there just for the idiots on our streets. Johnny B may not even know everything that's being brought in with this shipment. I don't think he does. Doesn't sound too bright to me."

"Our CI knows how we operate, even if he isn't the brightest bulb in the light fixture," Rikelman added.

LaBonge nodded in agreement. "The problem is there are a dozen cartels at war with each other for control. No one has all the power, but the Zetas want to change that. I don't think Bresani knows it. They're sending photos worldwide through social media of their mass graves containing the bodies of kidnaped officials, severed heads, and federal agents burned to death in the middle of a highway. Jesus, Americans used to go to Acapulco, but it's now one of the deadliest cities in the world. Bresani doesn't know who he's fuckin with!"

LaBonge was shouting now.

No one challenged any of that bit of wisdom.

CHAPTER 62

||||||||||||||||||||||||||||||||||||||||||||||

JUAREZ

Hamilton could see the respect Rikelman gained for LaBonge, but he also knew that Norman Bates still lurked in the background. No one was going to see Norman, not now anyway.

"So, I guess what you're saying is to go slow on this then, Mike?"

"Very slowly, Lieutenant. And we'll need some help on this from our team."

"I understand," Rikelman said, "and I do bow to your expertise in all of this, but we have to remember Bresani is our source CI, and he'll only talk to Officer Hamilton here."

"We understand that, Lt. but there may be a time..." he paused for that agonizing moment that everyone knew was coming, "...for now, sir, for now."

"Where do we go from here?" Hamilton threw out the anticipated question.

"Well, I wasn't completely done with my little class here," LaBonge retorted.

"Go on, go on," Rikelman prodded.

"The fact that the shipment is coming from Juarez is very bothersome to us."

"Why?" Hamilton, Barber, and Rikelman all asked simultaneously.

LaBonge settled into his lecture once again. "As I said, Juarez is the home base for the Zetas. It has been and probably always will be. Normally their shipments are made through the El Paso corridor. EPIC's Feds task force is effective in controlling the borders there, with a few exceptions. The Zetas have not, to our knowledge, been successful in compromising those borders, if you know what I mean."

"What do you mean 'compromising'?" Hamilton had to ask.

With a nod from LaBonge, Bonnie finally chimed in. "It means the Zetas don't have anyone on this side of the border on their payroll, at least not yet. Theirs is a billion - yes, billion-dollar organization. They wave millions in front of people to work with them. The problem is, if they don't cooperate, they not only threaten but carry out executions against their own employees' families."

Bonnie paused to let everyone know it was her turn on the lecture circuit. "Next to bribery, criminal extortion is third in line for these career criminals. It's an underground, corrupt economic system that has grown south of the border. Extortion by these drug gangs is what is killing the Mexican economy and why so many people want asylum here in the U.S." She looked around to make sure she had everyone's attention. She did.

"This is bigger than organized crime. It's become 'authorized crime,'" holding her fingers in quotes, "because there's extortion at the highest levels. The Mexican government won't confront it, so it just escalates. The gangs are the other government. Farmers are walloped with gangs manipulating the pricing of basic goods from fruits, vegetables, and other products. The cartel is controlling unions, and cab drivers are routinely killed for not paying protection money. And this is all coming from Juarez, right to our borders. Pepsi and Coke have closed their distribution centers, and tourist buses that don't pay the tariff are firebombed."

"But, and it's a big but," LaBonge added, "if they're making an entrance through San Diego, they may have somebody on their payroll, and this is a test shipment to see how it works. It could be Border Patrol or some unique avenue we haven't explored yet. They seem to move with impunity. With the cooperation of the Mexican drug enforcement units that we don't completely trust, they say that the tunnels have been secured, so we don't know what to expect."

"Here's the thing," Bonnie added, "the Zetas are the most brutal of the Cartels right now. They want total control of the drug and extortion trade. And not just in the States. They're now after the European market. They want the fresh new turf of France, Germany, and Spain, particularly

Spain. Just south of our borders, it's not uncommon to find the heads of the Zetas competition posted on sticks along the roadside. Seven to ten at a time. We've not seen that kind of brutality on our side of the border... yet. And don't want to."

"I can see we have your attention," LaBonge added, "and that's good because these guys have unique ways of sending messages. With their people, many times their enemies go missing."

He stood up to make his point again, "I don't want to repeat myself, but they'll kidnap high-ranking officials' relatives and send their body parts back to their offices in the mail. They'll chop up the bodies and put them in fifty-five-gallon drums and either fill them with acid or pour wet concrete in and toss them in a river or the ocean. We estimate that of the over fifteen thousand drug war deaths in Mexico, seven thousand or more occurred in the Juarez area that the Zetas now control."

"Jesus!" Rikelman finally broke the stillness that was in the room as the result of what they had learned.

"We have to regroup here a little. Can I get in touch with your boss to meet with him in your offices and go over what we need to do and what resources we need?" Hamilton had not seen Rikelman so conciliatory before. This was a first.

Orchard Hill had not seen anything like this in the past, Howard was thinking. *And never wants to.*

Elapsed time: 46 minutes

CHAPTER 63

||||||||||||||||||||||||||||||||||||||||||||||

REX

There was no such thing as normalcy anymore. Hamilton was gradually becoming a cynical, distrusting zealot about the safety of his community. He had been transformed from a small-town cop with very little to contribute to his community into a paranoid warrior.

Suddenly, he was not sure of anyone or anything. Who could he trust? His fellow officers, those who 'trespassed' in his city, or even some of his supervisors? His little world of driving by work on his way to raising a family, owning a home, and loving God had infected his environments like a disease.

The day-watch maggots had enveloped his very soul, influenced his wellbeing, and were starting to taint his view of the world. All in just a few months! He had been much happier being a guardian of his City and handling his shift work as if someone he knew lived down the street. He had taken pride in solving the problems in his neighborhoods, so they would not recur.

He would always ask himself and reflect on 'what would I do if my mother lived next door to this situation?' It made so much sense.

He needed a strong Clare fix. Downtime to talk this out. She was better than any Department shrink, and if anything, he needed time to sort this out. And then his cell phone rang.

"Couple things," Rex said with little preamble. "You ran one of your cases by me, and I thought I would make some inquiries, but first...have you given any more thought to that request I made?"

"What request?"

"About becoming a Eucharistic minister at St. Elizabeth's."

"Gosh Rex, I'm sorry. I was going to talk it over with Clare, and we never got around to that. Can you give me a few days?"

"Sure," Rex was quick on the draw with his response. "No pressure, just thought I would touch base. But that's not the reason for the call. Remember you asked about a case involving yoga?"

"Yes…"

"Well, Rampart dicks have an interesting case about an S&M, you know, sadomasochist type killing. It's not in my area of expertise but comes close. And yoga is involved."

"Tell me more."

"It seems this victim was phallocentric, passing himself off as a monk and giving classes that bordered on violence, but was just your typical S&M. They combined that in yoga classes for the wealthy with alternative lifestyles. Anyway, he was found dead and naked in the studio that was a horrors chamber for that crowd, if you know what I mean."

"Not really, not my area of expertise either, Rex."

"Glad to hear that!" he laughed. "Per the dicks, he was found in a building set up like a jail cell with shackles attached to the walls so that they could beat each other. He was naked on the floor, wrapped with yoga belts in what they called a modified lotus position, and get this, sucking his dick." Rex paused for effect.

"Jesus - I mean, sorry Rex - but are you kidding me? That's a hell of a picture!"

"I know Howard. There are a lot of weird things that go on in our world. We get to see it from our end. I heard about the case working something else and thought it might have some significance to your suicide, just because it was all yoga stuff."

"Do you do yoga?"

"No, but I'll do yoga with you if you become a Eucharistic minister. And one other condition."

"What's that?" Howard asked but thought he knew the answer.

"If your yoga doesn't include S&M!"

"Deal!" They both laughed.

"Do you mind if I pass this info along to the guy handling the case at our end? I won't tell him where I got it."

Rex was quick on the draw. "Leave me out of it too, but let me give you the contact at Rampart. The homicide D-3, or sorry, detective supervisor, over the case is Len Patterson. Good guy. He'll work with your guy...who is it?"

"Dieter Rollenhagen. Give Patterson a heads up, and I'll pass it along. Funny, I thought all the weird shit in LA was in Hollywood."

"According to Patterson, this building is on the northwest side of Rampart and butts up to Hollywood. It's in one of those buildings that look abandoned and boarded up. You go around to the back where the entrance is, and there's a small sign with the business name, "Rear Entrance." Get it?"

"No."

"Think about it. You will. Anyway, I saw the photos in the murder book, and it's a very elaborate setup with ultra-modern equipment and furniture, lounge areas, steam and sauna rooms, and a few jail cells. Well, TMI Howard, too much info. Have your guy get in touch with Rampart dicks and call me in a few. Oh, and Howard, one more thing...."

"Yes?"

"I only want to deal with you, not your Detective whatshisname. You're the go-between as I need to build a big wall on this one. No one knows I am talking to you. I'm your CI, and you're mine. Let's keep it that way."

"Roger. I promise not to lay you out. One more question before you go, Rex. My investigative questions are starting to rear up. By the way, did you say, 'butts up to Hollywood?" and I said, 'rear up and lay you out?'" They laughed again as the gallows humor took over.

"What did the victim do for a living, Rex, just teach yoga?"

"No, that's another thing. He was married to a wife and had two kids. He lived in the Hollywood Hills and was in the jewelry business. Dealt with high-end diamonds and lived a good life."

CHAPTER 64

IIIIIIIIIIIIIIIIIIIIIIIIIIIIIIIIIIIIIIIIIII

AGAIN

There was that discussion of a 'wall' again.

Hamilton flashed through his brain. He had been in police work for over seven years and had never heard or understood the term until recently. This was not going to be easy for a lot of reasons.

Would Rollenhagan buy not talking to Holcomb? He has no choice. Will he even consider all this or just keep the case as a suicide? Too easy, he thought, to just say no. Probably need to talk to someone about all of this, but who? Walker? No, Lieutenant Hospian? Big no. Sergeant Stevens? Hell, he has one foot out the door. Good grief, it must be Rikelman of all people.

Hamilton decided to sleep on it. That meant to talk to Clare about it but in more general terms. She didn't need to know all the graphic details.

The drive home was not nearly enough time to think everything through.

Now he understood how those guys who lived some jillion miles away from work could decompress better. They had alone time in the car and cleansed their brain of the days' work after they hung up their uniform in the locker. After ten hours of fighting the world at work and then an hour on the freeway, all could be right with the world. But not in less than ten minutes.

But... *Did I say but or butt? he laughed to himself.* ...he had Clare, Geoff, and Marcia, which made it so much easier to decompress.

In the standard cop dress of blue jeans, untucked t-shirt to cover his off-duty weapon, running shoes, and, oh yes, the sunglasses, he arrived home, plopped his keys on the end table, and was greeted ceremoniously by Clare with a hug and peck on the cheek.

"Nice to have you home at a decent time, Howard. Did you pick up Marcia at Beverly's as I asked?"

"Whoops," he muttered to the wall but loud enough for her to hear.

"Do I have to do everything around here, Howard, or are you a part of this family too?"

"Uh, oh," he thought, *"this isn't good!"*

"Never mind, I'll go get her. You just come home and put your feet up on the coffee table and have a glass of wine! You have no idea how much work it is to keep this house up." She was getting angrier by the minute now.

"Just today, I did three loads of laundry, vacuumed the entire house, paid some bills, went to a school meeting, and got my car washed and gassed at Costco."

Howard knew by now it was not a time to reason or even engage in a civil conversation.

"And you, all you did was go to work, dirty some clothes, and expect to be waited on!"

He was out the door after grabbing his keys.

Where the hell did Beverly live anyway?

CHAPTER 65

||||||||||||||||||||||||||||||||||||||||||||||||||

MARCIA

Beverly Toomey, Marcia's best friend, lived just far enough away that Marcia could not walk the distance. She was on the other side of Orchard Hill but still in the same school district. At twelve, Marcia was just starting to become a young woman. Next year would start her teenage years. Those ugly, defying, and yet defining years.

He arrived at the Toomey residence. It was a somewhat rundown or unkempt home. Music was blasting through the paper-thin walls. He didn't recognize the song or artist, but to him, the music of the day was just noise, no melody or message, a bit of anger wrapped in a beat with the potential of breaking an eardrum.

He knocked, then knocked again, just a little bit louder. The third time, he pounded the door, knowing they may not have heard him over the loud bass level.

The door slowly opened, and he was met with a familiar odor. From his training at the Police Academy to his time on the streets of Orchard Hill, the smell was all too familiar. Cannabis.

A boy somewhere between twelve and twenty answered the door with a drawl and slow welcome…."Yeah?"

"Would you send Marcia to the door?" Howard requested in an as calm but stern manner as he could muster.

"Marcia? Ahhh…?"

"Marcia Hamilton, buddy," Howard now demanded, moving his foot to keep the door open. *Fuck it. I'm not a cop here. I'm a Dad.*

165

He walked past the man/boy into the house, finding himself in the front room of a very small two-bedroom looking as messy as the front yard. He saw her right away, sitting in a chair by herself. And on her phone.

No words were exchanged because there did not have to be. Marcia walked out to the small front porch area, still talking on the phone. He turned and pointed to the door, indicating it was more than time to leave.

"Who are you talking to, young lady?" he demanded.

"To Mom. Where've you been? I've been waiting for you!" She started to become obstinate but quickly reverted to tears. "I didn't want to be there. I made a mistake coming over to Beverly's house. Sorry."

Hamilton grabbed her cell phone. "We'll be right home," and hung up.

He escorted his only daughter to the passenger side of the car without saying a word. She buckled in as he walked around the rear to the driver's side, trying to collect his thoughts before opening the door and getting more pissed.

He sat staring at the windshield, hoping the answer of how to handle this situation would etch or scroll in ticker tape across the glass. He was trying not to be a police officer. He needed to be a Dad.

How was he going to handle this?

Elapsed time: 23 minutes

CHAPTER 66

||||||||||||||||||||||||||||||||||||||||||||

DECISIONS

The silence was deafening. The car engine was not on. The only element of sound were other cars driving by in the background. His heart was beating too rapidly to get any words out. Marcia was holding her breath and trying vainly not to cry.

Both knew this was a defining moment in their relationship as dad and daughter. Neither wanted it to deteriorate into name-calling, shouting, or worse. But who would break the ice?

Howard had what he would call an okay relationship with Marcia, but he surrendered the role of parent to her Mom. He decided that after realizing he had more in common with Geoff than a frilly girl-girl like Marcia.

Clare had bonded well with their only daughter. Howard always felt that their relationship was enough for her to grow into adulthood, with him adding tidbits here and there. Maybe he was wrong and should have helped more in her life, making more of an attempt at influencing her thoughts and needs.

He reflected on a conversation with Mr. Coyle, whose daughter, Tac, he had a brief encounter that led to their friendship. Coyle told him that girls are great from birth to about twelve, and then they get to be a challenge. On the other hand, boys were tough to raise growing up to their teens and then become young men and much easier to parent. He was comfortable with Geoff and his maturity but had not paid much attention to Marcia's aging process. *Now maybe it was time.*

It was a decisive moment.

He reached over the center console of his Explorer and spoke rather softly. "Come here." In a mutual embrace, they clung to one another without a word being spoken. He knew he was communicating and hoped she knew her Dad was there for her, even if the words did not come.

"I was begging for Mom to pick me up but didn't want to let anyone know, so I didn't call," she finally blurted out. "I had no idea that Beverly's friends were going to be there, let alone do what they were doing. When I saw you at the door, I was so relieved."

"I'll bet you were," Howard said with a slight bit of sarcasm.

"Dad, don't you believe me?"

"I do, Marcia, but..." the word lingered out there a bit too long.

"Beverly is, was, my friend. But not a best friend, if you know what I mean. She seemed more mature than the other girls. We walked out of school together, and she asked if I wanted to come over to her house for a bit to listen to music."

"Uh-huh."

"Mom said she would have you pick me up on the way home. Things were quiet for a while at Bev's house, then some older boys I didn't know started showing up." She was trying to regain a level of confidence again.

"I wished that you would get off work early and come get me, but it seemed like a long time. Then the weird stuff started with this guy Jake. Other girls showed up, so I just went over to a chair and stayed away from everybody." Howard was still holding her hand as they were unembraced during her story.

"And, why didn't you just leave?"

"Beverly knew I was uncomfortable, but she just thought I was shy. She doesn't know what you do, and I haven't told her. I was hoping you would show up quicker."

A Father's lie detector does not work as well as a Mothers'. Mom's seem to know, but Dads can be bluffed or convinced their little girl has done nothing wrong. Howard's detection system was not trying to play games on him. He did believe or wanted to believe what Marcia told him.

Am I wrong to believe her, or should I put my cop hat on?

He was going to test her. "Who had the drugs?"

"Jake," was her one-word reply.

"Are you sure he was the one who brought them or were they already there at Beverly's house?"

"No, he brought them, I'm pretty sure."

"Why do you think that?"

"Because nothing happened until he showed up. Everybody was buddying up to him once he walked in the door, Dad."

"Who is he, and where does he go to school? He looked older than a middle school kid."

"I don't know." She turned to face him head-on once again. "I think Orchard Hill High, but I'm not sure."

"Can you get me his last name and where he goes to school, or better yet, where he lives?"

"Dad, are you going to arrest him? Do you know how much trouble I'd be in with my friends...if my Dad... arrested Beverly's friend? Dad, come on!" There was a slight sense of urgent pleading in her voice.

"I'll tell you straight out, Marsh. I don't know. I don't. I have to think about all of this a bit more." He paused as Marcia's cell phone rang.

"It's Mom," she said simply and put her on speaker. "Hi, Mom, we're on our way."

Howard added a "Hi Mom" to let her know they were together.

"Where have you been, you guys?"

He held up his hand to ensure Marcia didn't talk. "We've just been chatting, you know, dad to daughter stuff."

"What kind of 'stuff'?"

"Just 'stuff,' see you in a *few*." Howard hit disconnect on the phone.

He started the car and put it in gear. He could see Marcia's reflection in the driver's side window as he spoke into the glass, "let's just keep this between you and me for now, Marsh."

There was a break in the traffic and a break in the conversation, both only lasting as long as it took to get to the next subject.

When do we tell Mom?

Elapsed time: 23 Minutes

169

CHAPTER 67

||||||||||||||||||||||||||||||||||||||||||||||||||

HOME

Dinner was on the table, waiting for them. Howard and Marcia walked into the kitchen, trying to act as if nothing happened.

"Well," Clare said as she placed the salads at each of the four corners of the table, "thought you guys ran out of gas or something. I was starting to get worried."

"No need, Hon, we just took some time to catch up on a few things," Howard tried a lighthearted approach.

Marcia said nothing and merely smiled to no one in particular.

"Geoff, how was your day? That test go okay at school?" Howard was trying to work the room to the more typical family talk.

"Aced it!" Geoff said rather proudly. "It all came together, and it was everything I studied!"

Clare acted surprised at both the question and the answer. "Didn't know you had a test today, Geoff. How did you know, Howie?"

"What family do you think this is, Hon? I'm not just a drive-by Dad since I've been on days."

It was the icebreaker that both Marcia and her Dad needed to move the conversation.

With another catch-up on the past few days' events, dinner conversation moved to the following weekend activities. Beverly Toomey was now in the past.

Howard announced he had some office work to do and get back to a new Jack Reacher novel he found.

"Whose Jack Reacher? Clare queried.

"Just a character in some fiction novels that everyone is reading. And believe me, it is fiction!"

Marcia chimed in, "You ought to write a book, Dad. I'll bet you have some stories that are better than Jake. What's his name?" She didn't even realize that her reference to 'Jake' was a slip of the tongue.

"It's Jack, not Jake, Marsh, and it's Reacher, Jack Reacher. And it's something for Mom's and Dad's, not you kids. At least not yet." He and Marcia laughed as if only they knew the secrets hidden in that series of conversation. And they did.

Everyone went their separate ways after the table was cleared. Clare demanded that she be the one to put the dishes in the dishwasher. "You guys clear, and I'll stack them, my way, so out of the kitchen."

She didn't have to say it twice.

Howard took out the trash and eventually found his way to his cubbyhole of an office. It was his escape from the world that he found relaxed him as good as a dip in a jacuzzi. There was a serenity in a ten by twelve room that was no larger than a prison cell but with no lock on the door.

He left the door open to his office most of the time. As he approached his desk, he noticed a bright pink Post-it stuck to the middle of his computer screen. Clare was always leaving little 'love you' notes around in the most obscure places. But there were more words than the two he was used to seeing.

He looked closer and saw it was Marcia's handwriting. Jake Radshaw, not Jack Reacher.

CHAPTER 68

||||||||||||||||||||||||||||||||||||||||||||||

ROLLENHAGAN

It was time to talk to 'Sgt. Shultz.' aka Dieter Rollenhagan. While he knew they would not just give the detective position to him, Howard was not sure Rollenhagan was the best selection. But what did he know? He was just a street cop.

Rollie had already settled into his position and was dressed the part as well. The overtime in Homicide gave them more expensive suits, better gun belts, and just more bling to their step. Or was it the cufflinks? Anyway, he knew where the 187 dicks went for breakfast and thought he would catch Rollenhagan after his ritualistic morning session.

He sat in the parking lot of The Omelet Factory in Shop 885, just off Albion Avenue, to wait until Rollenhagan came out from his routine breakfast stop. His Peet's coffee in hand, he saw three obvious detectives pay their bill and come out the front of the diner. Rollenhagan was the one in the middle.

"Dieter, can we talk?" Howard asked.

"What do you need, Hamilton?"

"Just your time." Hamilton nodded to the other two detectives.

"My car's over there," pointing to one of the new plainclothes detective cars from Karsdon's Kars. Rollenhagan nodded to the other two detectives to say, 'I'll see you later,' then urged Hamilton towards the black Dodge Charger without saying anything.

"What's this about, Howard, that suicide? Or do you still want my job?"

"Yes and no, and in that order, Rollie. I might like your old job on the auto theft table, but Homicide is over my head right now."

"I'll keep that in mind. What's up on the Mason case?"

"Well," he hesitated, wanting to do this right. "I have a friend who happens to work LAPD. He and I talked about things, and the next thing you know, I was telling him about your case. He constantly jabs me that nothing goes on in Orchard Hill, and we have it easy compared to the war zones in LA."

"And?"

"I was telling him about the yoga belts that our victim used when he did the dirty deed of hanging himself."

"Go on... wait, how do you know they're yoga belts and not just straps?"

"I do yoga, and they're very much like what my instructor uses, and we use in class."

"You do yoga?"

"Yeah, with my wife, over at Yoga Bungalow, off Obispo." There was silence as Rollenhagan was deciding whether to make a not-so-positive comment. He decided not to.

"Anyway, LAPD Rampart has a homicide where the victim was wrapped up in yoga straps. He was naked and in what they call the 'lotus position' sucking his dick."

"What's the lotus position?", Rollenhagan was expressing some level of interest.

Hamilton described the position as well as he could without demonstrating in the middle of the parking lot.

"I get it. You think it's connected to Mason?"

"Don't know. Not my case, and I didn't pursue it."

"Where do we go from here, Howard?"

"Well, for starters, you might want to contact Rampart homicide, the D-3 there, Len Patterson."

"You seem to know a lot of LA guys, Howard."

"Don't even know him, Dieter."

"Who's your contact then?"

"Can't tell you or I'd..., well you know."

"So that's it?"

"Yup! That's all I got." Hamilton was taking a bit too much pride in being the keeper of information.

"Do you have Patterson's number?"

"Nope. You're the Detective, Rollie. Use those investigative skills that got you the job. And, hey, Patterson might be somebody to invite to Home Plate for a drink after this is over."

They looked at each other in a way that said, 'maybe we could get along, or maybe even be friends someday.'

"I'll let you know what I find out, Howard. It's worth a call."

"It is Rollie, it is."

They gave each other a half-assed handshake and committed to staying in touch if either got new information.

Got that off my plate, Hamilton said to no one as he walked back to his black and white. *Well, maybe for just a little while, anyway.*

Elapsed time: 23 minutes

CHAPTER 69

||||||||||||||||||||||||||||||||||||||||||||||||

BUSINESS

Bresani was working harder than when he was in the police department. It seemed like he never had a day off setting up this drug deal. Done right, it was going to give him an unlimited quantity to sell and branch him out to other business lines to launder the money into legitimate businesses.

He was ready to open the floodgates into the South Bay as the shipments came through Mexico from Juarez and up through San Diego. It was a roundabout system that he was convinced would work if only 'they,' his new partners, would let him into the inner circle.

He had to earn it, but he was well on his way to doing so because of Nicole. Since buying his Sprinter from her at the Mercedes dealership, they had started seeing each other. She might have thought they were in love, but to Johnny, they were 'fuck buddies.'

Mercedes were easy to sell, but Johnny was making it even easier. He became the link for his business partners to purchase new and used Mercedes for everyone in his latest venture. They all loved the MBZ look, the personalized clothing line that she provided, and the easy way to pass cash through a system that Bresani had set up. It was all so sweet! Nicole was 'hot,' had a good business head on her shoulders and a body that would not quit.

One of Bresani's responsibilities was to take a loaner car from Nicole's dealership, generally a trade-in of an older, non-Mercedes brand, and drive it on a back route from their headquarters in the industrial area of San Gabriel Valley to the Mexican border via Interstate-5. He would drive

Interstate-10, the 210, or 91 to the 15 and then head south to the border on alternate trips.

He would identify where the hot spots would be for California Highway Patrol Stations along the route or where Border Patrol stakeouts were likely to be located. He would also monitor patrol practices on the various freeways and major highways.

He would drive at various times of the day and night, often taking Nicole with him for a weekend stay on either side of the border. After October, he was by himself, as weekends for the end-of-year car sales would occupy her time at the dealership.

He had decided, however, that he was never going to transport their product. That was not his job, and he told them so. He also made it clear he would not get the 'mules' needed to carry the product. He could provide the cars, verify the routes and times of transport, and parallel the shipments during travel times.

Rather than balk at his demands, his new partners thought his plan of operation was more sophisticated than they had seen. They let him run with it.

Initially, he had a few run-ins with his new business partners. Blackie Sampson was a biker and former jock lineman with a few years in pro football. His sidekick was a hot-blooded Puerto Rican by way of New York, Carlos Fuentes. With Bresani's Italian roots from the Bronx, he and Carlos hit it off, talking about the old streets, cops on the take, and who knew who.

He couldn't warm up to Blackie. He was one of those overweight, and muscle turned to soft tissue types with arms as big as Johnny's thighs.

Bresani felt Blackie didn't trust him. He was not so sure he trusted Blackie, either. It had become a mutual distrust. Ideally, he would have run a record check on him to determine how bad an asshole he was, but it was too late now. No one, not even Hamilton, would risk their job to accommodate him.

If he needed somebody to stay close to, it would be Carlos. Blackie would have to prove himself, not the other way around. He had his expertise as an ex-cop, and he was going to flaunt that. Blackie thought he knew but didn't.

What bothered him the most about Blackie was the way he looked at

Nicole. It was business, all business, and Bresani wanted to keep it that way. He would make it a point to watch and listen. He made a mental note to ask Nicole if Blackie had tried to make a move on her. There would be a time when, if he even tried to get next to her, it would be his last.

CHAPTER 70

||||||||||||||||||||||||||||||||||||||||||||||

RAMPART

Dieter knew Hamilton was right. He needed to conduct a follow-up investigation on the Mason case, but he wasn't going to give him credit for whatever he found. He thought he had a good idea that Hamilton didn't want any acknowledgment for prompting him to contact LAPD.

Contacting Detective Patterson was the easy part. Finding Rampart was another issue. The Rampart police station was one of over 21 divisions of the LAPD. It's bordered by the LA River, the central area of downtown, the Santa Monica freeway, and Hollywood's streets.

His appointment was for today at 1000 hours. He had never driven to LA from the South Bay during peak traffic times, so MapQuest would have to get him there. With Orchard Hill having its own County Court building serving the South Bay, he rarely had to go to the Central Criminal Courts building downtown.

It took over an hour to get to the new Rampart Station on 6th Street. According to the plaque on the building entrance, the station had been on the site of an old receiving hospital to make way for a modern police facility. It was a new building that looked old already—typical LA.

With the Mason case file tucked under his arm, he identified himself to the desk officer and advised he had an appointment with Detective Patterson.

Patterson arrived at the appointed time and escorted him through the cavernous stacks of desks, tables, and paperwork. There were piles of boxes along the walls that must have some sense of order, but Rollenhagen couldn't see it.

They found a small interview room, not unlike the ones at OHPD, just a little dirtier. Patterson's shirt and tie did not match, but with his sidearm and ammo pouch askew on his belt, there was no mistaking him for an old-time detective. Of the best kind.

They both settled in with matching machine-made coffees. Patterson had the Murder Book and Rollenhagen his case folder.

Was it going to be 'I'll show you mine if you show me yours first?

"Let me tell you what we have, Dieter. We get one of these cases at least once a year. S&M homicide with a few weird twists. Our victim is a white male in his forties, married with two kids, and lives in the Hollywood Hills. By the way, how did you hear about this case? We've kept it out of the papers, far as I know."

Rollenhagen had anticipated the question and had a pat answer. "I think some of our guys hang out with some of your guys doing motocross, had some beers together at a watering hole called Home Plate, and it came up. I thought I would use it as an excuse to compare it with our suicide and expand my horizons. I'm new to Homicide, so anything I can learn would be good." Dieter thought he had sold it that way, and he was right.

"Yeah, guys love to talk about the more bizarre cases, I guess." Patterson took that at face value and continued.

"Anyway, our victim was a diamond dealer, and we initially thought it might be related to that. It turns out it probably had nothing to do with it, but we still don't know right now."

Patterson shuffled some papers around and reached for another stack. "He studied eastern ritual yoga and Buddhist teachings involving using manipulation for sexual pleasure. He was an instructor in this practice and used it to cultivate relations with his students, both male and female."

Patterson's matter-of-fact style made the storyline very believable. "So, we have a lot of suspects to sift through, and my guys are doing those interviews this week."

"Before we go too far, let me explain something. I'm a D-3, Homicide supervisor. The Detectives handling this case work for me. They have a few open cases, like ten or more, so I didn't want to tie them up with you until I knew what you had. My time is more flexible than theirs."

He paused to get some agreement and then continued. "If you can tell me a little bit about your case, maybe I can get one of them to look at it in more detail."

"That's a deal, Len, so here goes,"

It took about thirty minutes to walk Patterson through his case file and a bit of background on Mason. Patterson listened very intently and asked no questions until he was finished. Dieter let some silence pass.

"Can I see the photos?" Patterson quietly asked. "I made you a copy of the autopsy report on our victim, but it was pretty straightforward strangulation with the straps. No sex change or hormone injections were found.

He looked at them for what seemed a long time. "Do you have a close-up of those yoga straps?"

Dieter paused. "No, not right now, but I can send them to you. Why?"

Patterson opened his Murder Book to the photos and showed the close-up pictures of the belts used to tie up his victim. One eight-by-ten photo was a shot of the brown buckled end of the strap with the label reading 'Barefoot Yoga – 10.'

There were photos of the straps, or belts, uniquely wrapped around the victim and a video clip of how they were taken off the body. Other photos displayed shots of the external portion of the building, a sign Rear Entrance, a name that served several purposes.

Other photos depicted whips and chains, shackles attached to the walls of rooms that could only be called cells, adding to the bizarre.

"I'm not sure," Dieter said with some misgivings, "but I think my belts say 'Barefoot Yoga' too. I'll let you know." He felt a little foolish in the presence of a veteran homicide dick.

He now realized he was a bit over his head with Patterson and had much more to learn. Going from Auto Theft to Homicide was a big jump. A massive jump! Hell, he hasn't even been to Homicide School!

Elapsed time: 46 minutes

CHAPTER 71

||||||||||||||||||||||||||||||||||||||||||||||

STRAPS

Patterson and Rollenhagan agreed to exchange critical information regarding their cases but would both have to run it by their bosses. Patterson thought it would not be a problem at his end, and Dieter knew it could be at OHPD but didn't want to say anything.

"Have you done any kind of profile on your suicide victim yet?" Patterson asked, knowing the answer.

"Not yet," Dieter said with some level of evasiveness.

They agreed to stay in touch, but Rollenhagan felt he got a big lesson on death investigations. No one knew where he got the tips, and no one would have to. At least no one at OHPD.

And Hamilton was right. Maybe Patterson was somebody to invite to Home Plate when it was all over. The OHPD drinking spot was only known to a few other PD's, and he wasn't sure if LAPD knew about it or not. No doubt, they had their own. And more than one.

He drove back to Orchard Hill from downtown in the opposite direction of the commuters. He was back in his City in just thirty minutes with a list of things to do on a case he thought he had closed. *Just a few odds and ends, he thought, just a few.*

He walked downstairs to the evidence room. Sara, the CSI tech, was pregnant and reassigned to light duty in the evidence room to avoid chemical exposure in the CSI Unit. Dieter didn't know or want the details of that little scene, having only heard rumors from the dolphins about who the father was.

He completed the paperwork to pull the Mason case evidence box and take photos of the yoga straps in various stages. He glanced at them as she pulled the box from its shelf and, even without looking closely, knew they were the same as the LAPD case. *But yoga belts, or straps, were generic, right? And, what was Patterson's victims' name again?*

His department-issued cell phone chimed. He had an email message. That was quick! It looked rather lengthy so he decided to check it on his computer when he got upstairs. He did see it was from Patterson.

Sara let him know it would take her about an hour to photo the belts as she processed other items. "Do you also want any of the items from the case that were just booked as 'safekeeping'?" she asked. "I can pull that for you right now."

Sara knew Dieter was new to Homicide and probably didn't know which end was up yet. She was prompting him to be a little more thorough with his first death investigation.

"Oh, yeah, I was going to get to that," he said a bit sheepishly. Not wanting to be a complete fool, he took the box that held the various books from the storage area where Mason had been found and checked them out.

"I'll be upstairs in the conference room with these for a few hours, Sara."

"No problem," She said, "sign here and here, and I'll bring up the photos when I get them done."

He grabbed several envelopes to put items in for analysis and took the back stairs to the detective conference room. His phone chimed again. He saw the subject line from Patterson. It read, *Victim Profile.*

CHAPTER 72

||||||||||||||||||||||||||||||||||||||||||||||

PROFILE

Patterson's Homicide guys had done an incredible job with their victim profile of George Blankenship. Dieter looked it over and was very impressed with the format. Everything was filled in with essential information and in extensive detail.

Maybe they got the format in Homicide School because OHPD didn't seem to have such an extensive template.

He emailed Patterson's attachment to the conference room computer, locked the door, closed the blinds, and took a deep breath. *Let's go to school,* he thought.

Several boxes were taken from Mason's storage area, but Sara also gave him the yoga books and college annuals. He brought up the profile on Blankenship and continued to scroll down to see photos of the straps around his neck and the body in its initial stage of discovery.

The profile report indicated that the private yoga club members knew him as 'Geshe George.' According to the information provided by the Rampart dicks, a Geshe degree is one of Tibetan Buddhism's highest academic achievements and takes decades to attain.

Geshe George was a somewhat controversial figure in that he rejected many of the orthodox teachings of Buddhism and brought his version more in line with the sadomasochistic rituals of The Rear Entrance Studio. He had secretly broken his monastic vows by getting married, but no one at the Studio or in the world of Tantra Yoga knew. He had also fathered two children.

Blankenship was a world traveler and gave everyone the impression that he was going to various Buddhist retreats. He commuted to New York's diamond district, working for a company started by two Israelis. He quickly assisted them in growing into a two-hundred fifty-million-dollar manufacturer of mass-marketed jewelry.

His travels took him to South Africa and Russia. He learned branding diamonds with a birth certificate to trace their history from the mines to the retail stores, a system known as the Kimberly Process. At his busiest, he oversaw processing up to thirty-thousand stones a day.

Blankenship donated over half his wealth to his college alma mater. A portion also went to The Asian Classics Input Project, which transferred the decaying texts of Tibet theology into digital files for over twenty-five years. He was also in escrow to purchase the yoga studio and expand it to a 'Sampson and Delila' private club for alternative lifestyle men and women.

It looked like he was focusing on the high-end business and political world who desired an intimate and discrete meditation practice of Tantra Yoga and sadomasochistic bondage.

Rollenhagan continued to read Blankenship's profile with amazement. He practiced the pleasure/pain traditions, elevated his followers above their troubled place in life, and restored their spiritual confidence. Obedience and domination blended with the infliction of pain and ecstasy to produce an experience beyond what could be achieved through the routine practice of yoga. All with secret initiation ceremonies, altered states of consciousness leading to out-of-body encounters and intense orgasmic experiences.

Blankenship touted his monk-type existence. The conundrum was he was also in the process of purchasing a ten-acre piece of land in Tombstone, Arizona. He planned to develop a silent retreat house comparable with the Temples of his religion. Meanwhile, his reputation was being tainted by his yogi contemporaries; as he was known for creating orgasmic encounters with his closest students, commenting he wanted to 'embrace his feminine side.'

Rollenhagan skimmed the remaining part of the text, looking for anything he could tie into Mason, other than the yoga straps. And then he found it. *Jesus, Oh, my,* he uttered.

His breathing stuttered for a moment as he continued to read Blankenship's profile. Before his attendance at a monastery in India called

Sera Mey, he attended Ohio University in the mid-nineties and played basketball. He looked around the room, knowing he was alone, but wanting to tell someone.

His victim, Broderick Mason, had also attended Ohio University in those same years and played basketball!

Dieter moved to the box housing the college yearbooks and yoga texts. He grabbed the 1994 yearbook for the Bobcats and opened it to the athletic programs.

The team photo stood out like it was three-dimensional. There was the 1994 Bobcats Basketball Team, all nine of them, with their coaches. Standing next to each other were younger versions of Broderick Mason and George Blankenship, with their arms around each other's shoulders.

The phone intercom in the squad bay announced, "Rollenhagan, Detective Rollenhagan, LAPD on line two for you."

Elapsed time: 46 minutes

CHAPTER 73

||||||||||||||||||||||||||||||||||||||||||||||

EVIDENCE

"Detective Rollenhagan, can I help you?" he acknowledged, knowing who was on the other line.

"Hey, Patterson here. Guess what?"

"No," Rollenhagan said, "You guess what." They both laughed at each other's salutation. "You called, so you go first."

"Ok, talked to my guys, and they had the roster of 'Rear Entrance' membership, with all of their code names for obvious reasons. We found the charge card files with a search warrant, and guess what?"

"Broderick Mason, my victim is on it!" Rollie was pleased with himself for the one-up-manship on LAPD.

"How did you know?"

"Came back to the office and went through Mason's property again. Found his college yearbook for Ohio University and the Bobcat's basketball team. Guess who Mason's close buddy and teammate turns out to be?"

They both said it in unison. "George Blankenship!"

"I'm going to have my team contact you directly. I'll let them deal with you straight on. We need to re-interview some of the other players in this thing now that we have a connection with your case. If this is going where I think it's going, we owe you a drink or two. We'll need a copy of your coroner's report." Rollenhagan was sure that Patterson was always looking for a reason for a case clearance!

It's their case to finalize now. They agreed to stay in touch. Patterson would have Detectives Bobby Searles and Dana Tanner contact him for follow-up. "And Dieter, thanks for reaching out."

Dieter sat there for a long moment to savor the euphoria that bringing a case closer to closure does. He knew he had work to do. There were still questions that needed answers.

Was Mason a part of a more extensive S&M operation? What was his relationship with Blankenship? Who else needed to be interviewed to tie some things together? Did LAPD think his victim was their suspect? Of course, they did. Where the hell was Mason's autopsy report?

He grabbed his notebook and started making reminders of things to do. First, on the list, he didn't need to write down. Put the belts into an analyzed evidence envelope and seal it. Not sure when he would send it to the Lab, but he knew just enough to know there may be DNA on them.

He would go through all items originally booked in as safekeeping and available for release to any next of kin, and re-book everything in as 'evidence.' *Evidence in what he wasn't sure? An LAPD homicide?*

He needed to revisit the storage building where Mason was found and make sure they had not released it to someone else.

Did he put a hold on it with the manager there? Not sure…better check. The list of things to do was getting bigger. Should I put a Murder Book together? It was time to let the cat out of the bag.

He needed to talk to his homicide unit supervisor, Detective Sergeant Dave Niemen. Now!

He was wracking his brain for more things to put on his list. He thought of a few more things, like getting the photos of the straps for comparison to the LA case, and then…it hit him.

He owed Howard Hamilton, big time!

CHAPTER 74

||||||||||||||||||||||||||||||||||||||||||||

INTERESTING

Dieter Rollenhagan had spent over ten years on the streets of Orchard Hill and been a School Resource Officer at one of the local high schools. With four years in the Detective Division, he had worked the Auto Theft table but, as all new detectives, started with property crimes like burglary and petty theft cases. Going from the Crimes against Property Section to 'Crimes Persons' had been a big step in his career.

With less than ten homicides a year in Orchard Hill, there were not enough significant cases to keep the 187-unit busy. He would also be responsible for assault with a deadly weapon and other less than death-related investigations as well as suspicious deaths.

The tables for the squad of investigators were organized to share with the domestic violence or DV unit. It seemed that many of the OHPD homicides were domestic, or at least the victims and suspects knew each other. Not many stranger to stranger cases. He was convinced that no one in recent history had investigated a crime of this nature in Orchard Hill, and he was going to get first bragging rights.

His profile of Broderick Mason was sketchy. He knew it. After briefing Niemen, he asked about getting a search warrant for Mason's residence and just adding on the storage unit, just in case.

After his talk with Patterson and Neiman, he spent the remaining morning and early afternoon making sure his organization and paperwork could withstand the scrutiny of Niemen and the LAPD team.

As the clock moved quickly to just past 1400 hours, his desk phone rang.

He didn't want the call to roll over to the secretary if the LAPD detectives were calling again. Announcing to the world and the entire detective squad bay that 'LAPD was on the line for you, again, Rollenhagan!' wasn't going to happen.

But it was a very feminine voice that asked, "Detective Rollenhagan? This is Bobbi Searles, with Rampart Homicide. Got a minute?"

With a very tentative, 'yes,' he huddled over his phone to shield the caller's identity.

"According to my supervisor, I understand we may need to get together to talk about a case?" was the very matter-of-fact query.

He responded with a, "Yes, I think we have a case in common if you're talking about your Blankenship and my Mason."

"We're headed your way right now. Is it a good time?"

Rollenhagan looked around the half-empty squad bay and an open interview room.

"Sure, give me some time to put some things together for you."

"I'll be there in forty-five."

"Do you know where we are?"

"You found us, so I'll find you," was the immediate retort. And she hung up.

He knew he was not ready for the meeting but figured he had no choice. He let Niemen know what was going on and asked if he would sit in.

"Got a meeting with the Skipper in a few. If I get out and they're still here, I'll try to find you."

Rollenhagan thought about Hamilton. Was he even working today?

He contacted the patrol watch commander and found that Hamilton was indeed working but was almost EOW. He called dispatch and put in a call to have Lincoln 75 come to detectives, Code 2. *That should get his attention, he thought.* And it did.

Most of the detectives had a small squawk box on their desk to monitor dispatch calls to patrol and traffic units. It was a good way for everyone to know what was going on in the streets.

It also allowed detectives to respond quickly if additional units were needed in the field or heard something that another unit may need an assist. Rollenhagan heard Hamilton acknowledge the call.

Rollenhagan saw Hamilton come into the room, looking around for who may have called him. Dieter motioned for him to come over to his table.

"Hey, Howard, step into my office." He motioned to the interview room in his finest 'Sgt. Schultz's impression. "I have something you might find *verrrrrry interesting.*"

CHAPTER 75

||||||||||||||||||||||||||||||||||||||||||||

BOBBI

Rollenhagan escorted Hamilton into the interview room and immediately closed the door.

With a quizzical look on his face, Howard queried, "What's up?"

"First, let me say thanks for coming in from the street and helping this newbie. You were right, and I think I owe you an apology."

"What's this about, Dieter?"

"Well, you gave me heads up on that Mason case, you know, the suicide? putting his fingers in air quotes. "Your intuition may have paid off."

He led Hamilton through what he knew about Mason and what LAPD told him about their homicide. He explained his meeting with Patterson and the connection between their victim and Mason being on the same teams at Ohio University.

"My, suicide, I mean, our suicide, I mean yours and mine..." he stuttered, "It may be the suspect in their 187, Dieter said proudly. "Not sure yet, but I may know more in just a few minutes."

"What do you mean in a few minutes?"

"LAPD detectives are on their way here right now to go over what we have. After I met with Patterson, I came back here and went over some of the evidence we had downstairs.

"Hey, Dieter, can I interrupt you one minute?"

"Sure."

Is this going to take me to EOW or past it?"

"Probably."

"Well, I need to let the watch commander and dispatch know and phone home. Did you forget all that when you left Patrol?"

"No, sorry, just wrapped up in this a bit right now. Go ahead, make the calls."

Hamilton advised the watch commander and communications of his whereabouts and, most importantly, left a message on his home phone for Clare.

"Ok, where were we? Oh, yeah, the yoga belts are the same length and brand, and I have pictures in the yearbooks of our victim and their victim together. They played on the basketball team while in college. I think they were 'fuck buddies.'"

Just then, someone entered the room that no one was familiar with and asked, "Detective Rollenhagan?"

She was about five-four, petit, with short black hair cut in an androgynous style, reminiscent of Ellen DeGeneres. She had striking blue eyes, a military bearing, with an identification card clipped to her lapel that screamed LAPD. The white blouse, opened at the neck, beige pants with an open jacket showed a thick belt that no doubt held her on-duty weapon, cuffs, and an extra ammo pouch, or two.

Rollenhagan motioned her to the interview room as all heads turned in his and her direction.

"I'm Bobbi Searles, Rampart Homicide."

With the picture words of 'fuck buddies' fresh in their minds, Hamilton and Rollenhagan made eye contact with each other. They had difficulty stifling a laugh the best they could. Circumstances got the better of them as their inability to control themselves shown.

"What's so funny, expecting a guy?" Searles asked.

"No, I knew who you were, but my partner Hamilton didn't, and I think he was surprised." They made the best of a somewhat awkward situation until the door to Interview Room B closed. "Oh, this is Officer Hamilton," and introductions were made.

CHAPTER 76

||||||||||||||||||||||||||||||||||||||||||||||||||||

STERILE

The three of them made themselves as comfortable as could be for a ten by ten interview room. Soundproofed and furnished with a small wooden table and metal chairs, the space was designed to be uncomfortable for all who entered.

"Sgt. Patterson says he filled you in on some of the elements of our case, so let me bring you up to date on what we've been doing. I mean, Detective Tanner and I."

Searles got right to the point, covering most of what Patterson had already fed Rollenhagan. "My partner is interviewing some of the people we found on the confidential client list of the Rear Entrance membership. Your victim was on it, but we had trouble locating him, and now we know why."

"How much do you know about Mason?" Dieter asked.

"Not much, but we hear you have some good information."

"I'm still working up my profile on him," Dieter lied, "...but let me get some material that will hopefully explain a few things." Rollenhagan excused himself to retrieve the yearbooks and a diary written by Mason.

Hamilton was left alone with Searle and tried to make small talk. "How long have you worked Homicide?" he asked.

"How long have you worked Patrol?" She responded.

"Over seven years," he mumbled, feeling the press of control being lost in the room. "I was the first officer on-scene and stayed in touch with Detective Rollenhagan on the case, just out of interest."

"I see," was the sterile reply.

The door opened as Dieter carried in three yearbooks and a notebook ledger. He opened the books to the appropriate pages and displayed three years of the Ohio University Bobcats basketball teams from 1993 through 1995. Blankenship and Mason were next to each other in each photo, lined up with other team members, two coaches, and what looked to be a student manager.

"Can I get copies of these pages? And, the autopsy?" she asked.

"Of course," Dieter nodded. "Haven't got the coroner's report yet but as soon as I get it, I will send a copy. What have you learned so far from your wit's?"

"We're still sifting through them. There are over thirty members of this select group. The S&M crowd is a little different than most cross-culture groups. Their sexual activities are, most of the time very covert, and often stranger to stranger. We found that your guy and ours were the exceptions. But for the most part, it stops there."

Hamilton could not resist showing his naiveté, "What do you mean?"

"Nobody knew they knew each other. Blankenship was very secretive to the other Club members and even more so with Mason. He let Mason think he was a cloistered monk or something and never told him he was married and had two kids. All their contacts were at the Rear Entrance if you'll pardon the pun."

This was her first attempt at some semblance of humor related to the case, but neither Hamilton nor Rollenhagan bit on it.

"Mason had no idea that he was a diamond dealer, either. He thought he was this spiritual leader or Bodhisattva who had attained this enlightenment level. He convinced people he could go into and out of a death cycle and return when he desires. I know this is hard to believe, but Blankenship's clients, or members, believe he chooses to be in life to support them in their beliefs."

Everyone in the room took a breath at the same time. It was then eerily quiet.

"Can we get blood or another body fluid sample from you? How about DNA on the straps? May find something there."

"I've ordered it up," Dieter lied again.

"If you give me the Coroner's case number, I can take care of my evidence," Searles added.

"Sounds good," Dieter stammered. "I'll have my stuff sent to the County Lab, and we'll meet to compare results. What's your next step, Detective Searles?"

"It's Bobbi," as she looked at his business card, "Dieter. Do you have a card, Officer Hamilton?"

"Stay in touch with Dieter, Bobbi. It's his case."

"Oooookay," she drew it out to make sure that is what he meant. "So, here's what we have left to do. We've about another weeks' worth of interviews and, most importantly, have a lot of lab work to catch up on. Unless something drastic happens that we don't know yet, we hope the evidence leads us to your guy. If not, well, we'll cross that bridge."

She closed her notebook and distributed her cards with a few extras. "I'll be your contact. Dana is too busy at this point. We have two other cases going right now."

"I understand," Dieter acknowledged.

Hamilton was looking for a place to go, feeling like a fifth wheel at this point.

"As soon as I get some lab results, maybe we can clear this case and move on. I'll keep you posted. You can mail those photos of the yearbooks to me via snail mail. Eventually, we may need to have the original books, but I don't know just yet."

She paused for a microsecond as if she was trying to rattle everything off like a checklist. "There is one more wit we're still trying to locate, the receptionist for the place. Her name is Beth McAllister, and she's nowhere to be found right now, just in case you come across her. Later," and she was gone as quickly as she had entered.

Hamilton and Rollenhagen looked at each other with *an I'm not saying anything, and neither should you,* message.

Are we done for the day?" Hamilton asked with a smile.

"We are!"

Elapsed time: 46 minutes

CHAPTER 77

IIIIIIIIIIIIIIIIIIIIIIIIIIIIIIIIIIIIIIIIIIIII

YEP

He did it again. He'd pulled off the perfect end of watch. He just had one little thing to take care of, and he could get home. He stopped by the Narco Unit to see if Barber still in the office. He was.

"Hey, HH, what's up?" Sgt. Barber heard his name mentioned and stuck his head out of his office. "Come on in. We needed to chat, anyway."

"Good," Hamilton said. "Can I go first?"

"Sure."

"Not sure how to approach this, but..., well, I got some information about somebody dealing drugs at Orchard Hill High."

"What kind of drugs?"

"I think just marijuana, but I'm not sure." Hamilton now realized he might have made a mistake. But he was here and needed to dump this information on the proper unit.

"Got a name?" Barber queried.

"Yes, Jake Radshaw, I think he's a senior, not sure."

Sgt. Barber excused himself and came back with a high school annual for Orchard Hill High. He thumbed through the pages, stopping on the Junior class from the previous year, as the new annuals were not out yet. He pointed to a picture, "That him?"

"Uh-huh. That's him."

"Does he do it on campus or off?"

"Not sure if he does it on campus, but for sure off school grounds at some kids' house."

"Wait a minute, Hamilton, let's not play twenty questions here. Tell me what you know and how you know it."

Reluctantly, Howard told him the story of picking up his daughter, the encounter with Radshaw, and the information provided by Marcia. "Sarge, that's all I know. Do you want me to try and get more information?"

"No, Howard. I don't think so. You've given us enough work lately. I think we'll take it from here. You are a shit magnet, aren't you?"

"Seems that way at times. Do you know the name?"

Oh, yes, we do. I have heard that Jake could be involved with some other kids too. All we know right now is that he may deal in weed, and you just confirmed it."

"Well, my daughter Marcia confirmed it, but I'd like to leave her out of it, if possible. You know how that goes. Have kids, Sarge?"

"I do, Howard, and they go to that school."

"Is that how you know?"

"Yes," was the one-word reply.

"Then I guess you don't need another confidential informant, then, do you?"

Barber hesitated, "I need all of the CI's I can get on this one, Howard."

"Why? It's enough to move on him. He's still a juvie, I think."

"He is. Do you know what else, though? He's Lieutenant Hospian's stepson."

"Oh." There was a long pause. "...Oh, shit!"

"Yep."

CHAPTER 78

||||||||||||||||||||||||||||||||||||||||

CHARGES

It rapidly had become another one of those days. Hamilton didn't have many of them until recently. But they just kept coming of late.

Was Barber right? Was he becoming a shit magnet? Or, was this just what happens on the day shift. The maggots were in full bloom, he thought, on the short drive home.

He was not expecting what he found upon his arrival home. Clare was waiting for him, and the kids were nowhere to be found.

"We need to talk, Howard."

"Ok," was the terse reply. "Can I get one foot in the door and change clothes to put on something a little more comfortable?"

"We can talk while you change." She followed him into their bedroom, but not for anything intimate this time. As usual, their bedroom was immaculately appointed. The bed was made, pillows fluffed, and no clothes were strewn about the room. But none of that mattered right now.

Was it the Marcia and Jake thing? Did Marcia tell her and not tell him? That could be bad.

"Why didn't you tell me, Howard?" He was going to play this out without tipping his hand just yet. "Tell you what?"

"You know what!"

"If I knew what, I'd tell you, Clare?" This was as far as he could take it, and she knew it. "Is this about Marcia?" he finally asked.

"No, this is not about Marcia, but what about her?"

Damn.

I don't know, but I had her on my mind and was just wondering."

"This is about Dawn Kendall, Howard, and you know it. But what about Marcia?"

He was in a corner now and had to come out fighting. "What about Kendall?" he deflected.

"Your Department filed charges on her for hitting that boy, that's what! When were you going to tell me?"

"Because I didn't know. I don't work Traffic, you know."

"But your Department sent her a letter saying she was at fault. How come you don't know that? Everybody in town knows it but you!"

"Well, I didn't know and didn't want to."

"It was your investigation that did it, Howard, and now everybody knows." She glared as if trying to pierce the protective value of his deniability.

"Clare, I just did the preliminary investigation. Our Traffic dicks did the follow-up, examined the car, interviewed other witnesses, including the boy again, and did what they do."

"Well, we're getting the blame, Howard." Being called 'Howard' by Clare was equivalent to being called 'asshole' by anyone else. "Our entire family is being talked about."

"It'll blow over," he said, hoping it would.

"I hope it does. Now, what about Marcia?"

CHAPTER 79

||||||||||||||||||||||||||||||||||||||||||||

DEFLECTION

He finished changing clothes and, even though it was a little cool outside, decided on shorts and a t-shirt. He was thirsty, and Clare followed him to the kitchen for a bottle of water. He felt like a puppy dog with a new master.

"So, what about Marcia? And are we done with this Kendall thing? Some of the girls in yoga thought I knew all about it. Again!" she emphasized the last word for clarity.

"Let me nose around at work in the next few days, and I'll see what I can find out. I promise to do that but, and it's a big but... if I can't tell you, I won't. Are we okay with that?"

"Yes, dear, we are."

He thought he skirted the Kendall and the Marcia issue Clare had brought up but knew better, so he volunteered something he thought might work.

"And on the Marcia thing, you know that girlfriend of hers...what's her name?"

"Beverly Toomey?"

"Yeah, well, I don't think she's her best friend like you said. I think they know each other, but it's not like they hang out a lot with each other." He was now hoping to sound a little elusive so she would bite on his next little tactic.

"Well, she tried to tell me that she was her good friend, so I naturally assumed she was. I've never met her, and I guess we should have." Clare was now on the defensive.

He took a long drink from the bottle as he formulated his next strategy.

"I met her, and she seems like an alright kid. We had a dad-to-daughter chat, and she didn't know her that well. I didn't want to play 'cop' with her, just be a Dad, so I didn't push it. Just thought you should know."

CHAPTER 80

||||||||||||||||||||||||||||||||||||||||||||

FIX

Hamilton saw how when kids grow up, they bring many of the same struggles that he and Clare encountered. It was never his intention to be what they called helicopter parents, but neither did he want to be what the new trend was: a lawnmower parent. Thinking of always getting out front and ensuring that their lives were smooth with few challenges was not his idea of parenting. But he didn't want to have them fail, either.

It was time for a Guy Coyle fix, he thought. Maybe a person with a different perspective would help him through this phase. He was off the next day and placed a call for a meet at Peets. Guy was more than happy to accommodate.

He let Clare know he would be gone for an hour or so doing errands, purposely vague about his intentions.

◆◆◆

They met early in the morning after getting the kids off to school but before his and Clare's scheduled yoga class.

Hamilton arrived at the coffee spot to see Guy sitting there in his usual seat, with his usual dress of blue jeans, an untucked t-shirt, and running shoes. *Wonder if he still runs and carries an off-duty weapon? The best way to find out is to ask.*

"Greetings, Howard," Coyle reached for the gentlemanly handshake. He had not purchased his coffee yet, so they both waited in line to order. They disagreed as to who would pay and decided to each buy their own at the last minute. Howard was surprised when he did not see his personal barista, Sophia. The ponytailed, slightly overweight barista asked for his name.

"You mean I have to give my name to get a cup of coffee now, just like that other place?" The response from the name tagged Ted made him laugh. "It doesn't have to be your real name. Just make one up."

"Okay, I will," Howard chuckled. "Guy!"

"And for you, sir?" turning to Guy.

"Howard," was the one-word reply. The barista couldn't figure out what was so funny, so he retorted, "We get so busy here, it's hard to keep track of the orders, so we have to put a name on the cup. Any name will do."

When Howard and Guy were settled, the questions came in staccato fashion. "Yes, I still run, and no, I don't carry an off-duty weapon unless I'm going to the city." The simple things were easy, but Howard was loading up for a different series of questions.

"Reason I called was, some things have been happening of late, and I wanted your perspective on them."

"Thought there must be a reason for the coffee, but you don't need one, Howard. We can talk about anything you want. I'm all ears."

"How did you raise such great kids in this world of chaos, drugs, and other temptations?"

"I didn't do that great of a job, really, Howard. Can I call you HH?"

"Sure. And I think you did, from what you told me about your girls."

"I was a pretty absentee Dad, HH. The work got to me. I just had a great wife who kept pulling at me to be there when I could. She was the difference-maker, not me."

Coyle looked out the window as if to see someone he knew but only saw strangers. "Raising kids is not rocket science, but it takes a temperament that I didn't always have. Rosie, my wife, had it in spades. She was the family metronome. Keeping things going, dealing with the kids' problems and successes. I think I was just the checkbook and took out the trash."

"You don't give yourself much credit, Guy."

"No, I don't. You're a better Dad than I was. I see that in you."

"Well, I'm not so sure," Howard murmured. He then went on to tell about Marcia and what he found at her friend Beverly's house. He finished with the Radshaw/Hospian revelation without mentioning their names.

"That's not so uncommon, HH. We had a Chief whose son was a drugged-out burglar who couldn't stay out of jail. Another Chief's son couldn't make it through the police academy, and others whose kids came on the job and rose through the ranks or chose to be a good cop. Go figure."

"You're kidding?"

"None of my girls ever wanted to join our profession, but they carved out their paths with more than their share of bumps in the road. Hell, LA's former Chief has a son, daughter, sister, and niece on the job. Look at Mel Flowers. She didn't want to be around her dad at all. She loves him, but not the LAPD. I think she just saw the job satisfaction he got but wanted to earn her stripes. Everything you've told me about your family means that you're doing a great job, so keep it up."

While it was all good to hear, it didn't make his issues seem less critical.

"I hear what you're saying, Guy, but with the drugs in schools, this LGBT and transgender stuff with this case we have, it all gets to be a bit much."

"I don't want to sound like a preacher, but everyone, from presidents to chiefs, teachers, and firefighters, to you and me, our kids, we have decision points. Our decisions define us, from the spouse we choose, the choice of schools, careers, or departments we join. Within the PD's you have to make a decision which assignments you seek and those you turn down."

"Whew," Howard signed, "I know exactly what you mean. I enjoy patrol and have turned down some other assignments just because..."

"Well, be careful, Howard."

Coyle looked him directly in the eyes, "some of those are designed to advance your career. Remember you have over seven on now. Is this what you want to do for thirty years? Is it seven years in patrol, or, if I can speculate, one year seven times?"

Guy just threw the question out there like a softball, not expecting an answer. He was rewarded with silence but also a penetrating stare.

"Do you think I should look at detectives or Narcotics?"

"I think that's a very personal decision that you and Clare make together. They're different for a lot of reasons."

Guy was not about to make any decision for him. "The only ones we regret are those we didn't make and those where we failed. But they're all learning experiences."

"Yesterday, I met an LAPD detective on a case, and she had ten years on, but she'd been working in detectives awhile. She was already working homicide!"

"Well, LA has a lot of retirements at the senior ranks right now, so there are many younger detectives out there."

"She looked very masculine and overly businesslike. I just got the impression she was one of those pushy gays that made her way up on other issues, if you know what I mean."

"Where did she work, downtown Robbery-Homicide?"

"No, Rampart detectives."

"I worked Rampart awhile back. Who were you dealing with?"

"Well, because of the nature of the case, we were working with the D-3 Len Patterson. Know him?"

"Sure do! Len is a great guy when he's not in the bottle. Very knowledgeable. But you said you were dealing with a female?"

"Patterson sent her out because it's her and her partner's case. Detective Bobbi Searles. I met with her, but her partner is a guy named Dana Tanner."

Guy sat back, looking at his Peet's coffee cup, contemplating his following statement. "I know both. But Bobbi is straight, but her partner, Dana, is gay. And beautiful to boot."

"Are you sure? Dana Tanner is a female?" Hamilton said with a mild form of astonishment. "I can never get it right, so why should I have started?"

"Well, you screwed this one up, Howard."

"It doesn't matter if they do the job. And, I think they are. We're a little fucked up at our end, but I think we can work it out. We may have their suspect."

"That's good, HH, but you need to know something else before you step in it."

"Step in what?"

"Detective Bobbi Searles is your Chief's wife!"

"What did you say?"

CHAPTER 81

||||||||||||||||||||||||||||||||||||||||||||

RELATIVE

"What the...," Hamilton stared at Guy. "Did I hear right?"

"Thought you knew."

"Nope, I guess I don't pay much attention to that kind of stuff. But it does surprise me."

"I wouldn't spread it around. TheChief and Bobbie try to keep a low profile. That's why he applied to your Department. He was a Commander with LA, but even though we're a big department, it wasn't sitting well with everyone."

"I mean, I didn't even think that...well, you know. And, hey, she doesn't even use his last name?"

"Nope. Never has, to my knowledge. Doesn't want that label. Don't even try to figure it out. When you see her partner, you'll be even more surprised. She makes Mel Flowers look like an ugly third grader!"

Hamilton sat back, reflecting. "Relations are never what we expect them to be, whether it's between departments or people. Everybody thinks we all work like one big police network. They'd be surprised to see how independent we all are."

Hamilton was talking as much to himself as to Guy. "You've been a wealth of information today, sir, I mean Mr. Coyle, er, Guy, sir." Gee, I'm stumbling all over myself, again."

"No worries. Threw a lot at you. You're doing fine, just fine."

They agreed to stay in touch.

"How's the book coming, Guy?"

After getting a refill on the coffee, Coyle responded, "kind of hit a wall with it, but you know what? I think you just gave me more material."

"Glad I could help."

Hamilton walked back to his car through the maze of customers clamoring for one more shot of caffeine. He quickly replayed the conversation with Guy.

Was it seven years or one year seven times? That bothered him.

Elapsed time: 46 minutes

CHAPTER 82

||||||||||||||||||||||||||||||||||||||||

AGAIN

Rollenhagan walked out of Niemen's office with a refreshed sense of confidence. He had updated his supervisor regarding the status of his first big case and working with LAPD. Rather than be upset over giving LA anything, Niemen was complimentary of his investigation and the follow-up conducted to re-examine the case. There was no mention of Howard Hamilton.

A page over the intercom system from Janice chimed, "Detective Rollenhagan, LAPD on line two… again!" She made it a point to broadcast the 'again' with enough emphasis that all who were in the building heard it.

Janice's popularity was evident in his undertoned reference, 'Bitch.'

He then took a breath, speaking into the mouthpiece with a more upbeat, "Rollenhagan!" There was a renewed confidence and spring in his voice.

A somewhat subdued and sultry voice queried, "Detective Rollenhagan, this is Detective Dana Tanner, Rampart Homicide. Do you have a few minutes?"

"Yes, ma'am."

"I understand through my supervisor that we may have some things in common with our cases. My Blankenship case and your Mason case. Right?"

"I think so, yes."

"I have a meeting at the Rear Entrance to go over some files at two o'clock today. Is it possible that you could meet me there? I have a search warrant, and I think you going over their records with me would work to both of our advantages."

"I can be there, but how about if you and I meet in the parking lot at one-thirty to go over a few things. Oh, and who are we meeting with?"

"We're meeting with the property manager, Mr. Clyde Wexler. I'm told he has access to all we may need. Sounds good! See you at one-thirty."

She hung up, but Rollenhagan was sure he was in love. At least with a voice.

He grabbed the keys of one of the new plain Dodge Charger pool cars, just to make sure no one else would take it. He wanted to make an impression, and showing off their new fleet may do that.

Should he put a tie on? Sports jacket? First, he should organize his case file to meet LAPD's standards. Thank goodness he had plenty of time before his meeting. Where was the Rear Entrance, anyway?

CHAPTER 83

|||||||||||||||||||||||||||||||||||||||||||||

FRIDAY

Driving home from his meeting with Guy, Hamilton was reflecting on the multitude of topics and discussions. It had been a bit of an eye-opener for him. Not just about Detective Searles, but also about his career, decisions about what assignments he should consider, and what to talk do at home.

So, Detective Bobbi Searles was not only not gay, but she was our Chief's wife! I hope I didn't offend her in any way. Hell, I hope Guy didn't think I was some bigot or homophobic. LAPD was more open about all that sex stuff, but Orchard Hill PD, to his knowledge, had not dealt directly with those issues, at least not out in the open. And who knew that our Chief was married to another cop? Not sure I should say anything to anybody. Keeping your mouth shut was the best advice for now and maybe for a long time.

It was time to think about the rest of his day off. His Bluetooth phone connection activated, and he saw whose number it was.

"Hello, John," in an exasperated voice that sent a purposeful message.

"HH, things are heating up. Can we meet?"

"I'm on a day off, John. Can we do this tomorrow?" The exasperation was growing, but Bresani was oblivious to his frustration.

"Well, what is today? The fourteenth? I guess it could wait, but geez, I need to keep you up-to-date on what's going on."

"Can't we do it over the phone?"

"I suppose so, but Howard, the shipments are coming in big time." He said it with enthusiasm and nervousness that told Hamilton that something unexpected was going on. He also detected that Bresani was probably higher than a kite on his product. Again.

"The shipments have expanded."

"What do you mean?" Hamilton was now hooked into the conversation.

"Well, I can't go into details over the phone right now. There's gonna be multiple loads coming in from all directions. They're coming in from Juarez, through San Diego, and up to the San Gabriel Valley. They'll be caravanning with a bunch of different cars, maybe seven or more, zig-zagging all over the southern part of the state with at least five loaded with a lot of product. And not just coke."

"What are you trying to say, John," Hamilton pulled over to the side of the road to concentrate on what Bresani was telling him.

John's voice rose two octaves, "This is the biggest shipment the LA area will see since 94 when they took down MS 13." Jesus, HH, we gotta meet!" He was pleading now, and Hamilton did not like what he was hearing.

"OK, John. Listen," he raised his voice and deepened it at the same time. "Listen to me. We are not going to meet!" He emphasized getting his point across one more time.

"I will call you at eight o'clock sharp in the morning. Tomorrow, damn it. Got it?" He was now shouting over Bresani's ramblings. "Be where you can talk. I'll have the task force guys, Barber and the Lieutenant on this. You hear me, John?" His voice was now in a strong command presence that ensured his direction was going to be followed.

"When is all of this supposed to happen?" Howard returned to a conversational tone.

"On Friday, the 25th. So, we have some extra time."

"Ok, John, got it. Friday the 25th. That's fine. We'll talk tomorrow. Eight o'clock, exactly. Be available, hear me?" He was shouting into the windshield now. *And be sober* was the unspoken phrase.

"Ok, Howard. Thanks. Talk to you tomorrow." The reality and finality of Hamilton's words finally were sinking into Bresani.

"Tomorrow, 0800." The Bluetooth disconnected, and the news report resumed on the car radio:

"Retailers are gearing up for another blockbuster holiday season. Black

Friday is starting early. But for you purists, it won't start until November 25th, so shoppers, on your marks, get set, get ready for Black Friday, November 25th."

His radio must have been listening to his conversation with Bresani! *Black Friday?*

CHAPTER 84

||||||||||||||||||||||||||||||||||||||||||

PLANNING

Who was he going to call first? Rikelman needed to know ASAP. Tomorrow's meeting was going to be critical. He laughed to no one that he had the Lieutenant's phone number right there on the top of his speed dial.

"Rikelman," was the one-word salutation.

He filled him in as best he could. "Let me work on it, and I'll get back to you." There it was again. It was like Rikelman was reporting to him. "Are you working tomorrow in Patrol?"

"Yes, sir."

"Let me see if I can get you for a day or so just for the planning. I'll talk to Bennett." Once again, Hamilton could hear his brain churning over the Bluetooth. "Call me in about an hour."

Hamilton checked his work schedule on his phone calendar but already knew. He had done his holiday scheduling in advance, agreeing to work the Thanksgiving Thursday/Friday day shift to get Christmas Eve and Christmas day off. He could always have turkey dinner a little later.

The single guys didn't mind working on Christmas. There was a lot of peer pressure to give the Christmas holidays to those with a family. Things always worked out like that at OHPD. With this Chief, they viewed each employee of the Department as an extended family. There was an emphasis on a work-life balance and support for each other. Everyone contributed, and everyone sacrificed. Family first.

The key was to have him on loan to Narcotics for this case; tomorrow and on Black Friday. That may take some doing, but if anyone can do it, well, Rikelman ran this place.

By the time he pulled into his driveway, Rikelman had found him.

"They don't need you in Patrol to make minimums tomorrow, so I have you from 0730 to when we finish with Bresani. So just come in for briefing and show yourself out to my unit for a few hours."

The staccato orders were now in free flow. "Good news is I have you all day on the 25th. It seems they have a big deployment all over the city, particularly at the Mall. You won't be missed."

"Got it, sir!" Howard responded.

"I'll get other uniforms if I need them." Rikelman paused. "HH, I want you to file this away. I want you here in this unit. You're meeting the test with all this stuff, and we need you in this unit. You don't have to say anything right now but think about it. It's time."

"Sounds good, sir. See you at 0730!"

"Better yet, HH, just come in at 0700. It looks like we've got a lot to discuss."

It was typical Rikelman. More, better, faster, and sooner. No professional bullshit.

CHAPTER 85

||||||||||||||||||||||||||||||||||||||||||||||||

TANNER

Rollenhagan advised Niemen he was going to LA to meet Detective Dana Tanner at the location of their homicide. He pointed the new Charger north with a briefcase in hand and the makings of a decent Murder Book. Rollenhagan was ready for the big city detectives.

It was a 1330 meeting at The Rear Entrance, so he wanted to give himself plenty of time to get there. *It shouldn't take more than an hour.*

It only took forty-five minutes. Using the GPS on his phone, he found Meridian Drive two blocks off the Hollywood freeway. Just off Melrose, he turned on to Dagmar, drove about half a block to Meridian, and turned right.

It was a cul-de-sac with all industrial buildings boarded up and spray painted with graffiti. No one told him how creepy the neighborhood was. *This wouldn't fly in Orchard Hill. Our city manager would have a fit, let alone one of our community lead officers.* They were death on boarded-up buildings and graffiti. In LA, empty buildings just sat there and were the norm.

He found 4251 Meridian at the very end of the dead-end, buttressed up against the freeway. The building could almost use the overpass as its roof. He saw a driveway on the west side of the building and drove to the rear parking lot, slowly taking his new Charger through broken glass and trash sprawled over every inch of the passageway. The odor of urine and refuse permeated the air. There was one car in the lot, and it belonged to Detective Tanner.

She stepped out of the driver's side of what he considered a vintage

Crown Victoria. Her marathon runner look struck him by surprise. Close to six feet, she pulled back a blond ponytail and dressed in a fashionable rust-colored pants suit, with an open jacket that revealed her sidearm, ammo pouch, and the distinctive LAPD badge on her belt.

It took time for his gaze to even get to her face. If this were a commercial for something, he would have heard the music playing. She was striking in every way.

"Detective Rollenhagan, Dana Tanner, " she said with a purposeful extended hand.

As if he couldn't figure that out!

They did the ceremonial exchange of business cards. He printed his new title onto generically printed cards for the Sergeant rank and below. She mentioned she had not had time to get custom cards imprinted yet with her name and title, but soon. As if he cared.

Tanner brought him up to speed on the case. She had obtained all files from the business, including the membership data for their thirty confidential clients. She located the codes for each that revealed some prominent business people, local politicos, and of course, Broderick Mason. His code name was 'Bobcat,' a presumed reference to the Ohio University mascot he and Blankenship had in common.

She interviewed the wife only to find the woman had never been to the studio. She had just assumed it was a traditional yoga room for her husband to enjoy his passion for the sport. She did provide information about his diamond business. Tanner didn't seem to think the diamond business played an essential role in the homicide investigation, at least not yet.

"What about this business? This building? This location?" Rollenhagan queried.

Tanner smiled with a tossed-off, "don't you know? Of course, you don't. You're from down the freeway and Orchard Hill. In L.A., we have a lot of these types of businesses. Let's go in." She beckoned him with a somewhat come-hither smile as she pulled out a set of keys attached to an evidence tag. She unlocked the door and turned the handle.

"You first."

Rollenhagan stepped into a darkened room, pausing for his eyes to adjust from the cloudy sky outside. Tanner flipped the light switches illuminating the room in a subdued orange-tinted luminescence.

He was startled at what he was seeing. The dingy reception area was antiseptically clean but decorated quite simply with a desk, computer screen, keyboard, and one file cabinet.

"Keep walking" was her order.

He opened the door adjacent to the desk and looked in to see a cavernous room with faux rock walls, iron bars set up like mini jail cells, and side rooms with soundproofed doors.

At the very end of the hallway was a single room, approximately ten-by-fifteen. An exercise room. On the walls were open storage bins that contained yoga mats, blocks, blankets, and a box of yoga belts. All belts were labeled with the now familiar 'Barefoot Yoga Co.'

He quickly walked down the main hall, peering into each room and taking a mental picture of what he saw. Each of the four, eight by eight cells were outfitted the same. Bolted into the walls were four ornate gothic rings, mounted about shoulder height and width at the top, three feet apart at the bottom, and about one foot from the floor.

On the wall was an iron hat rack, each with three ornate hooks with a whip and several small chains hanging loose. A small box was in the corner containing an ampule of amyl nitrate, tiny clothespins, and a jar of Vaseline.

Dieter was getting a visual image he couldn't shake. He stood near the entrance for what seemed like an eternity.

Did they shackle guys to the wall? Facing front or facing the wall? Did they use those whips and chains, or was it just for show? I understand the Vaseline, but clothespins? Ouch!

"Do you know what they do here?" she asked.

"I think I do, but it doesn't take a graphic mind to see the possibilities. But do you know what happens here?"

"Unfortunately, yes, this isn't my first one. Butting up against Hollywood on our west side, we get a lot of spillover of this kind of kinky stuff."

It was a lot to take in. *Orchard Hill would never permit such a business enterprise.*

"Orchard Hill would never permit such a business like this, huh, Dieter?"

He was thinking what she was saying. That was scary.

CHAPTER 86

||||||||||||||||||||||||||||||||||||||||||

BAREFOOT

"I assume all this has been photo'd, and you're sending me copies?"

"I think my partner Detective Searles is doing that, yes."

"Where was the body found?"

She pointed to the yoga room. "Right in the middle of the room, here," she said, pointing to the center of the room. "His back was to the door. His head was facing the wall, and his face was in between his legs, in a lotus-style position. You'll see in the photos."

He wanted to visualize what the room was like on the day of the murder. Dieter found himself reenacting the scene in his mind, studying each section of each room.

Perhaps Blankenship was already in the lotus position, with his head between his knees. Did Mason walk up behind him and put the belt around his neck with his permission? Was it all about mutual sexual gratification gone wrong?

"Who discovered him?"

"The Coroner determined he died somewhere between 1900 hours to about midnight on the tenth. He was discovered by a cleaning crew that comes in about 5 AM."

"Are there any other rooms I haven't seen?" Dieter asked.

"Off to the left of the yoga room is a small sauna and steam room. Who knows what went on there," she said in a very straightforward fashion.

The entire building had a cold feeling to it. The steam room had not been used in a long time, still wreaking of a Lysol disinfectant that made it smell like a doctor's office. Dieter stuck his head in just to see the interior.

"There's a small closet up near the front reception area." They walked single file back to the front. The closet door was locked.

"Not sure I checked this. I think one of these keys works with this lock."

She tried it and quickly opened the door. A plaque was mounted on the wall high above a series of plastic shelving marked, 'Rear Entrance Store.'

The shelves contained various sizes of yoga balls, some in cellophane containers, netting to combine two, and others that required inflation. Packages of styrofoam yoga blocks about three by six inches were bundled in twos. Various sizes of yoga mats imprinted with *The Rear Entrance* name and logo of the back door all were neatly arrayed for ease of purchase.

On the top shelf was what he was looking for. The yoga belts were marked 'Barefoot Yoga Co.' in lengths of either eight or ten feet.

"Do you mind if I take one of these and book it into evidence at my shop?"

"What's the significance?"

"Well, my victim, your suspect, hung himself by belts that are identical to these. Not sure if we can prove this is where he got them, but everything else ties into this location."

"Yes, but these belts are sold to several yoga studios so he could have bought them anywhere. There's no indication they came from here."

"I know, but my victim is turning out to be a suspect in your homicide potentially, and right now, everything matters."

"I get it. Let me make a note, and you can send me a copy of your evidence report, just for the chain of custody. But remember, assuming he is our suspect, we won't be going to court on this. Oh, by the way, you owe us a profile of your victim. When can we expect it? And, about the belt? So..."

She paused for just too long for his comfort. "Can I say something? And I hope you don't take offense."

"Why would I be offended?"

"Well, hear me out. See, the public and the media think we don't give a shit about these kinds of people, if you know what I mean."

"You mean the gay, transgender thing?"

"Yeah. In our Department, we see so much of this. To us, it's just as important as, well, an ordinary homicide if there is such a thing."

"Go on," Dieter responded.

"Bottom line is that we work as hard on these cases as any of them because they're just harder to solve. We don't care if it's the mayor's daughter or some two-bit prostitute from South Central or Hollywood. It's a case we need to clear, one way or the other. These cases are a challenge where mom killing dad is way too easy." She was looking for just the right words to close the issue out.

"I want you to know I see how serious you've taken this case, and me, I mean we, appreciate it. We don't always see other agencies deal with them with the same, ah… energy."

"Hey, If I Can help LAPD, that makes us all look good. I can't take credit for clearing the case, but I'm learning on the job here. We can both feel good about this one with just a little bit more work. I'll send you our autopsy as soon as it comes in."

Dieter was beaming with what he hoped was the pride and satisfaction of clearing a big case.

"So, I can send you the profile tomorrow." He said, trying to bring some closure to a conversation that was way too heavy for his blood. "I have your email. But if this case gets closed, no civil suits or anything, I'll personally deliver this belt right back. But only to you."

"Why to me?"

"Why not? I don't get to come to L.A. very often. Would like to see Rampart station again and would get to see you again…" he dribbled the last part of the statement.

"Oh…" was all she could muster.

Elapsed time: 46 minutes

It took him over ninety minutes to find his way back to Orchard Hill. The traffic was miserable, but he didn't seem to mind. There was a lot to think about.

CHAPTER 87

||||||||||||||||||||||||||||||||||||||||||||||||

CONFIDENTIAL

The rest of his day off was a blur. Hamilton found himself spending way too much time on side issues of his job, not personal or family stuff.

Marcia was using her body language to tell him that Clare still didn't know anything about their encounter at Beverly's. Her unspoken look was more like; *I won't bring it up if you don't. And please, Daddy, don't.*

While he felt obligated to keep it between him and Marcia, it wasn't easy to keep *anything* from Clare. They both knew they were taking a chance. This was their very first dad/daughter surreptitious and slightly underhanded secret confidence. It was exciting for both.

He was at his assigned seat in the back of the briefing room and caught Sgt. Bennett's eye. They exchanged an unspoken acknowledgment that he knew Hamilton would be MIA for a period this morning.

The roll call was a training session regarding the on-body camera project done by Sgt. McGinty. Hamilton had played a small role in formulating the plan of action. According to McGinty, the hardware portion was out to bid right now, so it would be a month or two before they would be delivered.

Bennett could not resist. "We have a member of the Chief's committee with us this morning, Officer Hamilton. Care to fill us in, HH?"

You asshole! He wanted to say, but he didn't. But even Kip deserved the descriptor at times.

"I'll wait for the policies to speak for themselves. I think we had our

221

say. It's just a matter of what the Chief wants." Hamilton thought he put the issue to bed.

The roll call erupted in questions. "Is it going to be mandatory? What if I accidentally erased something? What if we break one? How long do they keep the recordings?"

Hamilton decided to take the opportunity to walk to the front of the room rather than have everybody turn around to see him.

"Just a reminder, I was only one of the members of the group. Meacham from the POA was on it and a bunch of other guys."

HH tried to be very matter-of-fact in his response. "The bottom line is, we gave our input and tried to come up with answers to all those questions you threw out there. They're coming, so get your head around that."

"Woooo...sounds like you kissed a little ass up there, HH!"

"It sure wasn't yours, and whoever said that, bite me." He would have grabbed his crotch to demonstrate his disdain, but there was one female officer in the room. Discretion was the better part of valor. The room erupted into laughter as he walked back to his seat.

'Kip' or Sgt. Bennett made his final announcement. "Don't forget to get tickets to Val and Harvey's retirement party...and... get a gun!"

Everybody knew what the last word meant. Get a gun off the street with a body, and you can get an early out. But only through Kip.

Probably not going to be me today, he muttered to himself.

CHAPTER 88

||||||||||||||||||||||||||||||||||||||||||||||

HORRORS

Hamilton walked out of briefing and worked his way up to the rarified air of the second floor and Detectives. *Was he in for a surprise! Need a bad cup of coffee, he decided.*

He was pleasantly surprised to see the coffee prep table adorned with a brand-new Keurig coffee maker, complete with flavored, regular, and decaf pods. Everything right out of Costco, including the pods and paper cups. There was also a small plastic bowl with a sticker that said, 'honesty bowl. Pay. Someone is watching.'

He treated himself to a coffee, with the only regret the machine would not make an au latte. He reminded himself to get some Peet's pods next time. *Keep them in my briefcase, and I only need their machine and water. Cool!* He looked around. No one was hovering. He left a dollar.

He was thinking about nothing special and entered the Narcotics office. Wow! It was full of bodies. Everybody from OHPD was assigned to the unit, and of course, there was Mike LaBonge from LA Deuce, but no Bonnie Carvin.

They had a good hour before the phone call with Bresani started, so everybody took their time chatting about anything but the upcoming event. The older narco detectives talked about their kids going to college, While the younger ones talked about buying a boat or a new car.

Without Bonnie in the room, the topic got down to sex. Don and Phil, their nicknames had always been the Everly's, were the only two bachelors in the group, extolling their latest escapades with a couple of court stenographers at the local courthouse.

When Rikelman entered the room, it became as quiet as a church. And, most of the language got cleaned up in the process. "Here's what we have, and this is how it's going to happen. Knock off the grab-ass," he directed to the Everly's.

"We have a CI we'll be talking to. I'll be in the next room and bring the information we get to you. Better yet, LaBonge, you already know some of it, so you sit in with Barber, Hamilton, and me. We'll record the conversation but won't play it for you."

"You," He waved his hand to reference everybody in the room but Hamilton and LaBonge, "do not need to know who we're talking to, is that clear?"

A few 'yes sirs' rumbled out.

"Things could change, but as far as we know, it'll go down on the day after Thanksgiving, Black Friday. They call it that for those of you who have wives who shop." There were a few chuckles, but very few. "Anybody have a problem with that?"

LaBonge spoke up by holding a finger to the ceiling, "We do, Lieutenant," with an apparent reference to LA Deuce, "but I'll talk to you about that after the call."

Since he was the only uniform in the room, side conversations were going on about Hamilton's presence. Rikelman picked up on it. "Oh, almost forgot, Hamilton is here because it's his CI, and he won't talk to anybody else, not even me or LaBonge, so he'll be part of the operation, but we'll do the planning. Everybody understands?"

There was a group consensus, but Don of Don and Phil interjected. "Hey, Hamilton, trying to get in the unit? If this works out, you never know. But you better get yourself a good divorce attorney." Everyone laughed, even Rikelman.

"No thanks. Not interested. I've heard the horror stories."

Don could not resist, "They're all true. Bye, bye love!" Everybody laughed again.

CHAPTER 89

||||||||||||||||||||||||||||||||||||||||||||||

TIME

It was time to make the call. Rikelman, Barber, LaBonge, and Hamilton moved to the next room while everybody else scampered to the coffee and pastries brought in from Starbucks for the big meeting.

Hamilton filled in LaBonge on his last conversation with Bresani. LaBonge just laughed.

"That's hilarious, Howard. We've been working on this from a completely different angle, and I was going to tell Lieutenant Rikelman that we were spread thinly on the twenty-fifth. But we have some information that ties in, so let's see what your guy knows and compare it with the info we have." Rikelman and Hamilton nodded in agreement, and both took a deep breath.

Some of the most tense and stressful times are not on the street. They are right inside the PD. Whether it's the building, the names on the doors, or the outside edifice, entering is at one's peril. *Today,* Hamilton thought, *was one of those days.*

The clock screamed eight o'clock, or maybe it just seemed like it. The recorder was set on the phone, and the speaker turned on, but not so loud as to carry outside the office.

He picked up on the first ring. "HH, how ya doing?"

"Doing Ok, John. Listen, before we get started, has anything changed since our last talk?"

"Not that I know of, but it's early in the game, so it could. If it does, I'll let you know." Rikelman and LaBonge nodded to proceed.

"John. I have the Lieutenant here with me, and we're recording this, but to make sure, we don't forget anything. You're protected, alright? Do you understand? We're not using your name anywhere on anything. Understand?"

"I do, HH. Hi, Lieutenant," was the most significant acknowledgment he could muster. There was no mention of LaBonge or Barber being in the room.

"So, now I want you to run through what you told me in our last talk. Step by step."

Bresani walked Rikelman through the expansion of the fleet to include the number of cars and how they would work. He added the locations they were using along the way and when they would arrive in the San Gabriel Valley. He also talked about what he had been doing in terms of laying out the routes.

That was going to be critical for surveillance purposes. It was pretty much what he had told Hamilton in their conversation.

LaBonge wrote a note to Rikelman. He nodded. "John, can you get us some names of the people you're dealing with?"

"I can, but not right now."

"Why not?"

"Because I can't," he said with firmness. "But soon. I'll give the information to HH."

Rikelman's jaws were getting tight. "What kind of weapons do they have? How about descriptions of the cars they're using? License plates or anything?"

"I'll work on it."

"Thanks, John," Rikelman said rather condescendingly, "we don't want to go into this blind, and you're our only source. This thing is big time, and you know the guys we have here. Can they do it?"

"I think so." He was not going to call him Lieutenant or 'sir' or anything respectful of his rank. Not now. He didn't have to.

Hamilton decided to probe a bit further. "What role are you playing in this, John?"

"What do you mean?" was the response.

"Are you transporting any product? Involved in doing any of the cutting and repackaging or handling any money?"

"No, I'm not doing any of that. We have mules to take care of that level of the work. As I said, I mapped out the various routes, identified some hotspots they should be aware of, and will probably end up at the industrial park in Irwindale when the shipments arrive. From there, I'm not sure yet."

Rikelman held up a hand to halt further questions from Hamilton. "John, how many people are involved in this operation? And I need to know what level of weaponry to expect."

"Good question." He hesitated, but neither Rikelman, Hamilton, or LaBonge could determine whether he didn't want to share that information or, as was more probable, he didn't know.

"I'll try to get a handle on it and let HH know," was the muffled reply.

Rikelman spoke up. "That would be good, John. We don't want anybody hurt. You understand?"

"I know," was the only response.

"Good, let's talk next Wednesday again at the same time. In the meantime, get as much information to Officer Hamilton as you can regarding the cars, names, and numbers of bodies."

"Ok," and then Bresani abruptly hung up.

"I'm uncomfortable with this right now," the Lieutenant said.

"Me, too."

"Me, too."

"Meeee, too."

Elapsed time: 23 minutes

CHAPTER 90

‖‖‖‖‖‖‖‖‖‖‖‖‖‖‖‖‖‖‖‖‖‖‖‖‖‖‖‖‖‖‖‖‖‖‖‖‖‖

REGROUP

The silence that filled the room was momentarily broken by loud noise in the outer office.

"Too much grab ass going on out there." Rikelman stood up, went to the door, and in his Norman Bates voice, ordered, "knock it off, you guys. We'll be out in a minute but keep the noise down."

'Ok, just so we're on the same page, here's what we need to do. Hamilton, I want you to pump Bresani as hard as you can. I want names, routes, guns, who got them, car descriptions if possible. Get the locations pinned down in Irwindale and the South Bay. I want it by next Monday." It was the Norman Bates rapid staccato in full order.

A quiet nod was all Hamilton could muster.

"Mike, I need to know how many guys from LA Deuce you can deploy on this. Maybe you should have your Lieutenant call me to discuss. What's his name?"

"Marsden, Darren Marsden. But if I could speak for a moment, sir."

Rikelman silently abdicated.

"I know how our Lieutenant thinks about this case. He may tell you that we're taking it over. We can use your guys and put them where we decide, but this has gotten so big that you may want to pass the baton to us."

There was another interminable silence in the room. "Way out of my pay grade, sirs. I'll wait for your decision on that," Hamilton said, trying to recuse himself.

"Let me talk to the Captain and maybe the Chief on this before I talk with Marsden, okay?" Rikelman reflected out loud. "I'm not opposed to it, but I think we have a big role to play here. "I'll get back to you by this afternoon, Mike, and maybe call Marsden to discuss."

The four of them looked around the room and felt a silent consensus as to the next steps. Barber finally spoke. "Hamilton, you and I need to keep in touch and work on the info we need from Bresani. As much as possible. We can't have this shit coming to the South Bay, so regardless of whose operation it is, we still need all the information you can get us. Got it?"

"Got it." Hamilton excused himself, advising he had to get back to the streets.

"We'll be in touch," Barber added.

"Lieutenant, before I get back to work, can we talk a moment in private?"

Barber and LaBonge quietly walked out of the room and closed the door. "This has nothing to do with Bresani and this caper, Ok?"

"What's up?"

"I need to know the status of this guy Jake Radshaw. Lieutenant Hospian's stepson. Barber isn't talking, and it's important."

"It's handled, Hamilton."

"How, may I ask?"

"No, it's just handled."

Hamilton was not going to settle for that. "What's that mean?"

"Bottom line is the family decided to send him to a military academy out-of-state. Maybe that'll square him away."

"Sounds like he got a break there."

"He did."

"Does the Chief know?"

"No."

"Okay..." he said with hesitation.

"Are we done, Hamilton?" Rikelman gave him his patented Norman Bates stare.

"Yes, sir!"

The streets were looking better and better all the time, was Hamilton's only thought.

Hamilton walked out of the interview room and passed the

scruffiest-looking group he had seen in a long time. He pointed at Don and Phil and sang, "hey, Bird Dog, stay away from my quail," he added with a flat note of the song. He got a 'Bye Bye Love' refrain back from both.

One more swing by the Detectives coffee table, and he headed for the comfort of Shop 885.

CHAPTER 91

IIIIIIIIIIIIIIIIIIIIIIIIIIIIIIIIIIIIIIIIIIIII

CRUISING

Rikelman was now thinking strategically. He knew the mission, knew what he had for a team, and just needed to dive into the details of this, his first big operation. Whether he had to be the strict Norman Bates character or just be his methodical self would be dictated by others.

"Just got off the phone with Lt. Marsden," LaBonge said. "Just as I suspected, he would want us to take it over, but he's on a cruise over the Thanksgiving weekend and beyond. Not available. Bresani knows too much about our patterns. We'll commit all our resources and our number two supervisor. I convinced him that we could work together on this and you could handle the operation. It was just too late for him to postpone his trip."

"Ok, listen, I think we need to sit down with your key guys, techies, and supervisor, along with Barber, and plan this out. I'll let the Captain and Chief know what's going on. Do we have access to an airship?"

"No problem there. We don't have our own but can always rely on LAPD or the Sheriff's." LaBonge and Rikelman were gaining confidence in each other as the events progressed.

"I'm counting on Hamilton to come through with Bresani, but you know what a flake Bresani is."

"We do. And don't trust him, not one bit," LaBonge said without hesitation. "This guy Hamilton seems to have a good relationship with him. As I recall, Bresani almost set him up for a big fall at the hospital, right?"

"Don't think it was on purpose, but, yeah. If we didn't know better, you guys would have taken him down."

"Good thing he had you on his side. Ever think of trying to bring him into the unit? Seems like a good fit from what I can see."

"Let's see what we get on Monday. And yeah, I'm working on him but not sure he's interested," was Rikelman's retort.

CHAPTER 92

||||||||||||||||||||||||||||||||||||||||||||||||

STREETS

HH took his coffee and almost ran to the first floor and out to the parking lot. The comfort of climbing into his mobile office was almost more than he could stand. As he drove out the gated parking lot, he drove past the station's front and looked at the entrance.

The brick and mortar sent the message of sturdiness, structure, and permanence. No one noticed the concrete planter balusters that zig-zagged up to the entrance to protect it from a car bomb. Nor did they know the bulletproof glass doors and windows that framed an otherwise stark public building were also protecting the secrets of an investigation that could have a disastrous impact on the South Bay and its population.

There were more confidences and mysteries inside this structure than anyone could fathom.

He advised dispatch he was clear and available for calls. Finally!

He readjusted his cellphone from mute and saw two calls from the same number but no message. And, of course, a call with a voice message from Clare. He decided to call the unknown number first. He thought he knew who, and he was right.

"Hello, Michael Alcazar," he said, trying to send a smile through the airwaves.

"Hi, sir."

"I thought I recognized the number. How are you doing?"

"Doing great, sir."

"I thought I told you, don't call me sir!"

"I know, Officer Hamilton, but a force of habit up here at the Academy. I just wanted to give you a heads up. We have another week-long ride-along coming up the week after Thanksgiving. You guys should be getting a notice soon. Graduation is scheduled for the sixteenth. Will I see you there?"

"Wouldn't miss it, Michael. How's everything else?"

"Really good, sir. I mean, Officer Hamilton. I'm enjoying the Academy but can't wait to get back to OHPD and the streets."

"I know what you mean. I'll make sure I calendar the graduation and see you after turkey day. Do we have a full week together?"

"I think so. It seems like everybody goes on vacation during the holidays. I think the Academy staff wants off too."

"Well, not everybody gets off, Michael. Some of us are working" They both laughed. "And you should get used to working holidays for a few years, so I don't have to." They laughed again.

"I'll work every day, sir."

"You're a good man, Charlie Brown. I remember those days," Hamilton joked.

"Whose Charlie Brown?"

CHAPTER 93

||||||||||||||||||||||||||||||||||||||||||||||||

TOMORROW

There are times when one can pack things into a mental suitcase and file them away in a separate compartment or storage area, never to be brought out until needed again. There was no such luxury in police work. It piled up, could only be stored temporarily, and always seemed to be hanging around. It was constantly up to each person to create a life-work balance that allowed time away, and if not, to pigeonhole the thoughts and information for a later time.

For Howard Hamilton, this was his time to tag certain information, make mental notes, and take the Scarlet O'Hara approach of *'tomorrow is another day, I'll think about that tomorrow.'* Hard to do, but so necessary, for today.

"Hi, Dad, can you call me at my lunchtime? It's about Jake." It was the voice message from home he thought was Clare. Cell phones had become the new parenting tool of the day.

Getting his twelve-year-old daughter her cell phone had been a hard decision. Her lunch break was at eleven-thirty. He would handle some radio calls and engineer his free time for the appointed call.

After a 'keep the peace' and suspicious person call that turned out to be someone who was just lost, he decided to return to Kensington Road once again to make his call to Marcia. "Hi, Babe, how're you doing?" he asked quite innocently.

"Okay, Dad, thanks for getting back to me. Hey, what do you know about what happened to Jake? He's disappeared. Did you have him arrested?"

He paused for a pregnant moment as the question caught him off guard. "No, why?"

"My friend Beverly said he just disappeared from school, and she hasn't seen him in the neighborhood."

"Well, young lady, I can tell you I had nothing to do with anything. But for sure, I didn't arrest him."

"You know how kids talk, Dad. They all know what you do now, and I just didn't want to be blamed for anything. Geez, these are my friends."

"As I said, Marsh, you don't need friends like that. Make sure no one takes his place in that group you seem to call friends."

"I will, Dad, but I had to know you had nothing to do with it."

"I didn't. Okay?"

"Okay."

The disconnect was mutual, but the thought process at each end of the conversation was different.

I wonder if he was telling me the truth? Marcia pondered. *No, he'd tell me.*

Howard blew out a deep breath. *If she found out Jake was Hospian's stepson, she may think I did make him disappear.*

CHAPTER 94

||||||||||||||||||||||||||||||||||||||||||||||||

PROFILE

Dieter finally made it back to the station. It was 1830, but he had no place else to be. He didn't want to go home, not just yet.

He would have to bring home something for dinner because she didn't like to cook for just two. Elena had been an afterthought as a wife. He had no misgivings, but their relationship had gone the way of many twelve-year marriages. He'd call and let her know he had a few more hours of work. It seemed alright with her. Everything was alright with her.

The evidence room was open until 1900 hours, so he had time to check out the box taken from the Mason storage locker. He had to get a victim profile done for Tanner, and there were still some other loose ends to tie up.

He took the box to the conference room off to the side of the evidence room and emptied it on a table. He copied the photos in the Ohio University Yearbook tied in Mason to Blankenship, but he needed more.

No one in Mason's apartment building knew him by other than a 'hi and goodbye, nice day.' They had never seen him dressed as a woman, nor did anyone ever see visitors, male or female, arrive or depart. He was a loner who harbored his lifestyle secrets that only a select few knew.

Dieter looked for anything more to tie him in with either the Rear Entrance or Blankenship. A half-filled journal Mason maintained only referenced work or school-related comments. There were no names or locations. It was almost like a line item to jog his memory about past events.

He kept seeing references to a 'Continental': was that a car? Mason owned a Mercedes, not a Lincoln. Later, that word seemed to morph into 'The League, or CBA.' What did that mean? He decided to google the two terms to see if there was any correlation.

Bingo.

The 'Continental' turned out to be a semi-pro basketball association with teams all over the country. It looked like the CBA folded in 2009 after financial difficulties. It had been made up of aspiring pro athletes, those whose time and talents had passed them by, and those who just liked to take part in strenuous physical activity and had a modicum of talent. Had there been a local league in L.A.? With the Clippers and Lakers, he thought, there had to be.

Tomorrow would tell the tale and give him another reason to contact Tanner.

He was putting things back in the box when he saw a small bundle of papers that looked like cash receipts, paper clipped, and ink fading on many. He laid them out for a quick look. There were three Staples receipts, two from Dick's Sporting Goods and three more from Victoria Secret. *Must be for the nightgown and panties*, he thought.

The older receipt was somewhat faded, but he knew right away what he was looking at. It was an itemized slip from The Rear Entrance for two yoga belts, one eight feet and one ten feet, two yoga blocks, and one set of two yoga balls with netting included. He looked at the date. Over two years ago. He'd have to see how that correlated with the membership records.

All this was making more sense, but there were still questions that needed to be answered. What kind of relationship was there between Blankenship and Mason? How long had they rekindled this relationship? Did anyone know that Mason was a cross-dresser or maybe even a transgender person?

Was Mason into diamonds? According to Tanner, Blankenship's wife knew nothing. Or did she?

An envelope addressed to him was sitting on his work desk. It was from the coroner's office and contained the long-awaited autopsy report for Mason. He scanned it and saw there was mention of hormone injections and a few other comments that would signal an attempt to modify Mason's sexual identity. He'd have to get Blankenship's autopsy report to compare notes.

Yes, tomorrow was another day.

Elapsed time: 23 minutes

CHAPTER 95

||||||||||||||||||||||||||||||||||||||||||||

DETAILS

Rikelman was not going to rest until his plan was in place. He and LaBonge would sit down and map out their strategies based upon what Bresani already told them. If things changed, they would change their Ops Plan, but they needed to brainstorm with Barber and determine their resources right now.

"How many airships do you think we need, and how many can we get?" Norman Bates was finally at work.

"I know we can get one, but let me work on another, Lieutenant." LaBonge was taking notes as fast as he could.

"We need to determine if we set up on them at the border, in San Diego, or at a checkpoint."

"Won't know that until we know if we have vehicle descriptions and plates."

"Sam, do we have access to the Automated License Plate Reader?" Rikelman asked.

"We do, but we need plates. We can start with B GOODE. Let me use some contacts at ICE. We need to have them aware of what's going on at the checkpoints. We don't know the routes for certain, and I don't want to set up shop in Irwindale and wait there. Never know. They may change plans on the fly."

"If we're going to get specifics on locations and cars, we're going to need GPS tracking. We'll need those search warrants all executed as quickly as possible. Let's see if we can get a DA assigned to this," Rikelman nodded to Barber.

Anybody special?" Barber solicited.

LaBonge and Rikelman chimed in together, "Carrie Wade!"

Wade had been the bulldog Assistant District Attorney on the Ginny Karsdon satanic cult homicide a few months back. Built like an NFL fullback and hungry like a tiger, she had become an endeared member of the OHPD detective teams. She not only put two suspects away, pending trial, but she also extradited the masterminds of the operation from Puerto Rico. It had to be her!

"Done," Barber said with a knowing grin.

Barber moved to the whiteboard with a black felt tip pen in hand. He started doodling with lists for equipment, teams by number, cars needed, and radio and technology equipment that may be required.

"How many teams can we get from the task force? I've got three teams of two here. Could get a few from detectives if we need to."

"We can get eight teams from the task force, no problem. I got two Spanish speakers if we need it and a bunch of gringos who think they know it."

Barber plotted the list of items in red. Cars were green, and teams were blue.

Barber threw out more questions. "How many cars do we need? Maybe we should rent a few just to be on the safe side." He was now asking and answering his questions. "I'll handle that. I'll reserve a frequency for us and the task force with dispatch. Will make sure we have plenty of hand-helds."

He rummaged through more papers. "If we can get a few names confirmed, I can feed it into our clearinghouse to get all the info we need. Do you think Hamilton can come through for us, Lieutenant?"

"If anybody can get it out of Bresani, Howard can. For some reason, they have a connection. I know Bresani owes HH a big one, but a lot will depend on how much Johnny B knows."

"I'm concerned that we find out how much armament they have," Barber said to bring the conversation back to what was necessary. "I don't want any of our guys hurt. I don't care if we dump somebody, but nobody gets hurt on our side. Anyway, I'll make sure all teams know that vests are not optional."

"Think we'll need a SWAT team at the Irwindale location?"

"If we do," Rikelman said, "We'll need more than one! But let's wait to see what happens on Monday."

CHAPTER 96

IIIIIIIIIIIIIIIIIIIIIIIIIIIIIIIIIIIIIIIIIIIIIIIII

WEEKEND

There's no such thing as a weekend or holiday in police work: just days off and days on duty.

HH was thinking about Geoff's final soccer game for the season, going to St. Elizabeth's on Sunday, and maybe even squeezing in a visit to the mall. Something was bugging him about this weekend, and he couldn't get it out of his mind. What was it he needed to discuss with Clare?

Friday night turned into Saturday morning, and he thought whether he should call Bresani or just wait for his call.

He'd wait. He had no idea the level of planning that was going on at the PD. His focus was only on getting as much information as Bresani to make sure the task force knew as much as they could.

Damn, he thought, *that bastard owes me!*

"This is Howard," he said after the first ring.

"Bennett here." It was not the call he expected.

"What's up, sir?"

"Need to move some days off around for the next deployment period. Are you planning on going back to PMs?"

"Not sure. Clare likes this shift, but I want to go back to what I do best."

"Happy wife, happy - "he was interrupted.

"Don't start on me too, please. These day-watch maggots are killing me! Whose side are you on?"

Well, I hear you're doing a great job there. Dolphins are talking."

"What do you hear?"

"Just stuff. You know I attend all those high-level meetings and, while it's all essential secret shit, I know who you're talking to."

"And?"

"Let me just say, if he gives you any trouble, you tell him he owes not just you, but me too. And he owes me bigger than he owes you. And he knows it."

"I may need that extra boost; he's a prick."

"That's just his character, haven't you figured that out?"

"Yeah, guess so. Mind telling me what he owes you for?"

"You don't need to know, Hamilton." The friendship was now set aside for the business at hand. "All I'll say is that it's bigger than yours."

They finished talking about the work schedule, and Kip signed off with a flippant, "see you in church."

That's it. Thanks, Kip. I needed to talk to Clare about being a Eucharistic minister at St. Elizabeth's.

CHAPTER 97

||||||||||||||||||||||||||||||||||||||||||||||||

BLACKIE

Where was Clare? He looked in the garage and didn't see her car. *Oh, well,* he thought. *Catch her when she comes in.*

Yard work and cleaning up the garage was on the list for today. He thought about the position of eucharistic minister and wondered what it entailed. When in doubt; google it. So, he did. He looked at the duties, requirements, and time away from the family.

How holy did you have to be? I'm not a bible thumper or anything like that. I don't want to be a reader or whatever they're called. Pick a Mass, distribute communion and don't drop the host or spill the wine. How simple is that?

He got the fundamentals of the position, and it didn't seem too time-consuming. *Heck, I already go to church.* Clare may know more about it.

He could feel his pocket vibrate and reached for his phone.

"Johnny B here, HH, "You said to get back to you when I had some more information."

"Do you?"

"Yes."

Why was he so coy? "Weeell?" he dragged out the word as if to ask for a more suitable response.

"Do you wanna meet up?"

"No, John, I told you. We don't meet. We don't see each other. We don't have coffee. We talk on the phone. That's it. We're not friends, got it? I want this case done, and you're the tool to make it happen, Okay?"

245

"Gotta pen?" He ignored the latest dig into what had been a friendship.

"Wait, one." Howard hurried from the garage to his office, grabbed a yellow tablet, and put Bresani on speaker. "What do you have?"

"Well, for starters, I have some names. Are you ready?"

"Go."

Bresani gave him the names and physical descriptions of Carlos Fuentes, Blackie Sampson, and three others.

"I'm working on the rest, but it ain't fuckin easy."

"Okay, does Blackie have a real first name?

"I think it's Gerald or Jerry, not sure."

"What else?"

"They're using seven different cars from Juarez. They have decoy cars through the border at San Diego. Only Blackie and Carlos know which cars are loaded."

"Any car descriptions?"

"That's the best part. We met yesterday, and they tricked out the cars that would make the exchange at the border. We built up false bottoms, framed the lining with lead. No dog will hit on it, and x-rays won't penetrate. These guys know what they're doing. Did I mention that it's not just coke? They're bringing in fentanyl, meth, and I think some tar H."

"Ok. What else?"

"Want the plates?"

"You got the plates?" Howard said, a little bewildered. "Jeez, John, how'd you do that?"

"Just did, man. Do you need to know how?"

"No."

Bresani read off license plate numbers along with the make and model of the car.

"I had some help," he said, not wanting to let him know about Nicole.

"Gotta ask…guns?"

"Shit yeah, everybody has a fuckin gun, including me."

"What kind? Semis, revolvers, AR's?"

"Yup?"

"You mean all of that?"

"Yup. They don't wanna get ripped off by other cartel members. They don't sweat the cops, they think they have this locked down, but they're not sure about the San Gabriel gangs that may get wind of what's comin' in. This is big shit, HH."

"I see that, John. Are you going to be okay on this?"

"I'm covered all the way, Howard, but why do you give a shit?"

"I don't. Just asking." There was a long pause between two people who used to be partners, on-the-job friends, and now at odds with their missions. Bresani sounded more like a street thug in every conversation.

"Well, I know you're going to check these guys out, but anything you can get me on Sampson would help. I don't know too much about him. And I'd like to."

"I'll check with the Lieutenant to see if that's possible, John. Not sure about that. Anything else?"

"If there is, I'll call you."

"Ok. Take care, John." There was a click. Had *he meant that last statement?*

"Honey, I'm home." Came Clare's greeting from the garage door.

Elapsed time: 23 Minutes

CHAPTER 98

||||||||||||||||||||||||||||||||||||||||||||||

INSURANCE

Hamilton had just dialed Sam Barber's cell number as he heard the familiar greeting from Clare. "Just a minute, dear," he yelled out as Barber picked up. "Not you, sir, sorry," HH here, sir."

"I'm pretty good at voice recognition, Hamilton. What's up?"

"Just got off the phone with Bresani. Got a bunch of additional info. Where are you?"

"I'm still in the office. Can you come by? Can't leave right now."

"Sure, be there in ten." He grabbed the yellow tablet and his off-duty handgun, told Clare he had an errand to run, and drove quickly to the station.

It took eight minutes, and he could not believe what he found driving into the station parking lot.

He couldn't find a place to park! He took a chance and parked in the service area for black and whites. The last time he parked his personal vehicle in the wrong spot, he got a ticket, and it eventually tied to the arrest of Bresani. That was a few months back. Well, he was on his turf now, so he took the chance.

He bounded up the stairs to the now-familiar closed door marked 'Narcotics/Vice.' He decided to knock.

Barber opened the door and greeted him like a long-lost brother. "Glad to see you. Come on into the chaos."

Hamilton looked over Barbers' shoulder to see at least fifteen different bodies he had not seen before, along with some of the OHPD regulars and, of course, LaBonge and Carvin.

Barber brought him over to his desk and pointed to a chair next to a computer. "Oh, Howard, let me introduce you to someone. This is Lieutenant Darren Marsden. He's the LA Deuce task force commander."

Marsden was about six feet, hundred and ninety pounds, and looked like a former sports athlete, but he couldn't figure out what sport. And, the name was familiar. They exchanged pleasantries.

"Thought you were going on a cruise, sir? LaBonge said you wouldn't be involved."

"That's what they have trip insurance for, Hamilton." Marsden said it in a somewhat sarcastic way that might as well have finished with; 'you dumb motherfucker.'

Barber pulled him away to get to the business at hand. "Thought I would introduce you. He runs Deuce, but he's a Lieutenant from Torrance PD. Not sure you know, but the task force is made up of PD's from all over Southern California. I think I mentioned it, but LaBonge is from Glendale PD and Carvin from Whittier. It's a two to three-year loan, and each agency splits the asset seizure money to help pay for these guys. The bottom line is they come from the different PD's narco units, so they already have the expertise. Marsden is one of the best. But he's also got a weird sense of humor. I think you figured that out, huh?"

"Yes, sir."

"Whatcha got?"

Hamilton went over the information provided by Bresani. He provided Barber with a list of cars, names, potential routes, and the expanded list of products to be delivered.

"Gotta tell you, though, sir, they all have weapons. Everything from handguns to semi-automatics and AR-15's."

"We kind of figured that."

"He also said they're not concerned with us, more concerned with the other drug cartels or gangs in the area."

"We've heard the same thing."

"What do you mean?"

Barber signaled Rikelman and Marsden into a small office and closed the door.

"Lieutenants, Hamilton here has given us plates, vehicle descriptions, names, and other intel from Bresani. I think it's time we tell him the rest."

Rikelman looked at Marsden for approval. He got a nod.

"Howard, the intel you gave us is invaluable. We know some of this, but we didn't have the level of detail you've given. You need to know that we have someone deep under in this group. All your info has been corroborated with our UC. You put the icing on the cake."

"Our UC couldn't get this level of detail," pointing to the yellow tablet, "because it would draw too much suspicion."

"My CI isn't your CI too, is it?"

"No," Marsden said flatly. "They know who each other is but neither knows what role the other is playing. And, for sure, your guy does not know our guy is a UC."

"This is getting a little complicated," Howard said exasperatedly.

Rikelman quickly said, "You ain't seen nothing yet! Come here."

They walked out of the office, leaving Marsden and Barber.

"We're eventually going to move everything to the Emergency Operations Center upstairs on Tuesday. Those guys - pointing to two males who looked like your typical computer geeks - are from Clearinghouse. They'll track all of the info you gave us, put it into a system and verify with ID's and vehicles, get photos, and develop a package on each."

Howard looked around at the mass of humanity that was squeezed into the three small rooms. He spotted a familiar face.

"Officer Hamilton, great to see you!" Carrie Wade grinned. "Are you involved with this case too?"

"Not really," he said sheepishly.

"That table there is working on all of the logistics with Barber." Rikelman was very animated as he pointed each group out. He was in his glory, and there was no sign of Norman Bates.

"Those guys are the ALPRS team that will be tracking the cars and this team..." pointing out a guy and girl slaving over hot computers, "...will be handling all search warrants and GPS tracking requests with Wade. We're going to try to find the cars used before 'D Day' and track them with GPS. There's a lot more going on, but you get the idea."

"Do I ever, sir," Hamilton said, again and again, shaking his head in amazement.

It was about time they took this case seriously.

"Wait till you see what happens on Tuesday." Rikelman said with more pride than Howard had seen. Ever.

CHAPTER 99

IIIIIIIIIIIIIIIIIIIIIIIIIIIIIIIIIIIIIIIIIIIIIII

TRANSFORMATION

His adrenaline was pumping. He had not been this excited about a case since the Karsdon homicide. What Rikelman had organized was nothing short of spectacular. But then again, it was Rikelman. There was no doubt that this would be a successful operation.

And how about that Lieutenant Marsden? He canceled a cruise with his family for this! That took balls!

Not sure that would fly at home, he pondered. It was apparent that 'the phantom' had gotten to Marsden.

HH had a theory about the Broadway play "Phantom of the Opera." The phantom was not a person. He merely represented the commitment needed to take one's talents to the next, higher level by sacrificing everything else. In the play, Christine was an opera singer who needed to devote more time and a higher level of obligation, dedication, and loyalty to her craft, if she was to attain her goals.

There was no doubt the phantom had reached out to Marsden; and got him! HH saw this as a metaphor for the need to devote time, effort, and energy towards a craft, much like doctors or other professionals do. It means sacrificing either personal pleasures, in some cases family and relationships, or Marsden's case, a family cruise, in favor of one's profession.

Howard could tell the Phantom was tugging at him as well. But it would not get him!

He pulled back into his garage and sanctuary. On the short drive home, he was replaying what he saw in the Narco squad room. It wasn't a

Saturday; it was just a workday. It wouldn't be Black Friday. It would just be a workday, just like every other.

Now, what was it he needed to discuss with Clare?

"Hey muffin," he chimed, entering from the garage to the hallway, "need to talk about something."

"In the kitchen, Howie and I need to talk to you, too!"

If there ever was a time to be straightforward and candid, it was now. "What do you think of me being a Eucharistic minister?"

"Where did that come from, as if I didn't know?"

"Yeah, Rex asked if I was interested in taking the classes and helping out at one of the masses each Sunday."

"Do you want to do that?"

"Well, I don't think it'll take that much time away from family, but I wanted to get your thoughts." He was trying not to show his hand. Not right now. He was waiting for the emphatic 'no' to his comment. By now, he knew the drill.

"I think it can help in a lot of ways. You know, the kids seeing you in that way may be helpful. But what about you, have you thought about it?"

"What do you mean?"

Well, think about it, Howard. Just being a Catholic cop is hard enough." She moved dishes around as she was preparing the fish and chips.

"A few years ago, your Department arrested our friend Ara from St. Elizabeth's at a pro-life rally where he beat up an abortion rights activist. And, your parents are divorced, and your Dad can't go to communion because he remarried. That might change, but not right now."

He looked at her with a newfound appreciation for assessing a situation. "The Church is against capital punishment, and we all know your position on that…it's not easy being a Catholic cop family. And think about this; would you give communion to an illegal immigrant who attends our church if you knew they were breaking the law by just being here?"

"I hadn't even thought about all those issues, but you're right. I just didn't want to take too much time away from family. You're right, though. It could add rather than take away. I'd have to give those other issues more thought."

"Why don't you get more details from Father Art or Rex, and we'll talk again. Or maybe even Father Mike. Being a Police Chaplain must have its contradictions. We have to consider if you go back on the night shift how that'll impact us and your new obligation, to boot."

"Maybe I'll talk with Rex again and see if we can't make it more of a New Year's resolution."

While he wasn't surprised by Clare's reaction, he never viewed himself as one of those who seemed so pious or holy.

He said 'fuck' and 'asshole' a lot, but only at work. Would he have to change and watch his language? What else would he have to change? Views on the death penalty? On immigration? Divorce? No! Did this have to be a transformation, or could he still be one of the guys and a good cop?

"Now, what was it that you had to talk about? The kids?"

"Well, I know you think it's all about the kids, but this time it's about me."

"Go on…I'm listening."

"Maru and I have been talking, and she's invited me to take courses to teach some beginning yoga classes." She paused to let it sink in.

She quickly broke the silence with, "it's a privilege to be asked. What do you think? She said it would take about two hundred hours of coursework, and she would sponsor me. That means she would pay a part of the costs."

"I'm not worried about the cost, Muffin. Just your time commitment."

"I was thinking that too. But the kids are getting older, and most of the classes would be while they're in school, anyway. She did say there may be a few three-day retreats I would have to attend and a few night classes, but we can work around your work schedule, don't you think?"

"Is this something you want to do, Clare?" He had to ask to make sure this was just not something Maru talked her into.

I do, Howie."

"Well then, that makes two of us that have to think about our New Year's resolutions, huh?"

CHAPTER 100

IIIIIIIIIIIIIIIIIIIIIIIIIIIIIIIIIIIIIIIIIIIII

LUNCH

Before he knew it, Monday arrived. Back to work. He thought about what lay ahead. Michael was graduating from the Academy in a few weeks, so he could put off thinking about that for a while. His first trainee. Exciting, he hoped.

Today, he needed to make one last connection with Johnny B to ensure the plan was still in place or get any necessary changes. He had planned to attend the updated briefing in Narcotics with the task force on Tuesday and give Rikelman, Barber, and Marsden any changes. He was working Thanksgiving, but, barring overtime, he would be home by four o'clock. It might take some engineering, but he could do it.

Out of briefing and set up with Shop 885, it would be a typical holiday week Monday. Chaos. The Mall would be filled with holiday shoppers and shoplifters, so there was no doubt he might get a call to transport someone arrested by the OHPD Mall Detail.

He was surprised to get a call at Della's Italian Kitchen, one of his and Clare's favorite restaurants. "See the manager regarding a 415 customer, disturbing the peace, 909 Toluca Way".

It was barely noon, and the lunch crowd was picking up. The manager, a middle-aged Italian with an early receding hairline and a gut that couldn't take one more meatball, came out to greet him. Because of the layout of the city, he was only five minutes away from anywhere but the Hills.

He chose a parking space about ten slots away from the entrance instead of blocking traffic in this relatively small strip mall.

"Hi, Officer...he gazed at Hamilton's nameplate. "...my name is Rick Guerra. I've got a lady in here that's been giving us trouble for the last, well, I'd say three or four months now."

"Ok, is that her sitting on the patio looking a bit angry at the world?" Hamilton saw a lady sitting tensely, grasping her purse with both hands and staring into space.

"It is. She comes in here twice a week or more and orders a big meal, lunch or dinner, and usually some wine. At least one glass, sometimes two."

"Ok..." Hamilton said, not sure where this was going.

"Then she walks out without paying or leaving a tip."

"Are you willing to make a citizen's arrest? I can't arrest her for the section of *defrauding an innkeeper,* but you can. The infraction wasn't committed in my presence."

"Well, that's another problem. She's done this, maybe twelve times, in the last few months. The first time she did it, her husband found out, came in, and made restitution. Then he asked if he could arrange to pay every time she walked out without paying. Well, to kind of keep the peace, and I agreed."

"So, she doesn't owe you anything except for today, right?"

"Right, but I have two problems. I have some of my other regulars who've seen the lady do this over and over. They brought it to my attention, and now I think I need to do something about it."

"Have you called her husband?"

"Yes, just before you got here."

"And...?"

"Well, the problem is, people have started to recognize her. You see, she's your City Manager's wife."

"*Eeeewww,*" HH muttered.

Just then, his cell phone rang, and he saw it was Bresani.

CHAPTER 101

||||||||||||||||||||||||||||||||||||||||||||

INNKEEPER

He had to let it go to voicemail. Hamilton continued the conversation with the manager as he articulated his adventures with the City Manager and his wife.

Before he talked with her, he decided that the best course of action was to get a Sergeant out here as soon as possible. He was advised by dispatch that Sgt. McGinty was on his way but was asking for him on the Tac frequency.

"What's up, Hamilton?" McGinty squawked into his earpiece.

"Would rather wait until you get here, sir."

"Why? Got another DB?"

"No, sir. You'll see. What's your ETA?"

"One minute," was the curt reply.

Hamilton casually walked to the matronly lady in her late 50's or early 60's. "Hello, Mrs. Rollins. My name is Officer Hamilton."

She was dressed age-appropriate. Even he could tell she shopped well. Her pantsuit was not Target or even J Crew. He had not seen anything like it, which meant it was expensive. He made sure they were out of earshot of the other patrons.

"How do you do, Officer Hamilton. I guess you know who I am," she said somewhat apologetically.

"Yes, Mam, I do. My Sergeant will be here any minute. I hope you don't mind waiting a few more minutes. Would you like us to call your husband?"

"I think the manager already did." It was a very whispered response, just in case someone was eavesdropping. She went back to staring out into space.

Sgt. McGinty rolled up and partially blocked the entrance to the restaurant. Hamilton quickly walked over to him and suggested he park in at least the handicapped slot, even though two black and whites would bring attention, anyway.

Away from the owner and patrons, He briefed McGinty on the circumstances. "Are you fucking kidding me?" McGinty looked up at Mrs. Rollins and the manager over Hamilton's shoulder as they talked.

"I think we can be assured he doesn't want to make a private person's arrest, but I'll get a verbal refusal anyway. Maybe by then, her husband will show up." Hamilton was just glad somebody with rank would relieve the pressure on him and make sure they followed the law, department protocol, and perhaps even a little common sense.

McGinty used his cell to advise the watch commander, who would, in turn, notify the Patrol Captain and the Chief. *Good grief, the world will know before too long,* Hamilton thought to himself.

HH saw the City Manager walk casually up to Guerra and have a brief conversation away from the crowd. Sgt. McGinty then walked over, shook the CM's hand, and the three of them huddled like in baseball when the manager goes to the pitcher's mound to bring in a reliever and brief the infield. They covered their mouths with their hands, so no one could try to read their lips.

Good grief, Charlie Brown.

McGinty came back to Hamilton. "This is your radio call, Hamilton, so stick around while this plays out. I think I know what we're going to do. I'll deal with the CM. You just stand by, okay?"

"Got it, Sarge," he said, relieved.

Ten minutes later, everything was resolved. Because Mrs. Rollins had not left the premises, there was no actual crime. She just had not paid yet.

Mr. Rollins advised Guerra, Sgt. McGinty and Hamilton that this had happened before in other business locations in the City. She would shoplift a dress or piece of jewelry, the proprietor would call the CM, and he would give them a credit card to charge it to, and all was well.

"That will now change," Mr. Rollins advised the trio of interested parties. "I'll be getting her some much-needed help. Thank you all for understanding." He was very subdued, embarrassed, perhaps even a bit angry. He beckoned his wife, and they walked to his car, arm in arm.

Hamilton's cell rang again.

CHAPTER 102

||||||||||||||||||||||||||||||||||||||||||

LADY

Hamilton took the call as he headed for his black and white. McGinty stuck around to smooth talk the manager and make sure there were no unanswered questions. Howard had already forgotten the call, entering into his mobile terminal the disposition of 'kept the peace.'

"John, sorry, was on a call. What's up?"

"Just checking in with you as we talked about last week, HH. All's well at this end."

"Any changes in the plan?"

"Nothing that you guys need to know. Can I ask some questions, though?"

"You can try, but I don't know much."

"What do you mean, you're involved, aren't you?"

"Yeah, but I'm not privy to all the details," he lied. "I'm trying to be your contact for this thing. Gotta remember, big John, I don't work narco, I'm just a lowly patrol turd, just like you were. But if anything changes, I need to know, got it?"

"I know. I just thought you might know when they plan to take everybody down? How many are on the team? Is it just OHPD?"

"Jeez, John. I don't know all of that. And, I don't want to. You and I'll keep in touch, but this is a one-way street of information. We don't tell you, but you tell us everything. Got it?" Hamilton decided to take a different tack. "Did some checking on your guy Sampson, John."

There was a silence on the other end.

"Do you want to know?" Howard was trying to respond to the silence.

"What you got?"

His radio chirped; "Lincoln 75, Lincoln 75, come to the station Code 2. See Admin."

"Roger that," he advised, "five minutes." They continued talking as he pointed Shop 885 in the direction of the barn. He had driven out of the parking lot when his phone switched over to Bluetooth and the car's speaker system.

"I'm not going to read you his rap sheet, John, but he's a badass. Did time for manslaughter, small-time dealing, and was drummed out of the NFL for drugs. He hung out with that guy from the Patriots, and you know how that all ended. I wouldn't fuck with him if I were you."

"Didn't know about the manslaughter case but pretty much figured out the rest."

"Might want to be careful around him. By the way, John, still got that dog?"

"Lady? She's right next to me, HH,"

"Got a question for you, John."

"Shoot."

"Where are you gonna be on Friday?"

"I don't know yet. Is that important?"

"God damn it, John, everything's important right now. You know that." He was getting a little heated at John's evasiveness.

"I'll discuss your requests with Barber and get back to you, but in the meantime, make sure I know where you're going to be on Friday. I think we need to touch base one more time. And by the way, Kip says if this goes well, you won't owe him anymore. What's that about?"

"That's between Kip and me, but how did he know about this HH?"

"What Department do you think this is, John? This takes a lot of planning, and certain people must know. Kip's one of those, but other than him, it's between the brass and Narco."

"Okay, but did he tell you why I owe him?"

"No. And quite frankly, Scarlett, I guess I don't give a damn."

The forced laugh at both ends of the phone was about to end the conversation.

"John, I just want to say, one more time, watch your ass with Sampson. He is a definite bad guy."

"I will, HH, I will."

CHAPTER 103

||||||||||||||||||||||||||||||||||||||||||

RARIFIED

Hamilton stood tall over Janet's desk but knew she outranked him in so many ways.

"Somebody up here wants to see me, Janet?"

"Yes, Officer Hamilton. I believe Captain Markham would like to have a word with you."

"Am I in trouble?"

"Have you done anything wrong?"

"I don't think so, but you guys think differently up here."

"Not everybody, Howard, just a few of them," she nodded toward the three Captain's offices.

"He's in his office, and it's okay to go in. He was expecting you."

Oh, that's not good, he thought. *Not good at all. I wonder what it's about? He thought about the use of force he disagreed with the Chief about? Bresani? Jeez, this day watch shit was too much. Maybe I can talk him into going back to PMs. This third floor is creeping me out!*

He expected to face Markham's typical scowl, but there was no grimace. There was an extended hand and as good a smile as a Captain could muster.

"Howard, great to see you. Sit down."

HH took a seat, reflecting on the conversation he had overheard between Markham and the Chief. He knew Markham had disagreed with the Chief's decision on his use of force but decided to let that go, for now. Only he knew Markham wanted the Chief's job and harbored a lot of resentment over not getting it.

"Just wanted to let you know that we appreciated the way you handled the City Manager's wife's situation today. You used good judgment in calling for a sergeant, and I understand you made the right call in advising the owner how the case was going to be handled."

"Just doing my job, sir."

"I know that, but not everybody here would have handled it the way you did. Both the owner and CM were appreciative of your empathy and to recognize a situation where someone needed help."

"Yes, sir."

"Just wanted to let you know because not everybody at city hall is our friend. We'd like to ensure that we at least have the backing of our CM, particularly when it comes to budget items. You don't need to know about all of that, but your handling of the situation helped the department."

There was no need to respond to that comment as he didn't understand it anyway.

"And, another thing. I've been watching your career and see that you've spent a lot of time on the night shift. I know it's great police work, but there are other things out there besides patrol work. We have our eye on you for career advancement opportunities and would like you to consider branching out and moving to another assignment within the next year. As you know, we make changes here around July to adjust for the next year's school calendar for guys going to college, so think about what else you'd like to do around here."

"I like the streets, sir."

"We all do or did at one time, Howard. Just a word to the wise, that's all. Think about it."

"I will, sir. If I may ask, how did you find out about this so quickly?"

"Well, Howard," - and he knew exactly what was coming- "what department do you think this is?" They both had a good laugh at the often quoted OHPD phrase.

"Is that all?"

"Yes, it is—great talking to you, Howard. Drop by up here occasionally. It wouldn't hurt to check out the rarified air up here."

"Yes, sir," shaking his hand once again.

And there was no mention of his use of force case. What does go on up here, he wondered?

Elapsed time: 23 minutes

CHAPTER 104

||||||||||||||||||||||||||||||||||||||||||||

DEBT

He was glad to slide out of the third floor without encountering anyone else he knew. Not suitable to be seen on the third floor by the guys.

He started down to Shop 885 by the back stairwell. He saw Dieter Rollenhagan coming up the stairs from the ground floor, heading back to Detectives on the second floor.

"HH, glad I ran into you."

"What's up?"

"Wanted to give you an update on the Mason case, got a minute?"

HH followed him back to his office desk, knowing he was still out to the Admin offices and dispatch would not be looking for him for a few more minutes.

"Not sure where to start, and I don't know if anyone else has filled you in, but…."

"No, have not heard anything since we met with Detective Searles of LAPD."

"Well, it's looking like Mason could be their suspect in the homicide at an S&M club in their area. They finally found someone who would talk about Blankenship and Mason. It turns out that Mason and their victim had a brief relationship while they were on the Ohio University Basketball team together, and Mason's lifestyle changed. He became a cross-dresser and was taking shots to convert to being female. I just finished shipping my profile and autopsy report over to Detective Tanner, Searles partner."

"Sounds like an interesting case, Dieter. From suicide to a homicide suspect. Wow!" Hamilton laughed to himself because it was his original idea that there was something fishy about the case, and Dieter initially balked.

"I know you had some suspicions, and I'm glad I listened to you. I guess I had a little tunnel vision on this one. But never again."

"You know," Howard said in a frank manner, "there is something to be said for the pleasure of finding things out and not letting your mind jump to conclusions."

"I know that now, HH. Hey, a couple of other things. You mentioned the belts Mason used to hang himself with."

"Yeah?"

"Well, as it turns out, they were purchased at this S&M club, and that's one of the key pieces of evidence that will help close this case. The Rampart dicks think Mason and Blankenship had rekindled their relationship. Mason eventually found out the victim was married with two kids and not just some yoga guru."

"That's good to hear. I recognized the belts because Clare and I take yoga. Never thought it would tie into a case like this."

"One never knows, HH. There is pleasure in finding things out." They both laughed.

"One other thing, and I 'll let you get back to the street."

"What's that?"

"I met Detective Tanner, and boy is she a fox. A knockout. She could be a homewrecker, if you know what I mean. If I ever had the chance, I'd jump her bones and take my chances at being caught."

"I'd stay clear of that one if I were you, Dieter."

"Why, you know something?"

"Let's just say that you shouldn't pursue the other one any further either."

"Care to tell me why?"

"No, and we'll leave it at that. I'd stay away from her and her partner if you know what's good for you. Oh, and Dieter, don't refer to them as Rampart dicks. Somehow it doesn't fit."

There was absolutely no way Hamilton was going to swim with the dolphins on this one. No way.

"Hey Dieter…" he said on his way out. "Save me a spot someplace up here. You owe me now."

"I know, HH, I know."

CHAPTER 105

||||||||||||||||||||||||||||||||||||||||||||||

UNKNOWN

Barber got the phone call he was expecting from Hamilton. Nothing had changed at that end, but plenty had changed inside the Narcotics office of OHPD.

It was a frenzy of activity moving the entire operation up to the third-floor Emergency Operations Center, or EOC. There was no way Operation BF, as it had been termed, could be run out of the small office used for regular, routine investigations. Repurposing the EOC as a 'war room' and the base of operations would be the key to the success of this case, and Barber knew how to handle it.

With minimal direction from Rikelman, Barber had opened the new phone and T-1 lines for communication, set up projectors to display GPS and Google digital mapping for every location and vehicle given by Hamilton. Barber tied into the ALPRS program with Border Patrol and CHP and displayed photos of all suspects and vehicles used.

They could track the movements of cars and people. Computers sprouted from tabletops. Encrypted satellite communications took the place of telephones. Strangers to OHPD sat at terminals with drawn faces, reddened eyes, and stubbled chins.

Not much talk, just focus on screens, the projection of data and intensity that only caffeine could quiet. It was right out of a futuristic television show, with the FBI-type war room.

Teams had been assigned to locate the cars early in the week and sit on them until the search warrants were obtained to secrete a tracking device on each. Barber also arranged for a radio operator from OHPD dispatch who borrowed overtime to control radio frequencies and relay assignments.

Barber and Rikelman made sure that at least one member of every agency involved assigned someone to the EOC for the week and track the movements of their people.

There was always the possibility that many of the vehicles would head south on Thursday or early Friday to rendezvous with the shipments coming across the border. Border Patrol and San Diego PD had been involved in the planning and agreed to let the shipments come north from their location.

Marsden decided, and Rikelman concurred, that as soon as three shipments arrived at the Irwindale location, they would take down everyone at once. Wherever the other suspects were located, those teams would stop simultaneous to the entry teams going into the industrial building in the San Gabriel Valley.

Based on traffic patterns and drive time, the estimated time for everything to go down was between 1400 and 1500 hours. Barber knew that this timing was critical. Everyone was convinced it could be done.

On Wednesday morning, Rikelman and Marsden called a quick meeting with LaBonge and Barber. "I'll be frank here, guys. I'm a little nervous about this thing. It's running too smoothly. What are we missing?" Rikelman tossed the question for response.

LaBonge was the first to speak. "What do you mean, Lieutenant?"

"You guys don't know our snitch. I do. He may be holding back on things that we should know or is feeding us info just to make us think we know everything. While he was here, I just never trusted the guy."

In typical Rikelman fashion, he stood up and paced the small room.

"Could never figure out how he knew everything that was going on in the streets. He's a conniver, manipulator, and an asshole to boot. We need to impress every team member to be careful, don't take things at face value, and think about alternatives. Got to be ready for the unknown. I would like to get out of this without a shot being fired."

Barber spoke up. "Hey Lieutenant, I think we should put a tracking system on the CI's Sprinter. Never know where that goes or where it may end up."

"Great idea, Sam. Add it to the list."

Marsden raised a finger to obtain the floor. "Agree. I'll get my team together and re-emphasize the need for being more cautious than normal. But, it's not our first rodeo."

"I know. But it's ours," Rikelman pointed to himself and Barber.

It wasn't war, but it was close to it. The enemy has been defined, targeted, and ready for attack. There is no room for surrender, loss, or even damage control. Only the necessity to stay on the offense and focus on the mission.

Everything was in place for Black Friday.

CHAPTER 106

||||||||||||||||||||||||||||||||||||||||||||||||

SANDWICHES

For just about everyone involved in Operation BF, Friday could not get here fast enough. Cram the turkey down with all the trimmings, eat too many slices of the various pies, and talk with whatever family was available for the thankful feast.

Whether single, divorced, married, or still living at home, members of the BF task force spent time working, surveilling, and rotating to be with family or friends. It took teamwork to make that happen, but for some reason, drug dealers do not celebrate the holidays. At least not like law enforcement.

Each team bedded down their targets and headed home, only to return at 0600 hours to be there for the wake-up call. At 0700 hours, everyone had checked in to the EOC, in place with their prey in sight.

Howard Hamilton reported to the EOC. At this point, his only assignment was to make himself available to Bresani and answer any questions posed by Barber or any other member of the team. As time progressed throughout the day, he would make his way to the San Gabriel Valley and circle around the target location in Irwindale.

At 0930, San Diego PD reported the products had crossed the border and were transferred to the cars on the monitoring system. The switch had been made in an abandoned warehouse right next to the Marine Corps Recruit Depot Training Center entrance. Cutbacks in military spending hit the city of San Diego hard. They were in the process of retooling much of the area's industrial parks that used to service the Navy and Marine Corps. Who these were leased to was something that SDPD would investigate.

The LA Deuce teams were well versed in surveillance techniques. Leapfrogging low-speed follows were coupled with alternating cars and sitting back to monitor with tracking devices. There were five cars suspected of transportation. Two took the direct route up the Interstate 5, while two spun off Highway 880 then to the 215 that went through Temecula on their way to the Riverside/Corona area. Hopefully, they wouldn't continue to Interstate 15 to take them to Baker and eventually Las Vegas. The fifth car stayed in the San Diego area warehouse after the others had left.

"What the hell is going on?" Rikelman asked LaBonge.

"Relax, Lieutenant, let me check with that team and see if they have eyes on them."

While LaBonge was checking with the team in San Diego, two other teams reported their target vehicles and suspects were already set up at the Irwindale location. Barber pointed out that Bresani's Sprinter was moving from his condo in Irvine to the Irwindale address.

By noon the fifth car left the San Diego warehouse. The team reported that several people lingered behind, but they couldn't get close enough to figure out why. Better to back off and be a bit patient.

Their patience paid off. Car number five left the warehouse and jumped on the northbound five, followed softly by the Deuce surveillance team.

As traffic became heavier, everyone seemed to be taking their time. Team One tracked their mark to a Denny's after they turned west from I-15 to the 91. Team Two followed their target past the 91 to the 215 to Highway 60, and they too stopped for eats.

"They must be talking to each other to ensure they all rendezvous at the same time," A-Team One member reported to the EOC. Barber was looking at the GPS map seeing where all known vehicles were deployed. By noon, everyone was back on the road.

"Hope everybody brown-bagged it with turkey sandwiches today," Rikelman announced to those in the EOC. To the person, everyone in the room lifted their lunch bags. A voice from the back said, "even fuckin' drug dealers eat better than we do."

Just then, the Chief walked in with Captain Pierson and Lieutenant Hospian. Hamilton got a little nervous. He could feel the temperature in the room, and sound decibels drop all at once. The combination of what was happening on the street and the Department's brass raised the anxiety level.

Rikelman took them aside and gave them a thumbnail sketch of what was going on. He told them the timeline and that things were going according to plan. He invited them to come back about 1330 or 1400 for the finale. They seemed satisfied and left after acknowledging to all how much they appreciated the work being done.

"Stay safe out there," the Chief said on his way out. "Don't want anyone hurt."

Rikelman assured him that things were under control and he would see them in about ninety minutes or so. As they left, the room temperature and decibel level resumed.

Team Three reported their subject vehicle had taken the split from the I-5 in Lake Forest at what was referred to as the 'Y' and turned northbound to the 405. Both Three and Four's people stopped for lunch and parted ways after about forty-five minutes, with Team Four continuing on the northbound 5.

"Looks like they're timing it to all arrive at the target spot by 1400, as planned," Barber reported to Marsden and Rikelman.

Marsden spoke first. "Yeah, but which cars have the product, and which are dummies? And, what's going on with Team Five?"

Barber raised Team Five on the Tac frequency. They could see the GPS still on the northbound 5 but slowly and methodically driving in the number three lane and not appearing in a hurry.

"Are they just sweeping behind? Looking for choppers or an obvious tail?" Rikelman asked Marsden.

"I think so. But the suspects could also be holding the product. Not sure. It's a late model Mercedes with a female and male. We got nothing on the female, but we know who the driver is."

Elapsed time: 184 minutes

CHAPTER 107

||||||||||||||||||||||||||||||||||||||||||

NOW!

Hamilton was in awe of the coordination and details of Operation BF. Everyone seemed to know what to do, and the electronics that supported this sophisticated surveillance were impressive. It was functioning like clockwork, at least from inside. The potential for problems in the field was still there as confrontation and takedowns had yet to be accomplished.

After attending a meeting with Marsden, Rikelman, Barber, and LaBonge for the umpteenth time, it was decided that Hamilton would go to the Irwindale industrial park location with LaBonge.

Rikelman and Marsden would meet them at a staging area that had been designated; the parking lot of the Santa Fe Dam, just blocks from the target location but secreted from public view. Barber would stay at the EOC to coordinate at that end. All were fully armed with body armor and raid jackets, clearly identifying them. Barber had the LA Deuce representative to the EOC notify Irwindale PD that the task force would be in their city.

"Keep it a bit nebulous. Just say we're doing a drug bust and will keep them apprised," Barber cautioned. "We'll call them if we need them."

The goal was to have everyone rendezvous at the staging area with Teams Three and Four, the OHPD Narcotics 6, and two teams of five LASO SWAT as the primary entry. Sgt. Wickstead, OHPD officer-in-charge of K-9's, would have two dogs with handlers as support. Barber had arranged for an airship from LASO, but high enough to not be detected from the ground.

Teams One and Two reported their suspects were fifteen minutes out from the location. Team Five was still about one hour away. Team Three and Four had already arrived at the target location. A prepositioned observation post, or OP, had reported they had seen Bresani's Sprinter go inside the warehouse at 1330. As the clock moved towards 1400, all but Team Five was ready to go.

Rikelman and Marsden quickly agreed that Team Five should call for a uniformed backup and, wherever they were, take their people down with a felony stop at the same time as entry by the SWAT Team in Irwindale.

SWAT and OHPD Narcotics, equipped with full raid gear, bulletproof vests, and AR-15's, plus handguns, quietly drove to the location, deploying on all four corners of the building. They gave themselves a five-minute window from the staging area to the target location on Miranda Road.

With exigent circumstances search warrants already prepared, they used a battering ram to knock the front door down and deploy as planned. The implosion rocked the building as flashbangs were deployed as a tactical distraction.

As SWAT entered the building from all sides, Team Five was making a felony traffic stop on I-5 with the assist of CHP at Disney Way. It would be tying up Disneyland traffic, but only for about thirty minutes.

Hamilton was right behind SWAT One as they made their entry in a slow, tactically advantaged manner. He crouched behind a long rifle marksman. With his Glock out and one in the chamber, he prepared himself for the flashbang to make sure his vision wasn't impaired.

There was movement directly to his front, just ahead of the scout member of SWAT. He extended his shooting hand to let his gunsight lead the way. He peered over the sight and saw a large male partially hidden inside an office. He had only a moment to mentally verify that it was Blackie. The cloud from the flashbang was diminishing, but the ringing in his ears and the unmistakable smell were a constant.

Hamilton stayed focused on Blackie. He heard a shot and saw him step back with a handgun and move towards the open office door. He was wearing a black hoodie with a Mercedes Benz logo that no doubt concealed a bulletproof vest underneath.

As Blackie walked from behind the desk, he raised his arm into a shooting stance. In the one second that transpired, Hamilton knew what he had to do.

Then, another shot rang out from his right front. The long rifle SWAT member had seen what he had seen and fired first. It was a headshot. Damn.

He heard a voice from one of the team members announce in staccato fashion, "Officer-involved shooting, one suspect down, rear of warehouse office, no officers hit," over the radio frequency. The SWAT Team charged into the room, and Hamilton followed.

The team moved into the far reaches of the warehouse office, securing the room from where Blackie had come out. Hamilton ran to the downed suspect, rolled him over on his stomach, and cuffed him from behind.

I don't care if he's dead or alive. He's not going anywhere.

Hamilton was transfixed on the back of the suspect's head. He grasped Blackie's cuffed hands and placed his knee in the small of his back. There was no resistance, and Hamilton could see the blood oozing from under the head. *Fatal and quick.*

Through his earpiece, someone made the announcement, "shots fired, one suspect down, no officers injured."

Within seven minutes, everyone was in custody, and a Code-Four, no further assistance was needed. It was over that quickly. Hamilton could still smell the acrid odor of the gunshots and flashbangs. It was a smell that only death could overcome. And, he was kneeling on death.

CHAPTER 108

||||||||||||||||||||||||||||||||||||||||||||||

KNEELING

Hamilton was frozen in time and space. He could not move from his control hold over Sampson. He saw a 45-caliber handgun in Blackie's right hand and focused on it, moving his vision from the gun to his head and back again.

Should I move it? Kick it away, or just leave it? His thoughts were focused but random. He was kneeling on a dead man.

Two plainclothes detectives moved into his field of vision.

"You okay, Hamilton?"

"Yeah, I think so."

"Did you put him down?" was a question from someone.

"No, almost, but somebody beat me to it. Not sure who."

"He's dead, so I think you can get up now," one of the detectives said.

Hamilton stood, but it was not easy. He was a bit unsteady on his feet but was not going to show any weakness now. Maybe later, but not now.

"One less asshole that won't see the criminal justice system," somebody muttered.

It was like being in the middle of a shooting range at monthly qualification. Gunpowder was in the air, and only two shots had been fired, notwithstanding the flashbangs. *Did he fire a shot? He didn't think so, but then again, maybe he did? Why didn't he know? Why couldn't he process this?*

He took a few steps and tried to clear his head. He walked around the small office, being careful not to touch anything. That's when two

SWAT team members met him. "One more down, here," pointing to a body behind a desk.

"Fuck!" Hamilton took one look but knew right away who it was. He didn't know if he expected it to happen or wanted it. Now that it had happened, he was conflicted, very conflicted.

Lieutenant Rikelman." he announced with a shout, "come in here."

CHAPTER 109

IIIIIIIIIIIIIIIIIIIIIIIIIIIIIIIIIIIIIIIIII

TENTACLES

Bresani lay crumpled in a small heap behind the desk. The top of his forehead had taken one .45 caliber bullet that did its job very quickly. The small pool of blood belied the damage to the brain. It was instantaneous and fatal. No pain, just shock was all he experienced.

Hamilton didn't know why, but he made the sign of the cross and tried to back slowly out of the room. He stopped. The long-haired, bearded, former police officer gone bad didn't survive his operation. Howard couldn't muster a tear, but the deep breath he took collapsed into an eight-count exhale that made his body tremble. Bile in his stomach was roiling, trying to come up.

It seemed like he was alone with Bresani for a very long time. There would be no medical treatment, no lifesaving attempts to resuscitate, no rush to the emergency room, and no church services to send his soul to wherever bad cops go. Hamilton was thinking all this as he stared into an eyeball that was not looking back. Johnny B was end of watch. Permanently.

Back at the EOC, Barber heard the 'shots fired' transmission. Anticipating the need for an ambulance, he had two on standby. It seemed the city of Irwindale was home to the largest ambulance provider in the San Gabriel Valley, AMR. Getting units to stand by was easy. He advised dispatch to make it happen immediately.

Several events happen simultaneously in an operation of this magnitude. Eleven suspects, including two females, were immediately cuffed and separated. Hamilton saw them all coming together at the same time.

Marsden and LaBonge advised Rikelman they would set up a long-term command post outside the rear of the warehouse door, out of public view.

The District Attorney's officer-involved shooting team was on the way. Irwindale PD was notified they had a shooting in their city and the nature and status of the investigation.

"The Chief is rolling your way, sir," Barber announced. "With Captain Pierson."

"Great," Rikelman mumbled to Marsden, "just fuckin' great!"

The Narco team of Don and Phil talked to one suspect that gave all appearances of being one of the people in charge of the operation. Hamilton overheard Carlo Fuentes immediately try to lay the entire operation on the dead suspect, Blackie Sampson.

"It's all about that Mercedes bitch, Nicole," he told the Narc, Don. "Johnny B's girl. Blackie wanted her. He and Johnny got into it. Blackie went through his van and found something, not sure what it was." He motioned to the dark gray Sprinter with the 'B GOODE' license plate.

Hamilton saw something on the desk. It was upside down, but he recognized it by the coloring and size. *Just look, don't touch.*

It was the old OHPD identification card with Bresani's photo and serial number. They had collected all the former Chief's issued ID cards, and the new Chief had redesigned their new one. "Everybody had to turn their old one in, didn't they, Lieutenant?" looking at Rikelman.

Rikelman merely acknowledged what Hamilton already knew. "What the fuck does it matter now?"

He heard Fuentes talking with Don. "He set us up, didn't he? He's a cop still, huh? Blackie found that fuckin card in his van, and that motherfucker set us up! Fuckin cop!"

"This was not going to be an OHPD investigation. Nor was it an Irwindale PD investigation. Everything had to be dumped on LASO and the D.A.," Rikelman advised Marsden and Hamilton. "Too many tentacles in this case."

———◆◈◈◆———

The LA Deuce mobile command post was in place to the rear of the building and out of sight from the public. The Chief and Pierson were given a walkthrough of the various crime scenes. Rikelman was designated to deal with the media. The less said about LA Deuce, the better. There was no need to let the world know of their involvement or even their existence.

Teams of follow-up investigators would be necessary to process the multiple crime scenes. It would take three days on-site to complete this part of the investigation.

The mobile crime lab would set up to process all cars in the warehouse after narcotics officers had searched them. With the assistance of the drug dogs, the investigators could locate all products that had originated in Juarez, Mexico, and arrived in Irwindale, an 800-mile journey.

Based on the intelligence provided by Bresani, they would have to dismantle the cars, piece by piece, to get at the product. Raw cocaine, tar heroin, fentanyl, and other precursors for meth, along with all cutting agents, were to be identified, packaged, printed and analyzed—all on the scene.

The search warrant called for opening every locked cabinet, storage area, or safe found on the premises. There would be no doubt they would find the money somewhere on the property. Perhaps millions.

Photos of every inch of the warehouse, cars, and equipment were taken to fill a library if printed. The cars would eventually be fingerprinted, impounded, and sent to a storage area to be auctioned and sold for asset seizure funds eventually.

An arsenal of every kind of weaponry was confiscated. Each of the key players was armed but admitted they carried to defend themselves against other drug dealers, not the police.

At last count, eight various models of Mercedes were seized, including the Sprinter. Over a million dollars, just in cars!

Hamilton looked at the array of handcuffed suspects and wondered if the other CI was in the mix. How would that be handled? Would they book him too? He had a lot of questions.

Hamilton called home to let Clare know he would be a while. No details.

"Can you and I take a drive?" he asked LaBonge.

"Where to?"

"Irvine."

CHAPTER 110

|||||||||||||||||||||||||||||||||||||||||||||||

IRVINE

After receiving an okay from Rikelman, it was after six o'clock when LaBonge and Hamilton left the Irwindale warehouse. Other than the Chief and Captain, they were the only two who left. There was too much to be done, but Hamilton and LaBonge were expendable, for now. Irvine, on a good day, was an hour away. On Black Friday night, it would take forever. Or at least it seemed.

There was a casual conversation as they started heading south on the 605 freeway.

"I have to ask," Hamilton said, "why do I know Lieutenant Marsden's name? I never met him, but he seems familiar."

"Years back, he was with the Los Angeles Angels before they were the California Angels or the Los Angeles Angels of Anaheim or whatever the hell they're called now. He's old, but he doesn't go as far back as the Hollywood Angels."

"Hollywood?"

"Yeah, I think that's what they were called. Anyway, Marsdon was a relief pitcher for them for about five years, messed up his arm, and...here he is."

"Ok, now that makes sense. My Dad was a big Angels fan, so the name is familiar. I couldn't get it out of my head. Thanks for clearing it up."

"Where are we going, HH, if I could ask."

"We're going to Bresani's condo, "Howard said quietly.

"Thought so. Think we'll have a crime scene there?"

"Not sure. But we need to check it out. I guess for some closure for me. You know John, and I used to be, well, not friends but close work associates, I guess you'd say."

"Did he have family or anything like that?"

"Had an ex-wife whose brother was on OHPD, but he passed away earlier this year. That's all I know. He had a girlfriend named Nicole, but I don't know much about her. That was who Sampson had his eyes on."

He wasn't emotional about losing this person he was trying to put a label on. He wasn't a friend by any means.

He worked with him, but Bresani went to the dark side with this drug dealing and excommunicated himself from being in the law enforcement family. He was still someone he knew that was now dead. And he saw him, dead.

How do you process that?

"One more question, if I could," Hamilton asked.

"Shoot."

"Was your CI in the group arrested?"

"Yup. Any other questions?"

Hamilton came right back with, "Nope." *Maybe someday, someone will clue him in.*

I got one," LaBonge asked. "Why aren't you in the narco/vice unit with Barber and Rikelman? It seems like you're a natural?"

"You too?" Howard responded in a laughing manner. "Everybody keeps harping on that. One of the Captains, Rikelman, and Barber have been all over me."

"Well?"

"Don't know about it yet. I haven't had a chance to talk about it with the real boss. Guess I should at least think about it."

"You should, HH. You should. Need guys like you in this drug business. Not guys like your CI."

"It's on my list to think about," Hamilton said and let it just stay out there in midair.

CHAPTER 111

||||||||||||||||||||||||||||||||||||||||||||||

HIDEAWAY

After over ninety minutes on the freeway, they arrived at Bresani's condominium complex. It wasn't gated, but it was clean, with lush landscaping on the common grounds and ample parking and walkways.

He recalled the address from the intelligence file and wanted to make sure this location had been accounted for in the final part of the investigation. He would provide whatever he knew to the LASO detectives regarding John's activities.

"Let's see if we can find a hideaway key somewhere." He motioned for LaBonge to look to the left while he looked to the right of the entry steps. There was a flower pot conspicuously sitting next to the front door, and as he looked through the ivy overhang, he heard a dog bark.

He was expecting to find 'Lady,' but he was stunned when the door opened.

"May I be of help to you?" Nicole asked.

"I'm sorry, I didn't know anyone was home."

Nicole could have been attractive when she cleaned up. Hamilton looked at a very disheveled thirty-something, dressed in jeans and a jeweled long-sleeved Mercedes Benz T-shirt with no shoes. Her dishwater blond hair was tied in a ponytail, with many strands missing the bungie that held it tight. No makeup, a pair of reading glasses dangling from her neck gave her the casual look of an out-of-work actress.

"Obviously!"

"My name is Howard Hamilton, from Orchard Hill Police Department."

He knew it was apparent as he still had his raid jacket emblazoned with the name across his chest and the word 'POLICE' on the back in bright white lettering. "This is Detective LaBonge. And, you are…."

"My name is Nicole Getty. This is my boyfriend's place, and he's not home right now."

"That's what we would like to talk about. May we come in?" She reluctantly stepped aside and motioned for them to enter. No one sat.

Lady rushed up to Hamilton as if she were seeing a long-lost friend. "Hello, Lady," he said, petting the top of her head and giving her a big hug. Both LaBonge and Nicole were a bit taken aback by the apparent familiarity.

"I introduced Lady to John."

"Are you his friend that he calls HH?"

"Yes, I am."

"I don't know when he'll be back, but you're welcome to wait," she said rather unconvincingly.

"He won't be coming back, Nicole." The words hung out there in space somewhere, waiting for a response.

"What do you mean?" She spoke softly and slowly but acted like she knew what he meant.

"I think you know what I mean."

There was silence, and she moved to an overstuffed chair and sat down, staring straight ahead. There were no tears. Not yet anyway.

"I told him, but he said this was the big one, you know. It would all be over after this one." There was a stiff silence hanging gently in the room.

"Do you live here?" LaBonge asked to move the conversation away from the bad news gently.

"Well, kinda. I work at the Orchard Hill Mercedes dealership and have a place up there. Since I met John, I've spent most of my time here. Or with him in the van."

"Is that where all of the different Mercedes came from? Your dealership?" LaBonge asked.

"Yeah, but they're all paid for. I got my commission because of John, and he brought me the buyers."

LaBonge spoke in a more authoritative voice. "The investigators on this may want to talk to you about all of that, Nicole. Do you have some identification?"

She reached for her purse, and LaBonge grabbed it from her. "I need to make sure there are no guns in there, sorry."

LaBonge inspected the interior and handed her an orange leather wallet from its contents. He pushed back two small baggies of white powder that he instantly recognized. He closed the purse and set it by his side, away from Hamilton's view. At the same time, he caught Nicole's eye. She knew he knew.

LaBonge took her personal information and returned her driver's license.

"Are you going to stay here in his place for a while?"

"I don't know." She paused to collect her thoughts. "Can I ask any questions? How did it happen?"

"Before we talk about that, do you mind if we look around?"

"It's not my place, I guess so."

They spend time in each of the bedrooms but didn't make a mess. There was no need. Hamilton spotted the clean blue police uniform, wrapped in plastic with the distinctive 'Orchard Hill Police Department' shoulder patches, hanging in the closet with his other clothes.

"We'll take this and book it into evidence," he nodded to Nicole. There was no response.

They looked in the kitchen.

Before they decided to go to the garage, Nicole said," I know, and you know what you're looking for, but you won't find anything here. That's not how Johnny operated. His home is a clean place, always has been."

"You know what business he was in, then, don't you?" Hamilton asked.

"Of course, I did. I'm not blind or stupid. We met after you guys fired him, and we hit it off. He was always good to me. I got nothing to say against him." It was a stern statement that just had finality written on it.

"You don't have to, Nicole," Howard said passively, "we know enough about him too. Any guns in the house?"

"Only the one he had with him. Didn't do much good. Did you guys kill him?"

"No," LaBonge said. "We think Blackie Sampson did. They thought he was still one of us and had set up the operation."

"Maybe. And maybe Blackie did it for other reasons. He was trying to get in my pants. I tried to tell him I wasn't interested, but he wasn't going to take no for an answer. I think John knew it."

Hamilton and LaBonge looked at each other in agreement. "We're done, for now, Nicole, but we need to stay in touch. Are you staying here? If not, we need your other address and contact info. And, will you be keeping Lady with you?"

She gave them her information and walked to the door. There were still no tears. "I think I'll keep Lady, at least for now, and I think I'll go back to my place in Orchard Hill."

"If you decide you can't handle Lady, would you let me know?" Howard asked. "She's special to me. I think I know someone who would take good care of her."

"I will, Officer Hamilton, I will."

CHAPTER 112

IIIIIIIIIIIIIIIIIIIIIIIIIIIIIIIIIIIIIIIIIIIII

REFLECTION

LaBonge contacted Rikelman and asked if they were still needed at the Irwindale warehouse. He gave him an update on the visit with Nicole Getty.

"We're taking all the bodies to County Jail right now," Rikelman said. "I have the lab still here, and some evidence techs are bagging up things. The D.A. and LASO Shooting Team will be here for a while. You might as well head back to the station and check in with Barber to see what he has for you."

It sounded like Rikelman was in full Norman Bates mode. "I'm going to need Carvin here with me till we get rid of the females. I'll make sure she gets back to home base."

Howard called home. By now, it was after 2100 hours, and Clare was getting the kids ready for bed. It would take another hour to get back to OHPD, so he gave her the estimate of midnight before he would be home. "Really, Howard? You have never been this late. Are you sure you're at work?"

"Yes, Clare, I'm sure." He wondered why she sounded so accusatory. He was a little embarrassed to have her on the car's Bluetooth for LaBonge to hear.

"It's been one of those days, dear. Hey, meet Mike LaBonge. You're on speakerphone. None of this has ever happened before, but I'll fill you in when I get home."

They exchanged greetings, and Howard could tell that Clare was getting the idea to be a little more personable. He disconnected and looked at LaBonge.

"Does your wife always want to know what's going on at work like mine?"

LaBonge paused. "Sometimes, you'd think I worked in an office or just went to school. She never inquires and is not involved in my work on the task force or back at my PD. She's so wrapped in her career, and with no kids yet, we just pass in the night. I think you have the better deal there," pointing to the dashboard that housed the Bluetooth.

"Well, maybe we can fix that. Have you and your wife over for dinner. I mean, we don't have many friends from the PD. Too much time spent with the kids to nurture something like that. I have beers with the guys, but that's about it."

"I think we'd like that, Howard," LaBonge said, staring out into the darkness that held too many secrets.

The rest of the ride back to OHPD provided the solitude each of them needed to reflect on what occurred this day. This Black Friday. Like no other.

Elapsed time: 276 minutes

CHAPTER 113

||||||||||||||||||||||||||||||||||||||||||||||||||

WHAT?

They arrived at OHPD just as Barber was shutting down the EOC. It was almost 2300 by the time things quieted down at the station. Barber asked both LaBonge and Hamilton to provide an after-action report by Monday.

He hadn't checked his emails or texts in a few hours and saw that they were piled up waiting for a response. Two were from Clare, of course, wondering when he would be home.

One was from Donny wanting an update on the Black Friday operation, and one was a lengthy email from Rollenhagan. It seemed that LAPD finally located a witness, the former receptionist of the Rear Entrance, who filled in the blank information on the Mason/Blankenship case.

The bottom line was what was speculated turned out to be fact. A long-standing relationship between Mason and Blankenship ended when Mason found out that his lover was married with two kids and living a double life as a yoga guru. He was going through the sex change procedures at the behest of Blankenship and somehow discovered his other life. Rollenhagan would fill him in on the details if he wanted to know.

Hamilton was pondering this piece of information when he heard another familiar voice. "Hey," Barber asked Hamilton, "were you planning on going to Val and Harvey's retirement dinner next Friday?"

"Yeah, Clare and I were going. Why?"

"It's been canceled. It seems it was just a charade. They're getting divorced, and Val took off with some contractor that had been working on their house. They were getting it ready to sell and move out of the

288

area to Idaho, Montana, or Wyoming, or wherever Sherman Oakes, that detective that worked upstairs, went. Now that's up in the air. Anyway, no retirement dinner, and if you paid, you'd get your money back."

"What the fuck?" Howard said to no one. "Sorry, just slipped out."

What is going on here? This isn't happening, is it? Is it still Black Friday? Can anything else turn my world upside down?

"We're back at the cop shop now, Howard, so anything goes," LaBonge laughed.

"What else are the dolphins saying, Sarge?"

"Well, it's been coming for a while. We're not sure if they've even been living together lately. You know this Peyton Place, Having your spouse work in the same Department can be, well, touchy. Easier to keep that shit separate as far as I'm concerned."

Barber was doing everything he could to get on his way and made closure with, "see you on Monday."

"What's a dolphin, Howard?"

Howard obliged with an explanation.

He still couldn't get his arms around the idea of Val and Harvey splitting up. He reflected on the night A.J. Johnson was killed and Harvey's struggle to stay focused. He was falling asleep and seemed to be rather sullen and staring off into space on other occasions. Being wrapped up in his crap, he never paid that much attention to someone calling out for help. And now, it was too late.

It sounded like the damage had been done over a long period. Hamilton respected Sergeant Harvey Stevens and liked Val, but how does something like this happen and he not notice?

Black Friday was accurately described for many reasons. Was there more to come?

CHAPTER 114

||||||||||||||||||||||||||||||||||||||||||||||

HOLIDAYS

Holidays in law enforcement communities throughout the free world are filled with a conflict of events that tax even the strongest hearts. At the same time, the families of officers make every attempt to prepare for that particular day, that special week.

Those who live alone work the holidays. Still, others have no place to go or no one to share it with, other than a bottle of something strong enough to make the pain go away.

Howard Hamilton reflected on his fortune that he had a family. Harvey Stevens had none of that. No wife, no kids. Hopefully, a brother or sister, but all he ever really had was OHPD.

The holiday season meant end-of-year suicides for those who carry the enormous baggage of despair. It would be a time of drunk drivers killing and maiming on city streets. There would be shootings that make no sense—family fights over everything from watching television to politics that would divide rather than bring together.

Celebrities and other famous people would pass away or enter *the ghoul pool* during holidays. Stores would set record sales for things that did not matter. Desperate people would steal or shoplift to satisfy their need to have stuff. Law enforcement would support retail sales by setting up shoplifting details at Malls throughout the country, taking those into custody that chose to take from others.

There would be neighborhoods in Orchard Hill that would set up extravagant Christmas light spectacles requiring the direction of traffic, barricading of streets, and controlling the flow so that children and somewhat inebriated adults could bask in the glow of what the holidays meant. Mothers would carry red Solo cups containing their favorite Chardonnay, Pinot Gris, or the new fad, Viognier.

Santa Claus would be in every place that young children would congregate. So would the pedophiles, the potential child molesters, or car burglars waiting for mom and dad to fill up the back seat and go back for more. Law enforcement agencies would weigh the needs of each of their communities and consider whether a DUI checkpoint would be in the holiday spirit or not.

If there were people in Orchard Hill that went hungry, Howard Hamilton didn't know of them; but that didn't mean they were not there. Food banks were at every church or Boys and Girls Club. People were lined up to take advantage of the generosity of those who could write checks, contribute cash, or package boxes with meals planned to last at least a week.

OHPD was planning its tenth annual Santa's sleigh ride through the neighborhoods, giving out candy to kids who didn't need it but later visiting families who needed food, clothing, and shelter. There was never a lack of volunteer officers to dress as Santa for the event. At this time of year, volunteering took on a whole new meaning.

Howard enjoyed the holidays and working a uniform detail. People acknowledged and waved; with all five fingers. It was a time to set aside whatever disorders, ailments, or squabbles were out there and focus on being thankful.

Next week Michael Alcazar and his classmate would graduate from the Police Academy to become part of the OHPD family. It would be up to Howard and the other training officers to mold them into the kind of police officer that the Department, city, state, and country wanted. Each hire would be significant, and their development to have a servant's mentality was uppermost in his mind.

He was thinking about the events of a very complex year when he received a radio call to go to the station.

What now?

He pulled into the police parking lot to see someone put a red nose on Sergeant McGinty's black and white hood.

He'd probably leave it on all week, Hamilton thought, laughing.

He saw Donny Simpkins from across the parking lot, dressed in a suit and tie, obviously coming back from court. They waved and approached each other. There was a brief guy-type hug.

"How're you doing, Donny? Sorry we haven't been in touch. You on nights and me still on days doesn't work that well, does it?"

"I'm good, HH. I'm getting through the divorce and checking in with Father Mike on occasion. Thinking about going to days, I don't know. Lot of shit goin' on right now around here. Heard about the Stevens'?"

"Yeah. Jesus, who would have thought. Are you getting one of the new boots out of the Academy?"

"Yup. Getting Tenery, the Marine. Looking forward to it."

Howard didn't want to ask how he and Pat 'the Wolf' Woford were doing if they were doing. Donny made the fatal mistake of having a relationship with his female trainee, but only Howard knew it. It would stay that way.

"You heard about Bresani?" Howard was asking to keep the conversation going.

"Yeah, he was a fucking asshole, anyway. Good riddance." Donny saw something in Hamilton's eyes he didn't like. "Wait a minute! You're not feeling bad about that dipshit, are you?"

Howard paused for just a second, too long. "Wait a minute, HH. He was a crook, dope dealer, and worse, he used to be one of us! That asshole got what he deserved."

"I-I know," Hamilton stammered. "It's just…it's just that I saw him that way. Dead, you know."

"Well, let it go. Good riddance. Hey, Heard about Biddle?" Donny asked, trying to change the subject.

"What about him? He's not dead, too, is he? Got in trouble for sexual harassment with Shirley, the records manager, right? That's why we had to take all those stupid classes."

"Yeah, and she got almost 300 K in a settlement with the City for it."

"So?"

"Turns out, someone spotted them together on the beach in Puerta Vallarta having drinks, holding hands, and molesting each other!"

"Are you shitin' me?" Howard said just before he burst out laughing.

And then they both couldn't stop laughing like teenagers; again. Howard remembered how close their relationship used to be and the last time they laughed that hard. He had caught Donny getting a head job by Woford in the workout room. Their experiences together were priceless, as was their friendship.

"Well," Howard said, trying to control his chuckling, "got to get in and see what the watch commander wants. I got a call to go to the station. How about tonight at Home Plate? Just for a few beers."

"Sounds good, HH. I'd like that. By the way, congrats," Donny said with a genuine smile.

"What do you mean? For what?"

"Go see the watch commander. He'll tell you."

"What do you mean, damn it? You know something I don't?"

"Of course, I do! What Department do you think this is?"

"OHPD!" they said in unison, laughing once again.

CHAPTER 115

||||||||||||||||||||||||||||||||||||||||||||

LINCOLN 75

He took his time walking into the station's back door. Someone had put a wreath on it with a bell that jingled whenever it opened.

Who does all of this?

Sgt. Bennett was just coming into work for the PM shift. "HH, hey, come here." *What was so hush-hush*, he wondered. He was about to find out.

"Are you Ok with how this thing with Bresani went down?"

"What do you mean, Ok? Shit happens, but yeah, it bothers me. He's dead, and I saw him."

"Well, hopefully, you can get past that."

"Any idea how he got to keep his old ID card? Thought all of them were collected?"

"I guess all but one was." It was not a casual statement.

"Who was responsible for collecting them?" Howard asked rather innocently.

"The assistant watch commanders for each shift."

"He worked for you, didn't he?"

"Yes..." There was another pause. "I knew he had it, just didn't do anything about it."

"Was going to, but after his bust, I thought it could just be something to bring him to justice, so I just let things happen."

"You mean..."

"I mean nuthin, HH, absolutely nuthin," and he walked away, leaving Hamilton speechless.

Some things need follow-up, and other things need to be let go. That needed to be let go.

Both Lieutenant Hobson and Sgt. McGinty were in the watch commander's office.

I wonder if McGinty knows he has a red nose on the hood of his car? Jesus, I love this place.

"Somebody wants Lincoln 75, sir?" he threw out to whoever was going to listen.

Lt. Hobson looked up from a stack of paperwork. "As a matter of fact, yes, HH." Just then, Captain Markham walked in and reached out a hand.

"Congratulations, Officer Hamilton! You and Dean Harris have been selected as the co-officers of the year for OHPD!"

"What? Is this a joke, or what?" Hamilton looked around for someone to laugh with. He was stunned.

"No joke, Howard. You and Harris will be recognized at a ceremony at the City Council, Chamber of Commerce, and the School Board. We'll be doing a press release and telling the world," Markham explained.

"For what?" he was now more puzzled than ever.

"For creating the School Student Valet program at 19th Street School. The program has gone District-wide, and it's all because of you guys. Everybody loves it. We've been getting inquiries from the Los Angeles Unified School District, and this thing could take off. Channel 7 wants to do a special on it. And you guys did it!"

"Yeah, but Officers of the Year? For that? I'm sure there was somebody much more *deserving*." Hamilton was trying to back off from his shock and trying to make sense of all this.

It wasn't even real fuckin police work.

Captain Markham spoke up. "It's been a tough year around here, Hamilton. We could have honored those who are no longer with us, but we need an uplifting, and the Valet program will do it. Just accept it, and let's have some fun with it."

He stood there somewhat incredulous and then looked at Markham. "Thank you, sir. Thank you!"

"And remember our little conversation, HH. You have a lot to think about."

"I do, sir,"

It had been a tough year. But on the day shift, the maggots just made it all seem much more complicated. He reached for his phone to call Clare. He got her voice mail and left a message.

"Hey, Babe, just getting off duty here. We have a lot of things to catch up on. I'll change clothes and be home soon. Just about 23 minutes."

ACKNOWLEDGMENTS

All writers have many people to thank with a kind word. Twenty-Three Minutes was a labor of love with encouragement from many.

Sandra "D" keeps encouraging me to tell more stories, mainly because I have them. But the stories come from all of my comrades, friends, and co-workers that filled a 40-year career with memories I can only sit back and reflect on.

That is what police work is now for those who started in the 1960s and evolved to the 21st Century…memories. Significant events were yesterday's headlines and tomorrow's memories.

We were there, yet the media portrayed it differently than we remembered. I can remember being at the scene of a notable story, only to read about it the next day and wonder if I was there. Who saw it so differently?

Why do we cheer the Dirty Harry's, Jack Ryan's, and Mitch Rapp's of the fiction world and chastise a forceful takedown from an incomplete video that saved injury or death to innocent people not seen by a viewer?

I thank all my colleagues over those years for giving me the experience of a lifetime on a merry-go-round that never stops 24-7, 365 days a year, year after year.

We all want to be like Officer Howard Hamilton;

we want to keep from getting our uniform dirty, stay out of the rain, not go hungry and go home safely. Is that too much to ask?

A special thanks to Tam Nguyen, my yoga guru, Bill Schilt for his encouragement, and George Gurney for prompting me to do a better editing job.

If you enjoyed this book, please go to my page on Amazon and complete a review that ensures someone else would have the opportunity to ride along with Howard Hamilton. Five Stars would be excellent.